Lady Gwendolyn Rowle was horrified when she learned that the enchanting stranger who had swept her across the dance floor was the same wild nobleman who had killed her young husband in a duel.

More horrifying still was her own secret desire to yield to this man with her husband's blood still on his hands...

MY LORD MURDERER
A Regency Love Story by
ELIZABETH MANSFIELD

Elizabeth Mansfield

My Lord Murderer

A JOVE BOOK

MY LORD MURDERER

A Jove Book / published by arrangement with
the author

PRINTING HISTORY
Berkley edition / July 1978
Second printing / May 1981
Jove edition / July 1986

ISBN: 0-515-08743-2

Jove Books are published by The Berkley Publishing Group,
200 Madison Avenue, New York, N.Y. 10016.
The words "A JOVE BOOK" and the "J" with sunburst
are trademarks belonging to Jove Publications, Inc.

PRINTED IN THE UNITED STATES OF AMERICA

Chapter One

ANDREW SEYMOUR VISCOUNT JAMISON surveyed the hall
with ill-disguised boredom. Dancing was not to Lord
Jamison's liking; in fact, it was he who had first been
heard to utter the now-famous epithet that dancing
represented society's sanction—in public, vertical
expression—of what were essentially private, horizontal
desires. (Fortunately, the remark had been so widely and
inaccurately repeated that its author's identity had been
forgotten.) He regretted already that he had let his sister
persuade him to attend her ball. The hour was still early,
but he had already discovered that the card games in the
side rooms were insipid (his sister never permitting
anything more daring than silver-loo), the buffet tables
were overcrowded, the champagne too tame, and the
dancing—well, enough said on the subject of dancing. He

1

should have known that his sister's annual ball would be no livelier this year than it had been in the past. But he knew he dared not take his leave for yet another hour.

Lady Hester Selby's balls were always popular with the polite world of London, Lord Jamison's views notwithstanding. Those who knew described them as "regular squeezes." Her ballroom was one of the largest in London, a tremendous, cavernous place boasting three enormous French chandeliers which hung from the high ceiling on long brass chains, sixteen windows set high on the side walls, and a dance floor made of the finest oak parquet. Two rows of graceful, fluted columns ran along two sides of the dance floor, separating the dancers from those who only wanted to watch, to sit and chat, or to promenade around the room. Well-laden buffet tables were set up at the far end of the room, and no less than six small alcoves were set aside for cards.

But although his sister seemed always to have made provision for the entertainment and satisfaction of her other guests, she invariably did something to render *him* uncomfortable. This time it had been a Miss Calisher. He had no sooner arrived when Hetty had taken his arm and pulled him to the sofa where Miss Calisher and her mother were seated. The girl was pretty enough, but she had an aggressive manner and a loud, too-ready laugh. He had been forced into an interminable country dance with her. And as soon as he'd restored her to her mother, Hetty was back again, urging him to meet another of her wallflowers. This time he'd been adamant.

"But Drew, why do you think I invited you?" his dear sister had asked. "I need you to brighten the evening for a few of these young ladies. There are never enough desirable bachelors to go around, and what's the good of my having a brother who's rich, single and so devilishly handsome that all the silly geese simper over him, if he won't put himself out a tiny bit to make his own sister's ball a success?"

"I'm not in the least concerned with the success of your

ball, and not a bit moved by what you probably think are flattering remarks," he had told her roundly. "And if you've invited me just to use me in this odious way, it's the last you'll see of me at your annual squeezes!" And he had turned his back on her and walked to the nearest card room.

Now, with more than an hour to go before midnight (when he could feel safe in taking his leave), Drew leaned his broad shoulder against a nearby column and sighed. He thought briefly of slipping out quietly without taking leave of Hetty at all, but he dismissed the urge. She would descend on him first thing tomorrow and subject him to more than an hour of recriminations. Better to stand here until midnight than to face her on the morrow.

He looked across the room. There was Hetty, greeting a newcomer at the doorway. Drew's boredom dropped away. Who was that *ravishing* creature his sister was welcoming? The lady at the door was taller by a head than his diminutive sister, and her hair had a bronze-gold color that seemed to glow from some inner, suppressed life. It was pulled back somewhat severely from a pale, oval face whose features were strong yet perfectly proportioned, mature yet youthful. She wore a darkly-colored dress— but who cared to notice the dress?—cut low across softly-sloping shoulders and an exquisitely-modeled bosom. When she turned her head to greet a few acquaintances who were beginning to circle around her, Drew glimpsed a warm smile and the sparkle of eyes surprisingly dark in that pale face.

Hetty was leading her across to the row of sofas and chairs that Drew secretly called the Dowagers' Circle. The two ladies were followed by a number of people who had recognized her and were hurrying over to greet her. Who on earth *was* she? How was it he had never seen her before, when obviously she was quite well known? He was almost tempted to cross the floor himself and demand that Hetty make him known to her. But no, he thought, she would probably turn out to be as insipid as the rest of this gathering. He would simply while away his enforced hour of attendance by watching her from a distance.

The lady seated herself. Hetty bustled about her solicitously, and the partly-deaf Lady Ogilvie, who was seated next to her, leaned close to hear the conversation. Now Freddie Knightsbridge was bowing to her. Drew leaned back against the pillar comfortably and grinned. It was not often that Freddie, prematurely grey and awkward in conversation with women, could be roused to play the gallant. Drew would enjoy watching him make a cake of himself on the dance floor. But the lady was shaking her head. She would not dance with him. Poor Freddie was bowing and walking away slowly, looking awkward and disappointed.

The lady was now smiling and chatting with Lady Ogilvie. Drew could see that her dress was a dark purple, much too dark a ballgown for such a young woman. Had she just come out of mourning? That would explain why she wasn't dancing. Now his brother-in-law, Lord Selby, approached her. Again she smiled and shook her head. Lord Selby bowed politely and turned to Hetty. Drew could see Hetty gesturing toward the dance floor. He could almost hear her: If you were willing to appear on the dance floor with someone else, why not with me? Drew laughed out loud as his portly brother-in-law shrugged and permitted his wife to lead him to the dance floor, reluctance manifesting itself in every step he took. It wasn't often that Hetty could so maneuver him, but fate had dropped him into her hands that time!

Good heavens, was that Lambie Aylmer approaching the lady in purple now? Not Sir Lambert Aylmer, the greatest fop, the biggest bore, the flattest flat in the room! The poor woman would be in for it now. She was about to be struck by "Lambie the Leech." Drew watched in amused fascination as Sir Lambert bowed and scraped and begged and wheedled to no avail. The lady remained firm. Sir Lambert pulled up a chair. Drew could almost feel, from his vantage point across the room, the restrained annoyance of the lady as she shifted closer to Lady Ogilvie and turned away from Lambie. But Sir Lambert leaned toward her, interrupting the ladies' conversation every half-minute. The lady made a gesture to the buffet table. Clever girl, thought Drew. She's sending him away to fetch her some refreshment. Now she'll get up and make her escape.

As he had anticipated, the lady rose. But Lady Ogilvie took her arm and detained her with a question. Before the exchange was over, Lambie was back with two glasses. The lady was caught again. Drew felt he could almost hear her sigh as she sat down again.

"There you are, Drew," said a voice behind him. "What on earth are you staring at with that stupid grin on your face?"

Drew turned to find his friend, Wystan Farr, looking at him curiously through his quizzing glass. Drew laughed. "I look a fool, do I? Well, never mind. Just cast your eyes over there, Wys, and see what Lambie Aylmer has leeched on to."

"Where?"

"There in the Dowagers' Circle. See him?"

"Oh, yes. Now, I—" Wys suddenly drew in his breath in a gasp.

"Yes, I quite understand," Drew said, amused. "She *does* take one's breath away, doesn't she?"

"Yes, but that's not why I . . . er . . . Drew, old fellow, don't you know her?"

"The lady in purple? Never saw her before in my life, I assure you. But never mind that now. Just watch our Lambie! She can't rid herself of him, try as she may."

But Wys was staring at Drew with a strange, arrested expression. Drew noted it with a flicker of surprise, but his mind was on the lady across the room. "Tell me, Wys," he asked musingly, his eyes on the lady and her comic tormenter, "shall I bestir myself and rescue the fair damsel?"

Wys shook his head in alarm. "No, no, Drew, please!

Not your affair at all. I wouldn't go near her if I were you."

Drew stared at him. "What's the matter with you, Wys? It shouldn't be too hard for me to find a ruse to separate her from her unwanted companion. What's your objec—?" But before he could finish his sentence, his eye was caught by a movement of the lady in purple. "Oh, she's getting up. I wonder if she's leaving? Look at that, Wys! The Leech is still after her! This is too delicious—I must get her out of this. I'll see you later."

"No, Drew, you can't! You don't realize who she is!" Wys called urgently. But Drew was already crossing the ballroom, out of hearing. Wys shook his head worriedly and followed as quickly as he could, skirting the dancers clumsily and treading on more than one offended toe.

The lady in purple was walking purposefully on the outskirts of the dance floor, closely followed by Sir Lambert, who was determinedly impeding her progress by asking her questions which necessitated her turning to answer them. Drew placed himself directly in her path, and when she turned back from Sir Lambert's last question, she found her way blocked by a tall, smiling stranger. "Ah, there you are, my dear," Drew said to her familiarly, taking her arm and placing it cosily over his. "I've been searching for you all evening!"

The lady started. "What?" she asked uncertainly.

Drew went on smoothly. "Now, I know you are not dancing, but you cannot have forgotten your promise to me the last time we met."

Sir Lambert, close behind her, looked at Drew with shock and anger. "My God!" he said in a choked voice. "Not *you*!"

Drew noted that Lambie's reaction was especially nonsensical, even for Lambie, but chose to ignore it. Smiling down at the lady, he asked, "You haven't forgotten, have you?" and gave her the briefest wink of his eye.

The lady's eyes sparkled mischievously. She flicked a

glance at Sir Lambert, then looked down at the floor demurely. "Forgotten?" she asked tentatively.

"Your promise! You said you would grant me a waltz the very next time we met. And, my dear, here we are, and I hear that a waltz has just begun. So, without further ado—" And with that, Drew swept her firmly toward the dance floor without a backward glance at the sputtering, apoplectic Sir Lambert who stood staring after them.

A moment later Wys was beside Lambie, shaking him. "Where are they, Lambie? Tell me, where *are* they?"

Sir Lambert pointed a shaking finger to where Drew, with smiling grace, was taking the lady into his arms for the waltz. Wys clapped his hand to his forehead in despair. "Too late!" he groaned. "Too late. We'll just have to let whatever happens happen."

On the dance floor, the lady in purple was smiling up at her handsome rescuer as he twirled her lightly around the room. "Do you always dance off so brazenly with strangers to whom you've not been introduced?" she asked in mock severity.

"Yes, always. I sweep them off their feet before they have time to think better of it," Drew answered with a grin.

"And for a *waltz*? It's infamous of you!"

"Why not a waltz? This isn't Almack's, you know. We need not have the permission of a patroness here."

"I think you deserve a good scold for your abominable manners, especially to Sir Lambert," the lady chided.

"Do you? I thought rather that I deserve a kiss."

"A kiss!"

"Yes, indeed! For ridding you of the man. I'd been watching you for quite a while, you know. Never have I seen a lady so in need of rescuing."

"I may have needed rescuing, I'll admit. And I'll admit to a sense of gratitude for your effective, if unconventional, action in my behalf—"

"Now, that's better," Drew interjected, grinning.

"—But I draw the line at being instructed in the nature

of the reward," she said with a saucy toss of her hair.

"Oh? Are you *not* going to kiss me, then?" Drew asked in a tone of deep disappointment.

"Certainly not," said the lady, laughing.

"Then I shall immediately restore you to the side of the charming Sir Lambert," Drew countered promptly.

"What an unhandsome thing to say," said the lady, laughter lingering in her eyes and at the corners of her mouth. "I see you have an unpleasantly calculating character."

"I'm afraid I have," Drew said unabashed. "If I can't have a kiss, what *will* you give me as my reward?"

The lady looked up at him with her mischievous glance. Drew felt an unfamiliar constriction in his chest and almost missed a step. The lady in his arms was something quite out of the ordinary. What a lovely ball this was after all.

"I'll give you my name. Is that enough of a reward for you, sir?" she asked.

"Your name? Nonsense, that won't do at all. I can get *that* from my sister."

"Your sister?" she asked, puzzled.

"Yes, my sweet innocent. My sister is our hostess, Hester Selby."

The lady stared up at him, her smile fading. "Hetty is your sister? Then you...you must be—!" She stopped dancing, thrust his arms from her and stood still, her cheeks white, her eyes shocked. "Good God! You're not...you couldn't be *Drew Jamison*?"

The dancers around them were staring at them. The dance floor was rapidly becoming a sea of murmurs and confusion. Drew tried to take her in his arms again. "Of course I'm Drew Jamison," he said with a puzzled smile. But the lady had turned into a frozen fury. Her arm swung up, and she struck his face with a resounding whack. "Murderer!" she hissed. "You vile, cowardly murderer!"

Drew stood speechless, his lips white, a wave of icy

tension gripping his chest. "Oh, my *God*! You're not ... *Lady Rowle*?"

She bowed, a deep, cold mockery of a bow. "May I present Gwendolyn Rowle, the widow of the man you so cold-bloodedly killed," she said icily. Then she stood erect and looked at him with loathing. "I ask only one thing of you, my lord Murderer. Only one thing. Never, *never* come near me again!"

And she turned quickly and ran from the floor, leaving Drew alone at the center of the crowd of dancers who were staring at him in embarrassed silence.

Chapter Two

IT WAS AN UNUSUALLY agitated Wystan Farr who hammered impatiently on Lord Jamison's door the next morning. Wys was a sensible, temperate, calm young gentleman who, like Aristotle, believed in moderation in all things. From his not-quite-reddish hair, cut in a conservative, not-too-short mode, past his shirt collars whose points were not quite high enough to mark him a Dandy, to his shiny top-boots which did not sport the extravagantly-flagrant bows on the cuffs favored by the fops of London but merely a couple of insignificant tassels, he was every inch a gentleman of modest taste and style. Only his extreme loyalty to his friend Drew could shake him out of his customarily tranquil demeanor. The repercussions of the events of last night had upset his equilibrium. Already spreading among the *ton* of London

10

were a rash of malignant rumors about his closest friend, and his loyalty to that association overrode his natural inclination to reticent behavior.

The violence of his knocking did not cause the door to open with more than usual dispatch. The staid and imperturbable Mallow opened it with no trace of having hurried. "His Lordship is in the breakfast room, Mr. Farr," Mallow said as Wys ran unceremoniously by him and up the stairs. Wys halted abruptly in the doorway of the breakfast room, amazed and annoyed to see his friend seated contentedly at the table looking very much at his ease in a green silk, frogged robe, calmly tapping the top from a soft-boiled egg. "Confound it, Drew, how can you sit there slopping up eggs," asked Wys in an aggrieved voice, "when all of London is gossiping about you?"

Drew lifted his amused grey eyes from his plate, looked at his friend and waved him toward an empty chair. "I do not 'slop' my eggs," he answered, returning his attention to his food. "Here, have some of this coffee. I have it roasted in a very special way, and I find it an excellent morning beverage. It seems to liven the spirits when drunk early in the day."

"No, thanks, can't abide the filthy stuff," Wys said, helping himself to a muffin, a slice of ham, some butter and the pot of marmalade instead. "Well, old boy, you really made a mull of it last night. You've got everyone saying you're a murderer."

"Rubbish! London is not Timbucktoo. We have law and order here. Everyone knows that Rowle's death was thoroughly investigated."

"But they don't know the circumstances. The scene last night stirred up the whole mystery again."

"What mystery? Everyone who was present at the duel knows exactly what happened."

Wys frowned at his friend impatiently. "That means only five of us—*five*! That's *all*! Pollard, who stood up for Rowle; I, who stood up for you; yourself; the doctor; and Selby, who was told after you were hurt."

"And the officials and the magistrates. Don't forget them."

"I don't. But you know perfectly well that they don't signify. As for the four of us, you made us all swear not to spread the story. And you can be sure Pollard won't say anything. He'll be quite content to let people think the worst of you. So it remains a mystery to everyone else who counts."

"Let it remain so. I'm not a bit interested in feeding the appetite of the curious for malicious gossip." And he tried to close the discussion by pressing on his friend another muffin.

"Aren't you at all interested in protecting yourself from being called a murderer?" Wys asked in disgust.

"Not particularly."

Wys shook his head. "You're mad! You won't be able to show your face at any social gathering. The women will ostracize you. You won't be invited anywhere—!"

"Don't agitate yourself, Wys. It doesn't suit you. Besides, I have a few good friends who won't desert me. As for the rest—" He shrugged.

"And how about your sister?" came a voice from the doorway. "Are you going to shrug *her* off too?"

Drew looked up to see his brother-in-law standing in the doorway, his portly frame filling its entire width. Selby stood leaning on his cane, his usually cheerful, chubby face darkened by a scowl. "Ah, Selby!" Drew greeted him. "Good morning. I suppose I should have been expecting you."

Lord Selby, realizing that his scowl and his dramatic stance in the doorway were being wasted on Drew, sighed and waddled into the room. He dropped into a chair with a groan of exhaustion. "Might have guessed that getting up early and racing over here would do no good. If Wys hasn't made you see sense, I don't suppose I shall either. Good morning, Wystan, old chap."

Wys looked at Selby with sympathy. "Had a bad night

with your wife, I expect," he said, nodding understandingly.

"Hetty's in a state, I can tell you. Didn't sleep a wink. Not a wink. Kept *at* me and *at* me to tell her the whole business. I tell you, Drew, I don't think I can hold out much longer."

Wys turned to Drew, a pleading look in his eye. "Can't you even let your *sister* in on the details?"

"A good question," agreed Selby. "Drew's an obstinate fool in this matter."

Drew looked at his brother-in-law contemptuously. "If I told Hetty, the story would be all over town in less than two hours."

"Think shame on yourself, Drew Jamison," said the mild Wys. "That's an insulting thing to say about your own sister. Next thing you know, you'll have *Selby* here calling you out!"

"Not likely, Wys, old boy," Selby put in ruefully. "Drew's absolutely right there. Hetty loves a good gossip, no matter who's involved, but if her precious brother is the *hero* of the story, there'd be no holding her back." And Selby sighed and reached for a plate.

An angry female snort from the doorway stayed his hand. He looked up to see his wife glaring at him in barely-restrained fury. "I've always heard," she said icily, "that men are worse gossips than women, and now at last I have the proof. Talking about me in that way! For shame! Wystan is the only one of you with a grain of sense."

Wystan and Drew got to their feet, but Selby merely put his head in his hands and groaned. "I might have known she'd come," he muttered. "I should have stayed in bed. I knew I should have stayed in bed."

Drew smiled at his sister, who stood barely five feet tall from the bottom of her high-heeled boots to the top of the high-crowned bonnet covering her curly auburn hair—every inch quivering with fury.

Elizabeth Mansfield

"Mallow must be in need of retraining," Drew said to no one in particular. "Everyone has simply materialized at my breakfast-room door like a series of unwanted poltergeists. I must speak to the fellow—and severely, too."

"Don't think to put me off with that hum," Hetty told her brother with asperity. "I told Mallow I would see myself up, as you well know."

"Nevertheless, he should not have permitted it. I cannot have my guests eavesdropping at my back, you know."

"Eavesdropping! Of all the insulting—! One would think I was skulking behind the furniture instead of standing here in the doorway in plain sight!"

"But there is so little of you, my dear," Drew said, smiling at her disarmingly, "that we quite overlooked your presence. But come in, Hetty, come in and have some breakfast with us. No earthly use your standing there sulking, you know. I'm aware that you're determined to have your say, so we all may as well be comfortable while you say it." He went to her, took her hand, and led her to the chair Wystan held for her. "I think there's enough coffee left to offer you a cup. Pass me a cup and saucer from the sideboard, Wys, like a good fellow."

Hetty allowed herself to take a seat at the table, but she accepted not a morsel of food and permitted herself no softening of the angry expression of her face. "All this attention and gallantry will do nothing to deter me from my purpose," she announced firmly. "I intend to get to the bottom of this, and I will not budge until I do."

"Wasting your time, my pet," her husband muttered, settling himself comfortably at the table and loading his plate with a sufficient quantity of foodstuffs to sustain him through the lengthy ordeal he knew would follow. "Your brother is as stubborn as you are. Neither Wystan nor I has been able to move him an inch."

"He may be able to withstand the two of you, but he

has *me* to deal with now," Hetty replied firmly, and she fixed a challenging eye on her brother.

"You have me all a-tremble," Drew said with a grin, and he returned his attention to his long-neglected egg.

"I don't see why you can't tell me what happened, especially since you are the *hero* of the affair," Hetty began.

"Hero?" Drew asked in distaste.

"I heard Selby say so," she persisted.

"I thought you said you didn't eavesdrop," Selby put in defensively.

"To eavesdrop is to overhear on purpose. I overheard quite by accident," his wife retorted. "Now, Drew, I want to know how you can be a hero and a murderer at the same time."

"A murderer!" Wystan said with a shudder. "You cannot believe that, surely."

"Of course I don't believe it. But all of London does, and I won't have it!" Hetty said passionately.

"Hang all of London!" Drew said impatiently. "As long as you all are convinced of my innocence, I don't care a fig for the rest of London. Can't we drop this fruitless subject? I'm finding this whole discussion a frightful bore."

"No, we can *not*! I'm not going to permit people to malign my own brother. If you are innocent, why can't we spread the true story and scotch these dreadful rumors?"

"Because," Selby explained patiently, "Drew feels that certain innocent parties will be hurt by the full disclosure."

Hetty looked shrewdly at the three men. "If it's Gwen Rowle for whom you're concerned, you needn't be."

Drew's eyebrows went up perceptibly, and his look sharpened. "Oh?" he asked carefully. "Why not?"

"Well," said Hetty, leaning forward confidentially, "she and I were well on the way to being intimates before her husband was killed. The fact that my brother killed him has dampened our friendship somewhat, but not completely. She places no blame on *me*, you know."

"I should hope *not!*" her husband said, scandalized at the idea.

"But I gather from little things she let slip that she and Lord Rowle were not getting on well. She gave me the strongest feeling that she was not happy—that she felt she'd made a horrible mistake in marrying him."

Wystan shook his head. "But her grief at his death! Why, it was the talk of London! And when I called on her to express my condolences, she was quite inconsolable. I found it almost . . . well, one hesitates to condemn a bereft widow, but I would say it was *excessive*."

"That's the very word I would have expected you to use," Selby said, with a knowing wink at Drew. But Drew's eyes were fixed on Hetty with a look of guarded speculation.

"You say she was not happy with him?" he asked intently. "Are you sure?"

"Yes, I am, despite her 'excessive' grief."

"Do you mean you think her grief was *feigned*? That she was only play-acting?" Wystan asked incredulously.

"No, of course not. I think it was a kind of . . . oh, dear, how can I explain what I feel? . . . a kind of . . ." and she floundered for a word.

"Expiation?" Drew offered, watching his sister's face with interest.

Hetty looked up at him gratefully. "Yes! Yes, that's the very word! As if she were trying to make up, by her grief, for the . . . *unwifely* feelings she had for him while he was alive."

There was a pause in the conversation while they all tried to imagine the strange marriage which had come to such a tragic end. Finally, Wystan broke the silence. "Do you think that this information relieves Drew of the necessity of protecting Gwen Rowle from the full knowledge of the details of her husband's death?"

"Yes I do. If Rowle's end—as I suspect—was as cowardly and ignominious as his life, it will come as no great shock to her."

Selby looked at his wife with admiration. "I think you're right, Hetty, for once. If a man is a loose screw and a rotter, his wife is bound to realize it before very long. What good are we doing, Drew, to protect Lady Rowle from something she already knows?"

Drew didn't answer. He was lost in a brown study, his lips curled in a small, secret smile, his eyes fixed on the middle distance. Wys watched him in annoyance. "Come now, Drew, you can't still refuse us permission to clear your name! Hetty has given us an excellent reason why secrecy in this matter is unnecessary."

Drew turned to him, forcing himself to apply his mind to the question just posed. "The reason still exists, Wys. I'm sorry, but I cannot release any of you from your promise to secrecy."

"But—?" Selby began.

"Rowle's *mother* is alive, and she's bound to hear the story. And we have only Hetty's *theory* about the relationship between Rowle and his wife. We could not take a chance on so unsubstantial a theory. I think it best to let matters rest."

The men sat back in their chairs, defeated. Hetty, seeing their complete collapse and knowing her brother well enough to realize that he was not likely to change his mind, resorted to her last means of attack. She permitted two tears to roll down her cheeks. "And I? Am *I* to be left in the dark, to face the accusations and the sneers of all my circle without even the inner knowledge of the truth to sustain me through the ordeal?"

Drew looked at her with a twinkle. "Come now, Hetty, you're doing it much too brown. You know perfectly well that I'm no murderer. That knowledge should sustain you quite adequately. It's only your *curiosity* that can't be satisfied."

"Quite right, Drew," agreed her husband. "He has you there, m'dear."

Hetty looked from her husband to her brother in disgust. "Very well, I *admit* I'm curious. I'm *bursting* with curiosity, as you both have guessed. And I intend to find out. I'm willing to give my word of honor not to tell a soul, if you insist, but I want to know the truth of this affair so that I can understand why all this secrecy is necessary. I shan't rest, nor shall I give any of *you* any rest, until you've told me the whole story. After all, Drew, I am all the family you have. Next to Selby, you are the dearest person in the world to me. Have I not the right to know the truth?"

Drew hesitated. Selby, taking advantage of that momentary lapse, put in quickly, "Tell her, Drew. Tell her, if you've any feeling for me at all. My life will be a nightmare if you don't."

Drew looked at Wys, who nodded his agreement. "Your sister has the ability to disturb *my* life too, I have no doubt," he said, with a rueful smile at the tiny but forceful Hetty.

"Very well," Drew sighed. "But, Hetty, you must give your word that the story will go no further than this room—that no matter how sorely you are tried, nor how many nasty things are said about your brother, you will be strong and refuse to reveal any information you learn today."

"Oh, but Drew, what if—?"

Selby cut her short. "Hetty!" he said, his voice filled with warning.

"Oh, very well," she pouted. "I give my word."

"Good," said Drew shortly and rose from his chair. "If you'll excuse me, I'll let Wys tell you about it. I'm going to dress. I have a call I wish to make this morning." With that, he left the room, but the others took no notice. They leaned toward each other, eager to review the fascinating particulars of the occurrence, six months before, when Edward Brockhurst, Lord Rowle, met his untimely end.

It had been a mildly pleasant evening at White's, Wys related, until Sir George Pollard had made his appearance, bearing with him his friend, Lord Rowle. Rowle, whose reputation as a gambler was unsavory, had never been offered membership at this the most reputable of the gambling clubs, but his admittance could not be refused if he came for the evening under the aegis of a member. This was not the first time Sir George had brought his crony along. Sir George himself was not popular among the membership, being a very clever player and a winner perhaps too often to avoid attracting suspicions concerning the honesty of his play. But no trace of dishonesty had ever been proved, and Sir George was therefore a member in good standing. He could be found almost every evening sitting in his accustomed seat, his ebony cane (a distinctive piece with a carved ivory handle, which he carried everywhere) propped up against his chair.

Wystan had been inveigled to join in their game and found himself winning heavily from Rowle, who was badly foxed. He'd tried two or three times to withdraw from play, but Rowle insisted on a chance to get even, and the play continued. Suddenly, Rowle's luck began to turn and he won two hands in quick succession. Wys again made a movement to end the game, but now that he was winning, Rowle insisted that Wys remain. Wys sighed and resumed his seat. Rowle continued to drink heavily. His cheeks were flushed, his dank blonde hair was matted with sweat, his eyes were wild. The bets went higher and higher despite Wys's attempts to keep them within bounds, but there was no reasoning with Rowle.

Drew's game at another table had ended, and he came looking for Wys, hoping for his company on the walk home. He paused behind Rowle's chair and watched the play. Suddenly, his hand swooped down, pinning Rowle's arm to the table. "What—? Who—? What're y'doin'?" cried the drunk Lord Rowle.

Without a word, Drew lifted Rowle's arm from the table. Under Rowle's sleeve rested a hidden card. A gasp went up from the men at the table and those standing near by. Rowle went white, and Wys jumped up from his seat. "I think you're a bit too foxed to play tonight, eh Rowle?" Drew said suggestively, giving Rowle the chance to say that he was too drunk to know what he was doing. "Pick up the pot, Wystan, and let's go home. I think Lord Rowle has had enough for tonight."

Sir George, who had been watching, felt a wave of relief. The man he had sponsored had been found cheating, and this would reflect on him, too. Lord Jamison had given them both a way out. Pleading drunkenness, they could apologize and make their escape with no reprisal other than a flurry of gossip which would soon die down. "Yes, good idea," he said quickly, shoving the chips toward Wys. "Let's get you some air, Rowle, old boy. Do us *both* good."

But Rowle's face flushed angrily and his eyes glittered with hate. He picked up his glass of wine and turned to Drew, flinging the contents in Drew's face. "Accuse me of cheatin', will you?" he muttered. "Nothin' for it but to make you call me out."

"Don't be a fool," Drew said quietly. "Get out of here before you make things worse." And he took out a handkerchief and calmly wiped his face.

Freddie Knightsbridge, who had been one of the players at the table, shook his head in disapproval. "I don't think you should let him get away with this, Drew," he said in a low voice.

"Do you want this to end in a shooting match? The man's drunk. Get him out of here, Pollard, and quickly!" Drew said.

"Come along, man, come along," Pollard said urgently to Rowle.

But Rowle was too far gone. "Won't go without m' winnings. Was my game. Mine! Would o' won if Jamison hadn't interfered. Ought to 'pologize or meet me." And he reached shakily for the chips lying unclaimed on the table.

Sir Reginald Travers, a distinguished, white-haired gentleman who had been a member of the club for longer than anyone else present, leaned over the table, put his hands over the chips and shook his head. He gave Drew a quick glance and shrugged, then turned his eye to Rowle.

"There will be neither winnings nor an apology to you, Lord Rowle. The game is Mr. Farr's."

The observers exchanged looks. Sir Reginald's meaning was clear. Rowle's chance of escape was no longer open. "No other way," whispered Freddie to Lambert Aylmer who had squeezed his way into the circle of men surrounding the table. "Rowle's gone too far." For Rowle now had no choice but to face the consequences of his act of cheating.

Wys glanced at Drew. "*I* shall meet him, of course," he said quickly. "Will you second me, Drew?"

Drew gave his friend a little smile. "Thank you, Wys," he said, "but it was *I* who had the challenge." And he showed the wine-stained handkerchief to support his claim. "You will second *me*, I hope." Wys made an unhappy but acquiescent bow.

"And I, of course, will second Lord Rowle," Pollard said curtly. "I shall see him home and call on you in your rooms, Mr. Farr." With those words, he led his drunken friend from the room.

The arrangements were made for the following morning, and it was a very pale Lord Rowle who descended from the carriage at a country inn ten miles from London. Wys surmised that Rowle's friend, Sir George, had made him painfully aware that he'd been a complete fool. First he had cheated at White's—in that unforgivably clumsy way—and then he had challenged the man whose accuracy with a pistol was legendary. Drew had given Rowle three opportunities to withdraw from the challenge, but he had drunkenly—or stubbornly—ignored them. There was only one hope for Rowle now—that Drew would delope.

To shoot wide, or fire in the air on purpose, was a practice forbidden in the *Code Duello*, but outside of Ireland the rule was often violated. Deloping was, in fact, a not-uncommon practice. Wys suspected that Drew intended to delope, knowing that his friend did not wish to inflict further harm on poor Rowle, whose reputation would be forever marred by what had happened the night before. Wys was therefore not very concerned about the outcome of the duel. When Rowle saw Drew raise his arm toward the sky, he was bound to do likewise, in relief and gratitude. The requirements of honor would thus be met, and no blood would be shed.

But the events did not follow the predicted pattern. Pollard and Wys checked the pistols, the participants were armed, the paces were measured, and they took aim. As Wys had surmised, Drew raised his arm skyward. Rowle, with a cry of relief, shot off his pistol before the order to fire was given. But he did not shoot in the air as Wys had expected. He had aimed right at Drew! The shot struck Drew on the underside of the arm that he'd raised in the air. With a wince of pain, Drew dropped his arm, and, having been about to fire, he unwittingly pulled the trigger as his arm fell. To everyone's horror, the shot gave Rowle a fatal wound.

With Rowle dead and Drew wounded, Wys had no choice but to call in the magistrates. Their inquiry was short and conclusive: with the evidence of the doctor who had been an eye witness, and the situation of Drew's wound—proof that he'd been about to fire into the air— Lord Jamison was completely exonerated. All the witnesses agreed to sign the statement that Rowle had shot too soon and had thus caused his own death. The case was closed.

In sympathy for the widow and the mother who survived Lord Rowle, Drew had immediately pledged the participants to silence, and Wys had carted him home. Selby, who by this time had heard rumors of the doings of the night before, was found waiting nervously in Drew's hallway. The sight of his brother-in-law, pale from the loss of blood and tense with pain, upset him considerably. He and Wys helped Drew to bed. Since Drew was too weak to discuss plans to hide from the world the fact of his wound, Selby was drawn into the group who were privy to the events of the morning. He and Wys concocted a story

about Drew's having left London to take care of some
business at his country estates; and while he recuperated,
they busied themselves in spreading the word that Rowle
had died accidentally. When no contradictory word was
issued from Rowle's family, the story had to be accepted,
and eventually the gossip died down.

Hetty sat back in her seat, her brow wrinkled in
thought. "There's something I still don't understand," she
said. "If the explanation of Rowle's death was not
questioned by Rowle's family, how is it that Gwen
accused Drew of murder?"

"I have no doubt of the answer to that," Selby said
bitterly. "Pollard!"

Wys shook his head mournfully. "I'm very much afraid
you're right. The man's a rackety loose screw, and sure as
check he told Lady Rowle just enough about the duel to
make Drew the villain of the piece."

"Dash it!" Hetty cried, shocked. "I won't sit still for
that, I can tell you!" And true to her word, she jumped to
her feet. "I won't have that man maligning my brother
that way! I'm going to tell Gwen the truth this very
morn—!"

"Hetty, sit down!" ordered her husband sharply. "You
gave your word, not one half-hour ago. You'll not break it
while I have a breath in my body. So take a damper!"

The willful Hetty stuck out her chin and looked at her
husband rebelliously. She met with a firm and quelling
stare. Wys watched in amused fascination while her eyes
dropped and she meekly lowered her head. Selby was not
such a milksop with Hetty as Wys had supposed.

"A bad promise, like a good cake, is better broken than
kept," Hetty muttered as she resumed her seat.

"Don't feed me platitudes," Selby ordered. "You are
honor-bound to keep your mouth tightly closed in this
matter. Is that clear?"

"Yes, my dear," she said with a small sigh.

Wys pushed away his teacup and leaned back in his

chair to face Selby. "It's all very well to keep your wife in line," he said, "but we have come up with no plan for clearing Drew's good name. With all this talk, the only thing we've accomplished is adding one small female into the select circle of people who know the truth. And she was on his side by act of birth anyway."

"Wys is right," Hetty said. "If you won't let me talk about this, how *are* we to clear his name?"

Selby shrugged. "Why look at *me* in that accusing way? What can *I* do? Drew is the only one who can do anything about this brangle, and he won't."

"Can't we think of anything else? Surely there must be something—?" Hetty asked in desperation.

"I've been up all night trying to think of something, but I confess I'm completely defeated," Wys admitted in complete discouragement.

"Don't lose hope," came Drew's cheerful voice from the doorway. "I have a plan of my own."

Three pairs of eyes turned to look up at him. He stood in the doorway leaning on his cane, dressed in a smoothly fitting coat of grey super-fine over immaculately-fitting white breeches. Even his soft leather boots and his dark curls brushed into a casual 'Brutus' proclaimed the ideal Corinthian gentleman. His sister sighed with pleasure at the sight of him; a man who looked like that could never be thought a murderer, she decided with satisfaction.

"Good! If you have a plan, we no longer need be worried," Wys said with relief and without a bit of curiosity. As long as his friend would not have to face social ostracism, he did not care about the particulars.

But Selby was not so easily satisfied. "And what *is* this plan, if I may ask? If you have some way to convince the *ton* of your innocence without revealing the story of what happened, you have more than a plan—you have a miracle!"

Hetty clapped her hands together in pleasure. "He's thought of something brilliant," she crowed. "I know he has! What *is* it, Drew? Tell us!"

"You'll learn in due course. But if you'll excuse me, I must be off," he answered indifferently.

"Oh, no, you won't," his brother-in-law declared, clumsily raising his bulk from the chair. "You'll *not* be excused. I won't permit you to treat us in this cavalier style. Here we are, the best friends and well-wishers you have in the world! Do you intend to leave us in the dark, after we've spent a sleepless night and a fruitless morning in your behalf?"

"That's *just* what I intend to do," Drew told him, a slight smile curling the corners of his mouth. "If you are foolish enough to lose time and sleep worrying over me, you must not expect *me* to feel responsible."

"You're a thankless, selfish monster," his sister pouted. "Where are you off to so rudely, if I may be permitted to ask?"

"I suppose you may ask," her brother retorted. "But I don't necessarily have to answer." And he turned and walked away to the stairs.

Hetty looked at Wys and Selby in irritation. "He's quite infuriating," she said. "I don't know why we bother about him at all." But she rose from her seat and ran out after him. Wys looked at Selby, shrugged and followed. Selby, shaking his head mournfully and feeling much put-upon, toddled after them.

Hetty had stopped halfway down the stairs and was observing her brother in the hallway below. Ignoring Mallow, who was handing Drew his high-crowned hat and a pair of grey leather gloves, she called out, "I insist that you at least tell me where you're going."

Unmoved, Drew put on his hat and, consulting a mirror hanging on the wall near the front door, adjusted it to a rakish angle. Then he turned to the stairway. There, in various attitudes of irritation or consternation, stood his three 'well-wishers.' He smiled broadly. "I'm going to pay a call on Lady Rowle," he said.

"Lady Rowle!" gasped Wys. "You're mad!"

"She won't let you into the house," Selby stated firmly.

"And if she did, I don't see what good it would do," Hetty added. "She'll only have you turned out and make you look a bigger fool than you did last night."

"Thank you, *dear* sister, for those comforting words," Drew answered with a sardonic bow.

"Of course," Wys mused optimistically, "if you've changed your mind and intend to tell her the story..."

"I have *not* changed my mind," Drew said firmly.

"Then damme if I see what good it will do you to see her," Selby muttered irritably.

Drew looked up at the three worried faces staring down at him and was forced to grin again. "Would it not solve everything to have the world see me everywhere in the company of Lady Rowle, her hand on my arm, her face gazing up at me in adoration?" he asked of his astounded audience.

Wys snorted and Selby choked. "In *adoration*?" Hetty asked incredulously. "Are you completely demented? You propose to convince her to appear on your arm in public, gazing up at you in—in—?" Words failed her.

"Told you he was mad," muttered Wys, shaking his head.

"*I'm* willing to be convinced," Selby said in a calm but skeptical tone. "How do you propose to accomplish this preposterous plan?"

"It's quite simple," Drew said with a twinkle. "I propose to *marry* the girl." And he touched his cane to his hat in a gesture of farewell and went quickly from the house, leaving the others staring after him, completely speechless at last.

Chapter Three

THE ROWLE TOWN HOUSE was the only property inherited by his widow after the estate had been settled, but it was an elegant legacy. Wide and imposing, it was set well back from the street, its circular driveway lined with aging shrubs and the front door flanked by an impressive row of fluted columns. The most impressive house on a fashionable street, it gave mute evidence of the wealth which had once sustained the family. That wealth, Gwen Rowle soon realized, was almost completely dissipated in paying the enormous debts that came due at the time of Rowle's death. Were it not for the generosity of the dowager Lady Hazel Rowle, who lived with Gwen and who had independent means, Gwen would not have been able to stretch her small income to sustain an establishment of that size.

Gwen had formed a close attachment to Rowle's mother from the first, and their mutual affection had been a solace to both of them during the months following Rowle's death. Each accepted with good grace the foibles and eccentricities of the other—Lady Hazel, with Gwen's blessing, saw to the running of the house, and although the older woman enjoyed surrounding herself with the pomp of liveried servants, gilt-edged dishes, and massive, old-fashioned furniture, Gwen did not voice any objections; on the other hand, when Gwen's parents sent her young brother Tom to live with them, hoping the seventeen-year-old would acquire a bit of town-bronze, Lady Hazel put up with his breezy, noisy informality without a word of complaint.

This morning, as Lady Hazel joined her daughter-in-law and young Tom at the breakfast table, she had every intention of provoking a quarrel. Gwen was behaving like a stubborn fool, and Lady Hazel had lain awake all night working up the determination to put an end to it. With a brusque good-morning, she gingerly lowered herself into her chair and reached shakily for the teapot.

"Are you quite well this morning, Hazel dear?" Gwen asked, looking at her mother-in-law closely. Hazel was a remarkable woman, her tall, spare frame belying her inner strength. Looking at her long, thin fingers and her tiny wrists, one would think that the slightest disturbance would cause her to break. But she had been a tower of strength to Gwen through her troubled marriage and its tragic aftermath, and Gwen had learned that—despite her fragile appearance and delicate manner—she possessed a character of sturdy stuff. This morning, though, Gwen detected dark shadows under Hazel's pale blue eyes and a more-than-usual tremor in her fingers. Her heart went out to Hazel in pain and guilt.

"Don't concern yourself with me, my dear," Hazel said reassuringly, "I didn't sleep very well, that's all."

"I thought as much. You upset yourself over our talk yesterday, didn't you?"

"I suppose so."

"What's the trouble, Aunt Hazel?" Tom put in. In the two months since he'd been living with them, he had become quite fond of her and had given her the honorary title 'aunt.' "Has Gwen been making a nuisance of herself?"

"Well, listen to *you*!" his sister remonstrated. "Who's the nuisance here? I suppose it was *I* who was more than an hour late for tea yesterday!"

"That's not what has upset you, is it Aunt Hazel?" Tom asked in a wheedling tone.

"No, of course not, dear. Only it *is* unsettling not to be able to serve tea at the proper time. You *will* see to it that you're not late today, won't you?"

"Well, perhaps you shouldn't wait for me at all. The fellows and I are going to take a ride into the country in Ferdie's new phaeton, and I'd rather not have to worry about the time."

His sister looked at him crossly. "Are you going out with Ferdie again? I don't like you to spend so much time with him."

"Why not?" he asked belligerently, but before his sister had a chance to answer the boy went into a paroxysm of coughing.

Hazel and Gwen exchanged looks. "If your cough is acting up again, Tom, perhaps you shouldn't go out today," Hazel suggested mildly.

"Humbug! This little cough don't signify," Tom answered, unconscious of having spoken disrespectfully to the dignified lady who was looking at him in concern.

"Don't bother to argue with him, Hazel. The boy never admits to being sick. Mama could never keep him in bed, even when he was little," Gwen said.

"Right," Tom agreed complacently. "But let's get back to Ferdie. What is wrong with my seeing him?"

Gwen shrugged. "I don't know. He just seems a bit rackety to me."

"Rackety! He's due to come into twenty thousand

pounds before long," her brother hooted.

"I've never heard that a big income gives a man character," Hazel murmured mildly.

"I say, Aunt Hazel, whose side are you on?" Tom demanded. "Didn't you just say that it was Gwen who upset you, not me? I don't want *my* hair combed because you're in a pucker over something *Gwen* said!"

"Really, Tom, I'm not 'in a pucker' at all! Wherever do you find such dreadful expressions?" Hazel remonstrated.

Gwen regarded Hazel with troubled eyes. "But you *are* in a pucker, I can tell. Is it about that dreadful Drew Jamison coming here again?"

Tom turned to his sister eagerly. "*Is* he coming here again? I say, Gwen, if he does, *please* let him in this time! It would really raise my credit with the fellows if I told them I'd breakfasted with 'Sure-shot' Jamison!"

Gwen whitened. "Tom!" she said, shocked.

Tom, realizing what he'd said, looked hastily at Hazel. "Oh. Sorry, Aunt Hazel. Sorry, Gwen. I didn't mean—"

"You're becoming quite incorrigible, Tom," Gwen said tightly, "and I'll thank you not to say things you have to be sorry for. In fact, it would be best if you did not mention that man's name in this house. As for my admitting him, I can assure you that I'll never do so—not while I have a breath in my body."

Tom shrugged and got to his feet. "I can't seem to say anything right this morning. If you'll excuse me, then, I'll take myself off." With a wave to his sister and a kiss dropped lightly on Hazel's head, he left the room.

Hazel looked across the table at her daughter-in-law in disapproval. Gwen was behaving in a decidedly unnatural—even unhealthy—way. The manner in which she had jumped on poor Tom, who hadn't meant any harm at all, was a sign of her oversensitivity on the subject of Rowle's death. She, Rowle's mother, naturally couldn't expect her own grief to have diminished by this time—she knew that she would always carry that pain with her. But Gwen had been Rowle's wife for less than a year. She was young and had her whole life before her. Surely it was neither desirable nor normal for Gwen to dwell so morbidly on the past.

Lady Hazel was a sensible and realistic woman, and she well knew what sort of man her son had been. Even as a child, he'd been spoiled and willful. Then he'd succeeded to his titles before he was mature enough to understand the responsibilities that accompanied them. He had been well on his way to dissolution and impoverishment when the duel took his life. Lady Hazel had never been able to control him, even when he was a boy, and had watched with anguish as the passing years had sunk him deeper and deeper into self-indulgence, corruption and debt. Her grief at his death had been somewhat tempered by the knowledge that, had he lived, his future would have held only misery for his family and himself.

But Gwen's grief, excessive to begin with, had turned to bitterness. Lady Hazel suspected that Gwen's excess was caused by hidden feeling of guilt about her marriage. It was quite possible that Gwen had taken upon herself the blame for Rowle's weaknesses. Lady Hazel sighed. Poor Gwen, married such a short time, had been left with a legacy of grief and guilt. Lady Hazel was determined to do something to prevent Gwen from poisoning her future with recriminations and bitterness. This business with Drew Jamison was the place to draw the line.

Lady Hazel had never met Lord Jamison, but she knew enough about him by reputation to be sure that he had not killed her son in cold blood, as Gwen was determined to believe. The murdering monster that Gwen had conjured up had no relationship to the sound, sensible, kind, and well-balanced young man she knew Jamison to be. She'd heard many stories of his generosity to his friends, knew that he was adored by his servants, that he managed his estates astutely, that he was *not* a hothead (there had never, until the duel, been a word of scandal attached to his name), that he was spoken of with admiration by all of society and (most revealing of all that his character was above reproach) that every woman Hazel knew who had a marriageable daughter would have preferred Drew for a son-in-law over any other man in London. Now, because of Gwen's rash behavior in Lady Hester Selby's ballroom, Lord Jamison's reputation was being ruined by rumors and whispers, and Gwen had withdrawn again into her bitter retirement. This nonsense had to stop.

Lady Hazel looked across the table and studied her daughter-in-law's frowning face. Gwen looked utterly lovely despite the fact that her bronze-colored hair was not yet dressed for the day, but instead framed her face and fell to her shoulders in appealingly-disordered waves, and that her dark eyes were stormy and her long fingers plucked nervously at the sleeves of her loose morning robe. Hazel loved this stubborn girl. In the year of her marriage to Rowle she had shown what she was made of, and in the terrible months after Rowle's death she had been Lady Hazel's only source of love and sympathy. While there was breath in Hazel's body, she would prevent this girl from throwing herself away on the altar of guilt. She took a deep breath and plunged again into the skirmish that had been taking place at their breakfast table repeatedly during the last few days. "Do you mean to say," she challenged, "that you intend to refuse to see him again today?"

"That's *just* what I intend," Gwen said waspishly, "if he has the effrontery to make another appearance at my door."

"Aren't you in the least bit curious? Don't you want to know what it is he wants to see you about?"

"I know what he wants. He wants to apologize. As if an apology can make amends for murder!"

"Gwen, I wish you would stop calling it murder. You must know perfectly well that it was nothing of the kind."

"What do *you* call the shooting of your own son?" Gwen burst out angrily. Then, immediately contrite, she reached across the table and squeezed her mother-in-law's hand. "Oh, Hazel, forgive me! That dreadful man is turning me into a thoughtless shrew. He's opened up all the wounds again."

"*He's* not to blame for that. All he did was to dance with a girl he'd never seen before. It was *you* who caused the upset."

"I don't want to talk about that any more. I only want to apologize to *you* for permitting Rowle's name to crop up so often..."

"Nonsense!" Hazel said with asperity. "I don't wince at the sound of Edward's name. You may talk of him as much as you like. In fact, I wish you would. What upsets me, my dear, is your stubbornness. It's so unlike you, you know."

"About *what* am I being stubborn? It's *that man* who repeatedly tries to see me—"

"There. You keep calling him *that man*. Why can't you call him Lord Jamison? That's a sign of stubbornness. And you're stubborn in insisting that the accident was murder."

"It was murder! What else could it have been?"

"If Drew Jamison had done anything wrong in that duel, he would have been brought before the magistrates—"

"A man with titles and influence doesn't have to answer for his crimes!" Gwen said bitterly. "Sir George told me—"

"Sir George is a...a...," Lady Hazel faltered.

"A what?" Gwen asked, looking at Hazel curiously.

"Never mind. I don't trust anything he says, however."

"I don't see why."

"Don't you?" Lady Hazel's faded blue eyes studied Gwen's face shrewdly. "Are you...er...partial to Sir George, my dear?"

Gwen shrugged. "He's witty and handsome and good company. He helps to take my mind off—" She cut herself off abruptly.

Lady Hazel had disliked George Pollard ever since he had befriended her son. She suspected that Pollard had encouraged Rowle to indulge in gambling and dissolute living even more than he normally would. Hazel certainly didn't want to see her beloved Gwen become attached to yet another loose fish. But it would not do to oppose her now. Now was the time to urge her to seek male companionship, not to encourage her to view all males with suspicion. "I understand," she said pleasantly, "and I'll say no more against him. I'm delighted to see you amuse yourself in male company. But ..."

"But?"

"If I were young," Lady Hazel added, giving her daughter-in-law a roguish glance, "I know whose company *I'd* seek ..."

"Whose?" asked Gwen banteringly, glad to turn the conversation from the serious and morbid to the nonsensical and light.

"Drew Jamison's, of course."

"Drew—!" gasped Gwen, her smile fading.

"Yes, my dear, Drew. I'm told he's the most handsome, the most witty, the most charming of all the bachelors in London. The very man you've kept cooling his heels downstairs for three mornings in a row," Hazel said, meeting her daughter-in-law's kindling eye without a blink.

"If you intend to keep harping on the subject of that *detestable* man, I shall leave the table," Gwen declared, pushing her chair back angrily.

Lady Hazel remained unmoved. "What?" she asked tauntingly. "Without even waiting for the footman to bring up his card, so that you can tear it and send it down again?"

"What makes you so sure he'll try again today?" Gwen asked.

"I'm not *sure* at all. I only *hope*."

"Hope! What a thing to say! Do you *enjoy* seeing him vex me this way?"

"No, not at all. But the man has something to say to you, and I for one am filled with curiosity." She looked up

at Gwen with a challenging and spirited sparkle. "Why
don't you go up to your room, my dear? Then, when he
comes, *I* can see him and find out what he wants."

Gwen put her hands on her hips and glared at her
mother-in-law, half in amusement and half in irritation.
"Oh, no," she said firmly, "I won't give you the
opportunity to invite that man in. I'll keep him from
setting foot in this house if I have to sit here all morning,
every morning, for the rest of my life!"

Lady Hazel hid her smile, looked down at her hands
and said demurely, "Whatever you wish, my dear."

Gwen snorted, glared at Lady Hazel and dropped back
into her chair, pouring herself a third cup of tea with a
huge sigh of resignation.

It was only a few minutes later when Lord Jamison
presented himself, for the fourth time, at the door of the
Rowle town house. Three times before, he had knocked
on the door, been admitted by the butler, and had handed
his calling-card to that overdressed, august personage.
Three times before, the butler had crossed the hallway to
the liveried footman waiting at the bottom of the stairs,
the two had conferred, and the footman had taken the
tray, and slowly mounted the stairs. After disappearing
for a moment into a room at the top of the first landing,
the footman had emerged, had slowly descended the
staircase, given the tray to the butler, and impassively
resumed his station at the foot of the stairway. The butler
had recrossed the floor with his stately tread and held out
the tray for Lord Jamison's inspection. On it lay his card,
torn in half. Three times the butler had bowed and said,
"It appears that her ladyship is not at home," and had
opened the door, clearly hinting that Lord Jamison was
expected to withdraw. Three times Drew had done so.

This time, however, Drew had had enough of the
charade. With a decidedly militant look in his eye, he
placed his card on the silver tray. The butler bowed and
turned, as usual, to take the tray to the footman. Drew

quickly crossed the floor and took the stairs two at a time.
"I'll announce myself," he called back over his shoulder.
Before the butler and his henchman realized what had
happened, Drew had reached the landing. And by the
time they'd recovered from their astonishment, he had
disappeared into the breakfast room.

Closing the door behind him and placing his back
firmly against it, Drew looked quickly about him. The
two occupants of the room were staring at him in
astonishment. One was a tall, imposing lady with iron-
grey hair and a pair of eyes that were both shrewd and
kind. She was undoubtedly Rowle's mother. As his eyes
met hers, her startled look was replaced by an expression
which Drew could only describe as glee. He gave her a
smile, a polite bow, and turned to look at her breakfast
companion.

With his first glance at Gwen, Drew found that he
himself was not immune to surprise. He had found
Gwen's beauty ravishing on the night of his sister's ball,
but now the sight of her caused him to miss a breath. Her
pale skin, the glowing hair falling loosely over her
shoulders, the curve of her breasts under her soft peignoir
and, most of all, her dark eyes which were at first wide
with shock and were now fiery with mounting fury—all
combined to stun him.

The sound of hasty footsteps on the stairs outside the
door brought him quickly to his senses. He turned to the
grey-haired lady who sat calmly regarding him with an
almost imperceptible smile. "Lady Hazel Rowle, is it not?
Your servant, ma'am," he said to her, an answering smile
hovering at the corners of his mouth. Then, turning to
Gwen, he made an exaggeratedly formal bow. "Ah, Lady
Rowle! I'm delighted to find you home *at last*."

"How *dare* you burst in on us like this!" Gwen hissed.

"Burst in on you?" Drew responded innocently. "I was
sure you'd be expecting me!"

"And so we were, my dear boy," said Lady Hazel,
rising and offering him her hand.

Drew raised her hand to his lips and then met her eye.

"Rowle was as fortunate in his mother as in his wife," he said.

"Thank you, my lord. But, will you excuse me, please? There seems to be a commotion in the hall that I must see to."

"Yes, please do," Gwen said between clenched teeth. "And ask them to come in here and remove this . . . gentleman."

"Yes, my dear, I'll see to it, I assure you," Lady Hazel said quickly, as Drew stood aside to let her pass. "I shall certainly see to it . . . in due course." And she left the room hastily, closing the door behind her.

Gwen rose from her chair in open-mouthed dismay. "In due course?" she cried. "I want him removed at *once*!" There was no response. The sounds in the hallway retreated, and it became quite clear to her that assistance from her mother-in-law would not be immediately forthcoming.

She stamped her foot in chagrin. Determined to take matters into her own hands, she crossed the room in angry strides, intending to open the door and call the servants herself. She found her way blocked by Drew, who had resumed his position with his back against the door. For a silent moment her eyes burned furiously into his. Smiling, he looked back at her, his eyes both imperturbable and appreciative. This only infuriated her more.

"Stand aside, sir," she ordered coldly, "unless it is your intention to keep me prisoner here."

"How can you be so foolish?" he responded, his voice warm and affectionate.

"Then of course you will let me by."

"Of course," he assured her. "I'm yours to command— as soon as we've finished our conversation."

"I don't intend to have any conversation with you. We have nothing whatever to say to each other."

"I don't like to disagree with you so early in our . . . relationship . . . but I have a great many things to say to *you*."

"Whatever they are, I don't wish to hear them. I must

ask you again either to leave this room or to permit me to do so."

"I think this is what is known as an impasse," Drew remarked conversationally. "You refuse to speak to me, and I refuse to leave until you do."

"You speak as though we're evenly matched," Gwen said, lifting her chin defiantly. "Don't overestimate the strength of your position, sir. Although you seem to have enlisted—heaven knows why!—the support of my mother-in-law, you should realize that I have but to scream to rouse an army of servants who will rush to my assistance."

"Scream, by all means," Lord Jamison said encouragingly. "However, I'd be much obliged if you could postpone doing so for a moment or two. In that time, I could have my say and depart content."

"I've no desire to aid you in achieving contentment," Gwen snapped.

"So it seems," Drew said wryly. "But even in wars, the opposing armies take time to parlay. If you give me my few minutes, I'll depart quite willingly, and you won't find it at all necessary to scream and create a vulgar scene."

Gwen glared at him for a moment. Then, with a shrug, she sat down at the table and propped her chin in her hand. "The 'vulgar scene' would be of your creating, not mine," she said, "but you're right in believing that I've no love of such display. Very well. Have your 'parlay' and be gone."

"May I sit down?"

Gwen merely waved to the chair nearest him. He sat down and smiled at her disarmingly. "Lady Rowle," he began, "since I have, albeit unintentionally, robbed you of a husband, I would like to make restitution."

"Restitution?" Gwen recoiled at the word. Was he suggesting some sort of financial settlement? "You cannot mean to . . . to *pay me off*?" she exclaimed, horrified.

Drew's smile faded instantly. "Good God, no! How

could you think such a thing! Hang it, I'm doing this very badly..."

"What *did* you mean, then?"

"Well, to be blunt, ma'am, I'd like to provide you with another husband."

Gwen gasped. "Another husband?"

"Yes, indeed. I have in mind a gentleman not quite thirty, vigorous, in good health, of acceptable birth and breeding, with an affectionate nature and a kind heart," Drew said, a mischievous twinkle evident in his eyes.

"Indeed!" Gwen said icily. "Pray, who *is* this paragon?"

"Far from a paragon, my dear, but I'm convinced you can turn him into a passable husband. It is *I*."

Gwen did not blink or react to this declaration with any sign of surprise or interest. She leaned back in her chair and surveyed Drew with eyes that glittered coldly. "You've had your little joke, Lord Jamison. Is *this* why you've assaulted my door these many mornings? It hardly seems worth it."

"Joke, ma'am? You call my offer a joke?" he asked in mock offense. "I offer you my titles, my estates, my wealth, *myself*... and you think it a *joke*?"

"Will you be serious?" she said in disgust. "You forced your way in to see me at the cost of considerable time and effort. You must have had *some* purpose other than this rather tasteless nonsense."

Drew met her look of scorn with one of straightforward honesty. "Sorry. My joke wasn't meant to offend. Besides, it expresses my intentions truly enough. I mean to wed you, Gwen Rowle. I haven't expressed myself well, I know. I started at the end. What I intended was to make a beginning here today. To ask you to let me call. To court you... with all of the pomp and formality and ritual you'd find pleasing." He rose and bowed. "May I have the honor of calling on you soon, Lady Rowle?" he asked with a smile.

Neither his words nor his smile had caused her expression to soften, but now her eyes began to smolder, and she leaned toward him with a look of burning scorn. "I knew you were cruel and murderous," she said venomously, "and now I see the *arrogance* that breeds the rest!"

"Lady Rowle—!" he said, startled at the vehemence of her dislike.

"You are surprised I think you arrogant? What else but arrogance would lead you to imagine that I'd even consider marriage to the man who murdered my husband?"

"The accusations of murder that you've hurled at my head so repeatedly are a definite impediment to our budding relationship," he remarked, unruffled. "It would help the development of our intimacy in great measure if you tried to accept the fact that I did *not* murder your husband."

"Intimacy! I've not the slightest desire to develop an intimacy with you! And as for accepting the fact that you're not a murderer, why *should* I accept such a lie? Did you not, a few moments ago, admit that you deprived me of a husband?"

"Yes, Lady Rowle. To my everlasting regret, I did. It was an accident, not murder."

"So you would have the world believe. But I am not fooled."

He looked at her keenly, the smiling glint in the back of his eyes fading. "My word means nothing to you then?"

"Less than nothing."

Drew, nonplussed, tried to plunge ahead, although the difficulty of his task was beginning to be apparent. "Nevertheless, I've offered myself to you. Even a murderer, I trust, may make amends. And may be turned into a worthy man by the love of a good woman."

"Perhaps. But the tendency toward violence in a man is completely repugnant to me. As repugnant as your suggestion that there could ever be anything between us."

And she stood up to indicate that his few minutes had come to an end.

Drew rose, circled the table, and confronted her squarely. With the disarming smile that Gwen was beginning to find rather disconcerting, he lifted her chin. "I hope you change your mind, my girl," he said softly. "There's an attraction between us that should not be dismissed so summarily. It's not often that two people are suited in as many ways as we are."

"Suited?" she asked scornfully, making no effort to pull her chin from his hand. "In what ways?"

"I think you know as well as I. For one thing, our minds seem attuned—each one follows the other's thinking so easily. For another, we laugh at the same things. For a third—" He paused.

She couldn't help asking, "A third?"

"Yes," he said. "For a third, this!" He pulled her into his arms and kissed her, holding her close against him until they both were breathless. When at last he let her go, he turned quickly away, picked up his hat and cane, and went to the door. Just before opening it, he turned back, his eyes again appreciative, his smile warm. "I'll see you again, Gwen Rowle. I don't give up so easily. But you may relax at breakfast in future. I'll find some other, less violent way to secure your company." And he bowed, put on his hat, and was gone—leaving Gwen staring at the door, her breast heaving with several confusing emotions she did not dare identify.

Chapter Four

GWEN OPENED HER EYES to the sound of the wind blowing the autumn leaves against her windowpane. She knew it must be early; there was no sound of household activity, and her abigail had not yet scratched at her door. Not quite awake, but not wishing to go to sleep again, she sat up, plumped up her pillows, and settled herself against them. For a while her mind drifted aimlessly in that state between sleep and waking where the dream can't be remembered but the feelings of the dream persist. What had she dreamed that had left her in this wistful mood?

Her eyes absently noted the streak of sunlight on the ceiling, sunlight which had stolen in through the gap of her window curtains. In that narrow streak of light the shadow of the leaves outside her window danced enticingly. It will be a beautiful day, she thought idly, the

kind of day that pulls one out of doors: a day to stroll
through the woods, to smell the tang of the air, to feel the
wind tingle the hairs at the back of the neck. If only one
had someone with whom to share the day...

Inevitably, as it had every morning for the past three
weeks, her mind turned to Drew. He would have made an
exciting companion on a ramble through the woods, if
only... if only... She shook herself in annoyance. How
irritating it was to find him in her thoughts so constantly.
He had shot her husband in a duel, he had embarrassed
her in public, and he had invaded her home and her
privacy. He was a violent, overbearing, unfeeling
creature, and she debased herself by thinking of him. Yet
at unexpected and frequently-recurring moments, she
would find herself remembering his eyes with their glint of
amusement; or her face would redden at the recollection
of the strength of his arms around her and the pressure of
his lips against hers; sometimes the sound of his voice
came back to her: "I'll see you again, Gwen Rowle. I don't
give up so easily."

Three weeks ago he had said those words, and she had
not heard from him since. She was relieved, of course. Of
course. Still, it was surprising that he had declared himself
so vehemently and then dropped from her life. Perhaps
he'd reconsidered—regretted his impulsive behavior and
realized that it would be useless to persist. Gwen admitted
to herself that she felt disappointed at his withdrawal. He
should have put up a stronger fight for her. Oh, she would
have enjoyed refusing him again!

She had imagined that he would pursue her all over
London, and she had pictured several delightful scenes in
which she would revenge herself upon him. He would
approach her at Almack's, and she would give him the cut
direct. And all the dowagers would snicker at him behind
their fans, and his friends would turn away from him in
embarrassment. Or he would ride up beside her in the
park, and she would send him away with a sharp rebuff,
turn her horse, and gallop off—leaving him red-faced and

miserable in a cloud of dust. Or he would find her alone in a side sitting-room of the house of a mutual acquaintance, and he would fall on his knees before her and plead his case, but she would merely laugh scornfully, and he would stumble out of the room and run from the house in despair.

These were childish imaginings, she knew. It was far better that he'd withdrawn from the campaign. The best course for her was to put him firmly from her mind. She whipped the covers off with an air of determination and jumped out of bed. From this moment on, she would banish him from her life and her thoughts. And for that, she needed to arrange for herself a very, very busy day.

Lady Hazel had also arranged a busy day for herself. She did not often leave the comfort of the house, but today she determined to pay a call. She told Gwen that she was going to pay a call on Lady Ogilvie, although she had no such intention. Gwen kindly offered to accompany her, but this would interfere with Hazel's plan. Lady Hazel knew, however, that Gwen found Bess Ogilvie a dreadful bore, so it was not difficult to urge her to remain behind. Hazel had never before lied to Gwen, but she hoped the end would justify the means.

It was a little past eleven when she knocked at the door of the Selby house in St. James Square. When the butler opened the door, she saw Lady Hester standing in the hallway tying on her bonnet. "Oh, dear," Hazel said in obvious disappointment. "You are going out."

"Lady Rowle!" Hetty exclaimed, running to the door and grasping Hazel's hands. "How lovely to see you!"

"Thank you, my dear, but I don't want to keep you . . ." Hazel began.

"Nonsense. I was only going to call on that detestable brother of mi—" Hetty said unthinkingly, then stopped in embarrassment.

Lady Hazel patted her hand. "Then of course you must

go. I won't have you keeping that charming young man waiting on my account."

Hetty looked at Lady Hazel in surprise. "Do you *know* my brother, ma'am?" she asked hesitantly.

"I had the pleasure of meeting him briefly a few weeks ago, when he came to...er...call on my daughter-in-law. I must admit I was quite taken with him."

"It's very kind of you to say so...under the circumstances," Hetty said with appealing frankness.

"Not at all," Lady Hazel said crisply. "We must not permit a tragic accident to cause unnecessary bitterness between our families."

"Oh, Lady Rowle," said Hetty, reaching up and hugging the older woman impulsively, "you are so good! So good!"

"But you must hurry along, Lady Selby. I believe I hear your carriage at the door."

"I shall send it back to the stables, of course. I can visit with Drew at any time. Please go into the drawing room, Lady Rowle, and I'll join you in a moment."

"Well, if you're sure Drew won't miss you..." Hazel murmured in relief, and turned to do as she was bid.

When, a few minutes later, Hetty joined her guest in the drawing room, she found Lady Hazel looking about the room with interest. Hetty, always pursuing the latest styles, had had her drawing room decorated in the new Egyptian mode. The wall panels were painted white and edged with gilt, with Egyptian figures painted in the center of each. The gracefully-curved sofa had clawed feet, and a round table in the corner was supported by a pedestal which was ornately carved to represent two huge, winged beasts. All the furniture was upholstered in pale silks which, combined with the white walls—which were reflected in the large mirror over the fireplace—gave the room a surprisingly bright appearance. Lady Hazel, whose tastes ran to the dark, massive furniture of an earlier day, found herself rather uncomfortable in the midst of so much gilt and brightness.

"Won't you sit down?" Hetty asked, indicating the sofa.

Lady Hazel lowered her tall frame gingerly and sat uncomfortably on the edge of the seat.

"I'm afraid you don't think much of my Egyptian drawing room," Hetty grinned.

"Well, I..." Hazel began. "You see, it's all a bit too bright for me, my dear."

Hetty laughed. "What you mean is that you find it vulgar."

"Oh, no, my dear, of course not," Lady Hazel said hastily.

"You needn't be embarrassed. Selby and my odious brother agree with you. But I don't mind. There must be a terribly vulgar streak in me—I love this room!" she said in her endearingly forthright way.

"And so you should, Lady Selby, for I am sure it is...er...all the crack!"

"Thank you, Lady Rowle. But I'm sure you didn't come to see me to discuss my horrible taste in furniture," Hetty said, pulling up a chair with gilded arms, the ends of which were carved to form lions' heads. She perched lightly on it and looked eagerly at her guest.

"Well, my dear," said Lady Hazel, uncomfortable about broaching the subject so abruptly but plunging in anyway, "I've come to see you about this bumble-bath your brother and my Gwen have got themselves into. May I be absolutely frank, my dear?"

"I wish you will be. This whole affair has given me many a sleepless night," Hetty said, leaning forward with interest.

"Well then, without roundaboutation, I must tell you that Gwen has convinced herself that Lord Jamison is guilty of murder, and her mind will not be changed. Nevertheless, his visit a few weeks ago seems to have had a profound effect on her—"

"*Had* it?" Hetty asked eagerly. "I've tried and tried to

learn what happened that day, but Drew won't tell me a word about it."

"Gwen will not discuss it either. Believe me, my dear, I was sorely tempted to listen in at the keyhole that morning," Lady Hazel admitted with a twinkle, "but my old-fashioned conscience wouldn't permit me."

"If only *I* had had the chance!" Hetty grinned. "I have no conscience at all when it comes to eavesdropping."

Lady Hazel laughed briefly and then sighed as she returned to her subject. "Gwen has not been quite the same since Lord Jamison's visit. She mopes about the house, broods too much and goes off into a daydream in the middle of a conversation. Not at all like her. She is usually so...so..."

"Purposeful?" Hetty supplied.

Lady Hazel looked at Hetty gratefully. "Yes, the very word. Purposeful. And there is something else...troubling me about Gwen. I'm afraid her marriage to my son was not very happy, yet since his death I think she has been blaming herself for...well, for having failed to..."

Hazel was finding it difficult to speak frankly of her son. Hetty leaned forward and squeezed her hand. "I understand what you mean. I noticed myself that Gwen's reaction to Rowle's death was...strange."

Lady Hazel nodded. "You are very easy to talk to, my dear. Now, I come to the reason for this visit. If we are agreed that Gwen and your brother would both benefit from an end to their hostilities—"

"Oh, I would agree to more than that!" Hetty asserted, her enthusiasm causing her to forget her manners. "I want to see them *married*! Nothing less will satisfy me." She glanced at Lady Hazel quizzically. "Have I gone too far, Lady Hazel?"

Hazel smiled, but shook her head. "We mustn't hope for too much," she cautioned. "It will be enough to see Gwen overcome her bitterness and to restore Lord Jamison to the good graces of society."

"I suppose you're right," Hetty said, sighing. "But I

don't see how we're to bring even *that* to pass."

"Well, you see, I've thought of something."

"Have you?" Hetty said, delightedly clapping her hands. "How wonderful! We all—that is, Selby and Wystan Farr and I—have tried endlessly to find a way. What on earth have you thought of?"

The grey head leaned close to the curly auburn one, and a delightful hour passed in plotting stratagems. The plotting continued over a hastily-arranged luncheon of baked salmon, coddled eggs, country ham, cold roast beef, hot biscuits, stewed tomatoes, a ragout of veal, and a number of creams and jellies. By the time the two conspirators kissed each other goodbye, it was past two o'clock. Hetty saw Lady Hazel to the door, and, swinging her bonnet by the ribbons, she almost danced up the stairs to her sitting room where she spent the rest of the afternoon at her desk composing a number of carefully-worded notes. Meanwhile, Lady Hazel walked home with a decidedly youthful spring in her step, and a secret smile hovering at the corners of her mouth.

Lady Gwen Rowle had been persuaded by Sir George Pollard to join him and a couple of lively friends, Lady Flora and Sir Richard Warrenton, for a gay evening at the Covent Garden theater and a late supper afterwards at the Warrentons' table. Gwen had at first refused the invitation, for Lady Flora seemed to her a silly woman who responded to every remark with a giggle, as if everyone's purpose for speaking to her was to tease, and Sir Richard was a court-card who often rendered Gwen uncomfortable by staring at her decolletage through his quizzing-glass. However, Sir George was persistent, and Gwen had determined to keep herself busy, so she agreed at last. Now, sitting in a box at the theater at intermission time, she was glad she had come. The famous Mrs. Siddons was most affecting as Constance in *King John*, and Sir George had done everything to see to her comfort, even taking a seat between her and Lady Flora as if he understood that she did not enjoy having that lady giggling in her ear throughout the performance.

This intermission was the first moment he had permitted her to be alone, the Warrentons having gone off to visit with some acquaintance they had spied in another box, and Sir George to find her some refreshment. She leaned back in her seat and fanned herself contentedly. She let her eyes roam over the other boxes, and suddenly her fan ceased moving. Looking at her with his hint of a smile was Lord Jamison, comfortably ensconced in a box only two removed from her own. She stared at him coldly and turned away with a decided toss of her head. She hoped that the insolence of her gesture made it clear that she would not in any way acknowledge his presence.

To her chagrin, her pulse began to race in a most alarming way, and her cheeks became noticeably hot. She fanned herself rapidly and began to wish for Sir George's return. She did not like to be observed by *that man* while sitting here alone. She felt awkward and self-conscious and found herself strongly tempted to glance in his direction to see if he was still watching her, but of course she could not permit herself to do such a thing. After an endless moment, the door of the box opened, and she turned gratefully to welcome Sir George. But it was Drew who stood smiling down at her.

"Good evening, Lady Rowle. Are you enjoying the play?" he asked comfortably, seating himself beside her without leave. She turned her head away from him in annoyance. "A number of people have seen us," Drew continued smoothly. "Do you want to set the tongues wagging again?"

Gwen turned to face him, trying to keep her expression calm. "It is very like you to cause this awkward scene and then to blame *me* for the result. If you didn't want tongues wagging, why did you come in?"

"It's been some time since I've seen you. I couldn't resist the opportunity to pay my respects and tell you how dazzlingly lovely you look tonight."

"Perhaps that was your intention, but instead you accuse me of setting the tongues wagging! Do all your intended compliments end by being insults, sir?"

"I sincerely hope not," he said ruefully.

Gwen glanced around the theater and noticed the many faces staring at them, accompanied by much surreptitious whispering behind programs and fans. "Oh, dear, they *are* watching," she said, dismayed.

"We are an interesting drama in ourselves, I'm afraid— to some, more interesting than the one on the stage. If you cry 'Murderer!' and order me out of the box with a large gesture of your arm, everyone in London will know by morning that I have accosted you again," Drew suggested, his eyes smiling into hers in that irritatingly disconcerting way.

Gwen raised her chin proudly. "I am not as vulgar as you seem to think! I do *not* enjoy being part of a public spectacle." She glanced around again, uneasily. "What can we do to prevent their whisperings?"

"If you but nod and smile at me in a friendly way, they will have little to gossip about," Drew suggested.

"If I nod and smile at you, will you leave?"

Drew grinned at her broadly. "My dear, if you nod and smile at me, I'll go to the ends of the earth for you," he said extravagantly.

Gwen's lips twitched. "There's no need to go quite so far," she said. "Back to your box will do." And she gave him a dazzling smile, permitting her face to be seen by as many observers as possible, and held out her hand to him. He rose, took her hand and kissed it, then looked at her with a twinkle.

"As you wish, my dear," he said. Still holding her hand, he added softly, "Do you see now that it is quite easy to behave kindly to me?"

"Easy!" she exclaimed, carefully keeping the false smile on her face. "I find this the most difficult thing I've ever done. What I'd *really* like to do is...is..."

"What, my dear?"

"Push you over the railing!" she said, withdrawing her hand from his but keeping the smile fixed on her face.

"You really are utterly enchanting, you know," he said. He went to the door but turned back before leaving. "Was *that* a proper compliment, ma'am?" he asked. But she didn't turn around.

George Pollard came in at that moment, a glass of champagne in each hand. He stopped short on seeing Lord Jamison and gaped.

"Good evening, Pollard," Drew said politely, then bowed with a flourish and went out quickly.

"Good Lord!" Pollard exclaimed. "What was *he* doing here?" He crossed the box quickly, spilling champagne heedlessly as he walked. "Damn the man! Has he made a disturbance here?" he demanded, his black eyes glinting coldly.

"No, no, I assure you," Gwen said, surprised and a little perturbed by the hate in Pollard's eyes. "He was quite polite, really. There's nothing to disturb yourself about." She took a glass of champagne from his hand and sipped it calmly. "Sit down, Sir George, or you'll have the tongues wagging again."

Pollard reseated himself, put down his drink, and picked up his omnipresent ebony and ivory cane. He swung it thoughtfully, smacking the ivory handle into the palm of his left hand with, Gwen thought, irritating regularity. His eyes still smoldered. "I suppose *that* was his purpose in coming here," he said.

"What?" Gwen asked, not following.

"His reason for accosting you here. To win back his place in the world by forcing you to acknowledge him," he said shrewdly.

Gwen's eyes flew to Sir George's face in surprise. It had not occurred to her that the careless raillery with which Drew had entertained her could have been calculated. "Do you think so?" she asked, aware of a sharp pang of disappointment cutting into what had been a very pleasant mood. "I suppose you're right," she sighed. "Yet he seemed rather indifferent to the gossipers. That is . . . yes, I'm sure you must be right. That *dreadful* man has used me again."

When the play resumed, Gwen found herself too depressed to follow it. Sir George continued to swing his cane. "Must you do that?" she whispered impatiently.

Pollard leaned close and whispered sympathetically, "Jamison *has* upset you, hasn't he? Would you like to leave, my dear?"

"No, of course not," Gwen whispered back. "The Warrentons seem to be completely absorbed. We mustn't disturb them."

Sir George nodded, put down his cane, and let his arm fall over the back of her chair. With his other hand he lifted her chin. "Then smile, my dear, smile," he said softly, his face close to hers. "I want you to have a merry evening."

Made uncomfortable by the intimacy of his attitude, Gwen's eyes stole to Drew's box. Somehow she could not bear to have him see George Pollard leaning over her this way. But Drew was not there.

Later, as he drove her home in the Warrentons' phaeton, she could not refrain from questioning him about the subject most on her mind. "I've been wondering, Sir George, why you've never told me the details of Rowle's duel."

Sir George frowned. "You needn't know the details. They're not a woman's business."

"But I must know," she urged, "if it was a fair fight. Did Lord Jamison give Edward a fair chance to—?"

"How could it have been fair?" Pollard interrupted brusquely. "Everyone knows that Jamison is a crack shot."

"Yes," Gwen sighed, "but even so, if everything had been done according to the rules . . . ."

"You mustn't ask me to reveal any secrets concerning Jamison or that duel. Having been a participant, it would not be honorable to do so. All I can tell you is that the entire affair made a mockery of the word 'honor.' But no good can come of this talk. You must put the business out of your mind."

"I will try. But one more question, please. Are you hinting that . . . Lord Jamison did something dishonorable? Did he truly murder my husband?"

"I can only answer that by suggesting that you deduce what you can from the facts. Here was a man whose ability to handle a pistol is unquestioned, facing a green boy whose hand was unsteady with sick fear. What do those facts tell you?"

A sound of agonized pain came from Gwen's throat. "It would seem . . . that he is . . . indeed . . . *guilty* of . . . murder . . ." she said in a choked voice.

"Then what more can I say?" Pollard said blandly. "Best to forget it all, my dear. Best to forget it."

"I wish I could," Gwen said quietly, as a wave of utter misery washed over her.

Chapter Five

TOM, ALREADY DRESSED FOR the day in a neat double-breasted blue coat and fashionably tight breeches, emerged from his 'aunt' Hazel's bedroom with a conspiratorial smile lingering on his lips. He looked up and down the corridor and, satisfied that no one was about, returned quickly to his own room. There he stripped off his coat, put on a rather shabby dressing gown, and studied himself in his shaving mirror. Making an exaggeratedly miserable face, he coughed several times in a pitiable manner and then smiled at his reflection as if he were quite pleased with himself. This strange behavior seemed to satisfy him immensely.

Still smiling, he emerged from his bedroom and made his way down to the breakfast room. Before he entered, however, he carefully re-arranged his expression to duplicate the miserable one he had practiced in the mirror. In the manner of an actor making an entrance, he opened the door. "Good morning, Gwen," he said in a tired croak, and took his seat with a sigh.

Gwen looked at him with raised eyebrows. "Not dressed yet, my dear?" she asked. "I thought you were engaged for riding again this morning."

"Changed my mind," Tom answered gruffly, reaching for the coffeepot. There he stayed his hand as his chest shook in a spasm of coughing.

Gwen looked at him sharply. "Aren't you feeling well?"

Tom shook his head vehemently. "I'm fine, fine. Don't kick up a dust over a little cough."

Gwen was about to remonstrate when a knock at the door interrupted her. Mitching, the butler, entered carrying several notes on a tray. "These arrived this morning, Lady Rowle," he said, and placed the tray beside her plate.

"Thank you, Mitching," Gwen said absently, her eyes still on her brother. Mitching, about to withdraw, opened the door in time to admit Lady Hazel, who looked bright-eyed and cheerful in a flowered morning dress. "Good morning, my lady," the butler said with a bow. He stepped aside to let her pass and left the room, closing the door behind him.

Lady Hazel smiled at her daughter-in-law and Tom. "Good morning, good morning. I see you have both risen before me today." She took her place and looked across at Tom. "Not yet dressed, my boy? Is anything amiss?"

"No, no," Tom said in very convincing annoyance. "You two fuss over me like a couple of old hens. I'm just a bit tired, that's all. I think I'll go back to bed after . . ." And he coughed again, a good long spasm.

"We may be a couple of old hens," Gwen said shortly, "but that cough of yours doesn't seem to be getting any better."

"It's nothing, I tell you," Tom said and began to cough

again. He felt Hazel kick him under the table and cut the spasm short.

"It's just as well that you're returning to bed," Hazel said calmly. "I think it's going to rain before long. Nothing is more chilling to the bones than an October rain. A day at home in a nice warm bed will be good for you."

Tom only grunted and sipped his coffee. Gwen sighed, shrugged and began to leaf through her messages. "Here are some for you, Hazel," she said, handing them across the table. Watching Gwen from under her lowered lids, Lady Hazel opened her notes with feigned eagerness. Gwen looked at one of her notes with surprise. "This is from Hester Selby! I wonder what she—" Gwen broke the seal and scanned the note quickly. Tom gave a quick cough, but she didn't look up.

"Nothing is wrong with Lady Selby, I trust," Hazel remarked.

"No, no. She only says she would like to call on me today and hopes I'll be at home. It's as if she were afraid I'd cut her!"

"Well, you *did* cut her brother, after all..." Lady Hazel murmured.

"That's very much beside the point," Gwen said defensively. "She *knows* I don't blame her for her brother's behavior. I wonder what she wants to see me about."

"You'll find out soon en—"

But Lady Hazel's words were interrupted by another paroxysm of coughing. Both ladies looked at Tom with concern. "Listen to him," Gwen said, troubled. "I think we should call Dr. Blackman, don't you?"

"I don't want to see any pill-peddler," Tom said grumpily. "It's nothing. Nothing. I think I'll just lie down for a while." And he went to the door, the merest totter in his step. As he passed Lady Hazel's chair, his back to his sister, he gave Hazel a broad wink.

Gwen looked after her brother with a troubled frown.

"He doesn't look at all well. Hazel, do you think I should send for Dr. Blackman?"

"Tom will be so cross if you do. Besides, I've found that doctors are quite ineffective in cases of inflammation of the lungs."

"Inflammation of the lungs!" Gwen cried, alarmed. "Do you think—?"

"No, no my dear, I don't think he's seriously ill. That is, not yet. I only fear that if his cough persists..."

"Well, what am I to do? He won't keep to his bed for long, I know that. He *does* love to engage in sporting activities with his friends, so he's bound to be up before long. And with the weather becoming worse..."

"We shall get him better, never fear. Don't worry so, my dear. I'll go down to the kitchen right now and make him some of my special herb tea," Lady Hazel said, rising and going to the door. With her hand on the knob, she looked back at Gwen with a sigh. "It's too bad that Brockhurst House is no longer ours. A couple of weeks in the country would have been the very thing for Tom. The very thing. Oh, well." And with another sigh, she left the room.

At the Selby house in St. James Square, Wys was staring at Hetty across the breakfast table with considerable suspicion. "I don't know, Hetty. Does Selby know what you're plotting?"

"I tell you, Wys, you are troubling yourself over nothing. Selby has been trying to wheedle me to agree to go to Suffolk these past two months. He says he's neglected his duties at Stonehaven for too long."

But Wys was not taken in. It was clear to him that Hetty was hoping to avoid facing Selby with the details of this preposterous plot she was hatching. "That is not an answer to my question. Does Selby know whom you're planning to invite?"

"There is no point in telling him until she accepts the invitation, is there?"

"Yes, there is," Wys said firmly. "By the time Lady Rowle agrees, it will be too late for Selby to put a stop to it."

Hetty glanced at her guest mischievously. "I see you have a basic understanding of the situation," she said with a giggle.

"Hetty!" Wys said, rising and frowning down at her in disapproval. "How can you use Selby so! I won't be a party to it."

"I'm not asking you to be a party to it," Hetty declared vehemently, her smile fading into a petulant pout. "You're behaving as if I were doing something reprehensible. I'll have you know this is not at all the case. I am merely making plans to rusticate for a few weeks at the manor house in Suffolk—something Selby has been urging me to do for the past age—and I mean to ask a friend or two to join us there. I'm certain Selby will see nothing objectionable in *that*."

"Yes, my dear," said Wys, feeling quite uncomfortable at the thought that Hetty was sharing with him the very information she was withholding from her husband. "But *tell* him first." He leaned toward her in earnest appeal. "I'll do whatever you ask of me if only you'll tell him first."

Hetty fixed her eyes on Wys coldly. "I'm sure you *mean* well, Mr. Farr, and I know you are an old and respected friend of the family—"

Wys sighed. "Now, Hetty—"

"But that does *not* give you the right to advise me on how to handle my own husband! Marriage is a subject about which you know absolutely nothing!"

"Through no fault of my own, I assure you," Wys murmured.

"Of course it's your own fault! I've put half a dozen wonderful young ladies in your way in the last few months. One was too shrill, and one was too plump, and one too silly, and one too bookish..."

Wys colored. "We were talking of another matter, I think," he suggested mildly, not any more willing to discuss his private affairs than he was to discuss Hetty's silly plan.

Hetty subsided. "You're right, of course. We were. That is, *you* were interfering in my marital affairs."

"I beg your pardon," Wys said amicably.

Hetty got up and began to pace about the room. "You are a most irritating person to quarrel with, Wys. You never get angry."

"I have nothing to be angry about," Wys said mildly. "May I have a bit more of this ham?"

Hetty, realizing that he was trying to change the subject, pouted. "You'll be as stout as Selby one day," she muttered.

"I suppose you're right. Well, then, I'll take my leave. If I remain here at the table, I shall be tempted to gorge myself." And he stood up again, a gleam of hope that he could escape from the whole affair brightening his eyes.

Hetty scurried up to him, the top of her curly head as high as his shoulder, and pushed him back into his chair. "Not until I have your word that you will bring Drew to Stonehaven by the end of the month!" she said stubbornly.

"Even if I were to agree, I don't see how I'm to manage it," he objected.

"I've *told* you how. You are to invite him to your shooting lodge in Melbourn. There you will become queasy and dispeptic, and suddenly it will occur to you that Selby and I are in residence at the manor, a mere two hour ride. You will suggest to Drew that you will get some proper care *chez nous!*"

"I don't see why you can't invite Drew yourself. It would be so much simpler."

"I can't very well assure Gwen Rowle that he won't be there if I've already invited him! Do you want me to *lie*?" Hetty asked with perfect sincerity.

"Your *scruples* are beyond me," sighed the put-upon Mr. Farr. "You're expecting *me* to lie to *Drew*, aren't you?"

"Yes, but if you do this *my* way, both Gwen and Drew will believe his arrival to be accidental. Only you and I will know..."

"And Selby, of course."

Hetty stamped her foot. "Dash it, Wys, leave Selby out of this! He's completely incapable of any sort of dissembling. He would stammer and cough and act uncomfortable. Believe me, the less he knows, the better our chances."

"I'm not particularly good at dissembling either, you know. Perhaps you ought to find another way to get Drew to Stonehaven," Wys suggested, still hoping to find a way out of this fix.

"You are not going to refuse me!" cried Hetty desperately. "You are my only hope!" She dropped down on her knees beside his chair and grasped his hand. "Please, Wys, please! You say Drew is your closest friend. You want to see him happy, don't you? You want his name cleared, don't you? You can't turn your back on him now!"

Wys looked down at the pert little face turned up to his. Her eyes were filling with tears. Selby and Drew had often laughed at Hetty's talent for making her eyes water at will, but Wys could not keep himself from being affected. Having been deprived of a mother at an early age, he was inexperienced in dealing with women. The least sign of tender emotions on a woman's face rendered him helpless and miserable. "Don't cry, Hetty, I beg you," he urged unhappily. "I'll do as you ask, I promise, but *do* get up, and don't cry!"

Hetty jumped to her feet, smiled at him sunnily and clapped her hands. "Dear, dear Wys! It will all work out beautifully, I know it will!"

An hour later, Hetty—wearing a high-crowned bonnet adorned with enormous, sweeping ostrich feathers dyed a bright shade of green—was ushered into Gwen's drawing room. Gwen, entering behind her, was quite unprepared for the sight. She gaped at the bonnet in some dismay. "Good heaven, Hetty, what a hat!"

"Don't you like it?" Hetty asked in consternation. "I paid a fortune for it, I can tell you. I've been afraid to show Selby the bill."

"Oh, it's quite magnificent. In fact, it's . . . it's as tall as *you* are!"

"Oh, dear," said Hetty, turning to the mirror over the mantelpiece and staring at herself critically, "I was *afraid* it would be too overpowering. I said those very words to the milliner, but she assured me I could carry it off."

"And so you can," Gwen said, smiling at her fondly. "It makes you look quite imposing."

Hetty looked at her friend dubiously. "Do you really think so? Well, I shan't trouble myself about it, since I'll be leaving town before having an opportunity to wear it again."

"Leaving town?" Gwen asked.

"Yes. Selby must go to Suffolk to see about the estates, and he *insists* that I accompany him. It's such a bore. Night after night with no company but a few Suffolk provincials."

"Sit down, Hetty, and let me give you some of this ratafia. There. Now, dreadful girl, tell me why you are complaining about a trip to Suffolk. Surely a few weeks in the country, basking in the lovely autumn sunshine, tramping through the leaves, breathing all that crisp country air, need not be considered such a trial?"

Hetty smiled at Gwen eagerly. "Do you really feel that way about the country?" she asked delightedly. "I'm so glad, because that's why I've come."

Gwen raised her eyebrows. "To hear my views on country life?"

"No, silly, of course not. To ask you to come *with* me."

"Come with you?" Gwen asked in surprise. "But why on earth—?"

"I would *so* enjoy your company. It's quite lonely at Stonehaven, you know, at least for me. Selby is closeted

for hours at a time with his bailiff, or he goes riding about
the estate seeing to the farms and the livestock, and what
have *I* to do with myself all day? But if you were with me,
we could take long walks and have some good gossips
over the embroidery frames, and play hearts and read to
each other... oh, all sorts of things..."

"Hetty," said Gwen wistfully, "it is lovely of you to
invite me, and I should truly enjoy spending a few weeks
with you, but..."

"But what, my dear? Surely Lady Hazel could spare
you for a while?"

"Yes, of course. But there are several other things that
would make it impossible. Thank you, Hetty, but—"

"What things?"

"My brother, for one. He's been looking a trifle out of
curl, and coughing a bit. I couldn't leave him now."

"He's not seriously ill, is he?"

"No, but a cough like that may worsen, you know, and
I'm terrified of his developing an inflammation of the
lungs."

Hetty nodded in sympathy, and the two sat in
thoughtful silence. Suddenly Hetty clapped her hands
eagerly and bounced up and down on her chair. "I have
it," she cried. "We'll take him to Stonehaven with us! A
few weeks in the country should do wonders for him.
Rustication is the very thing!"

Gwen surveyed her friend speculatively. "Isn't it
strange," she mused, "that Lady Hazel said those very
words this morning?"

"What words?" asked Hetty, blinking her eyes in what
she hoped was stupid innocence.

"That a couple of weeks in the country would be the
very thing for Tom." Gwen rose and paced back and forth
before the fireplace. "A couple of weeks in the country
would no doubt be good for *both* of us. Hetty, you *do*
make it all sound so tempting. I scarcely have the strength
to refuse you. But no, I couldn't accept. I couldn't. What
if...? I mean, suppose...?" Gwen sat down and twisted

her fingers in her lap. "Please don't be offended, my dear, but I cannot bring myself to visit you any more." And she lowered her head in embarrassment.

"Oh, I *see*," said Hetty. "It's Drew, isn't it. I was *afraid* that dreadful duel would come between us."

"Don't say that, Hetty. It needn't spoil *our* friendship at all. You may visit *here* whenever you like. I shall always be delighted to see you. But if I come to you, I run the risk of meeting your brother, and you understand that I must avoid that, don't you?"

"I suppose I understand. I've been reproaching myself for *weeks* about the occurrence at my ball. I was a fool to permit such a thing to happen."

"It was not your fault. You *had* to invite your brother to your own ball."

"Yes, but I didn't wish to cause you any pain or embarrassment. I truly believed that at such a tremendous squeeze—you know, there were at least two hundred people present—one could easily avoid anybody one wished to. I didn't know that you and Drew had never met and could not recognize each other."

"Hetty, don't blame yourself. Who could have foretold that he would ask a perfect stranger to dance with him—without an introduction!—or that I would be fool enough to permit him to do it."

"Well, it certainly was an unfortunate evening," Hetty sighed. "But nothing can be done to erase it. However, I shan't dwell on it, so long as you assure me that our friendship has not been destroyed."

"I promise you that it has not."

"Good," said Hetty with alacrity. "Then there's no reason why you can't come with me to Stonehaven."

"But, Hetty, you shatterbrain, I just explained—"

"I know, but you will not meet Drew at Stonehaven. He *never* goes there. It's Selby's place, after all. Not that we wouldn't welcome him, of course, but he has his own lands at Abingdon, and he usually can be found *there* when he's not in London. And there's another family estate in Devon, you know, so one can scarcely expect him to spend time at *our* place. Managing estates as extensive as his requires quite a bit of time, and Drew is very conscientious about his responsibilities, you see."

"Is he? I wouldn't have thought—! But never mind. Do you mean to say that he's never visited you at Stonehaven?"

"Of course he has, when he's been expressly invited. He spent Christmas there once, I remember. But he has not been invited this time, I promise. Believe me, my dear, you will be quite safe from him in Suffolk."

Gwen looked at her friend contritely. "Hetty, you must think me dreadfully rude. He *is* your brother, after all."

Hetty leaned over and pressed Gwen's hand. "No, I don't find you at all rude. I understand perfectly. But you will say you'll come, won't you?"

"Gladly," Gwen said with a warm smile, and the two sealed the bargain with a hug.

"So she hopes to diddle me, does she?" Selby asked, looking into his brandy glass, an angry sparkle in his eye.

"I didn't put it that way," Wys said uneasily. The two friends were seated in a corner of the lounge at White's, Wys having tracked Selby down for the purpose of revealing Hetty's plan. "I feel like a tattling old chubb telling you all this."

"And so you are, dear boy, and so you are. No point in roundaboutation: a tattler is a tattler."

"Would it have been better if I'd have gone along with her tricks?" Wys demanded defensively. "I *had* expected a bit more of gratitude from you."

"Why should I be grateful? Here I was, playing cards in complete contentment, not a care in the world, and you bring me news that my wife is entangling herself, and all of us, in some wild imbroglio."

"Do you mean to tell me that you would rather not have known?"

"Of *course* I'd rather not have known!"

Wys shook his head in stupefaction. "Hetty is right. I don't understand a thing about marriage."

"Yes, she is. You don't."

"Nevertheless, I can't believe you'd prefer to be an ostrich—not knowing what's going on around you!"

"What's the good of knowing what's going on? If one *knows*, it follows that one must *act* on that knowledge. *Now*, you see, I must *do* something about all this."

"Naturally," Wys nodded in agreement. "Don't you *want* to do anything about it?"

"No, I don't. I'm much too lazy to enjoy taking action. And action against one's wife is particularly wearing— there are so many ways a wife can get back at one. You've quite cut up my peace, you know."

"I'm sorry," Wys said, chastened.

"Well, no need to look so glum, old fellow. We shall brush through it. No point in making more of a hobble of the matter than it is."

"Do you think you can stop Hetty from inviting Lady Rowle?"

"Probably not. If I know my wife, she has invited her already."

"Then what's to be done?"

Selby drained the last of his brandy, put down the glass, and sat back in the deep winged chair. He clasped his hands across his belly and shut his eyes. Wys watched him in fascination. The only sign that Selby was alive was a slight movement of his lips, as if he were involved in a debate in a dream. A few moments later, Selby's eyelids flickered. His eyes opened, revealing an alert brightness that proved he had not been sleeping, and he sat bolt upright. "We'll do it," he said chortling. "We'll proceed exactly as she wishes."

Wys gaped at him. "You don't mean it! You intend to permit her to take Lady Rowle to Suffolk? And you want *me* to lure *Drew* there? And in that underhanded, secretive way? I can't believe you're in earnest!"

"I am perfectly in earnest," Selby said placidly.

"Have you thought this through carefully? Only *think* what can happen! Lady Rowle, who is not a fool, will see through the plan in a moment. Then, being a woman who in my view is lacking in moderation, she will very likely fall into a fit of hysterics or wild fury. This will cause Drew to feel far from pleased at our interference in his affairs. We shall then suffer the wrath of both of them. We shall have to endure a veritable *storm* of villification and abuse about our heads. We shall lose Drew's friendship, gain Lady Rowle's enmity, and all for nothing."

Selby looked at Wys admiringly. "You should definitely stand for Parliament, dear boy. You present your case in such commendable style: a gifted mixture of the factual and the dramatic, well seasoned with verbal pyrotechnics of a high order. Yes indeed, you must certainly consider standing for Parliament."

Wys regarded him with a cool stare. "Thank you. Is *that* all you have to say to the purpose?"

"What else shall I say?" Selby shrugged and heaved himself up from his chair with great effort. "If your prediction is correct—and I have little doubt that it is— Hetty shall get no more than she deserves, and I hope it may teach the saucy chit a lesson to be less interfering in the future. If, on the other hand, your forecast proves to be inaccurate, and the two victims of these devious machinations do not fall *out* but rather fall into each other's arms, we shall have the satisfaction of having done a good deed." With that, he patted his protruding stomach with satisfaction and turned to leave.

"And do you expect me to go ahead with the dishonorable and dastardly plan that Hetty has concocted to get Drew there?"

"My dear boy, don't look at *me* so accusingly. I don't care what you do. *You* are the one who promised Hetty you would do it, not I."

"Yes, but...you see, she had started to cry..."

Selby grinned. "Well, you can't say I didn't warn you about Hetty's tears. Talented little minx, ain't she?"

"Are you going to let her think she's pulled the wool over your eyes?" Wys asked.

"Don't know yet," Selby answered, signaling a waiter to get his hat and coat. "I'll see. I'm going home now to play a little cat-and-mouse game of my own." And with a cheerful wave of his chubby hand, he left the room.

Wys watched him go with an expression of bewilderment. "They're quite right," he muttered dazedly. "I don't understand a thing about marriage."

Hetty had dismissed her abigail, donned a lovely and expensive new nightdress made up of yards and yards of filmy blue gauze, and sat brushing her auburn curls to a shiny luster. At the sound of Selby's knock, she dropped her brush and ran eagerly to the door. Selby, resplendent in a maroon velvet dressing gown held together across his bulk by several pairs of frogs woven of gold cord, had no sooner stepped over the threshold of her bedroom and shut the door when Hetty jumped up on her toes and flung her arms around his neck. "Here you are at last," she said, chiding him affectionately. "I've been waiting for you this *age*!"

"Have you, my dear?" he asked fondly. "I was under the impression that I'd left the club rather earlier than usual tonight." And he settled himself in an easy chair and drew her onto his lap. "What is this?" he asked, fingering her nightgown. "Another new gown? I hope the size of the bill won't spoil my delight in looking at it."

"You *do* like it!" Hetty said, pleased with herself and settling herself snugly against his shoulder. "I'm so glad you do, for the bill is shocking, I warn you."

Selby sighed. "You're a shameless little chit. Whatever am I to do with you?"

Hetty, recognizing his mellow mood, giggled and nuzzled his neck. "Don't lose patience with me, for I have some news which will please you. I know you'll be delighted to hear that I've decided to accompany you to Suffolk after all. I'll be ready to leave next week, if that pleases you. So you see, I'll be quite removed from all the London shops and the dressmakers, and thus won't be spending your money for a while."

"You've decided to go to Suffolk? After being quite adamant about it only a few days ago? How am I to account for this sudden change in plans, my girl?"

"Well, you see, I'm growing quite bored with London these days. Ever since the ball, I've had the feeling that people are avoiding me. I may be imagining it, of course, but I see no reason why we shouldn't leave town for a while."

"I'm delighted that you want to go, my dear," Selby said blandly. "We'll make arrangements to do so quite soon. If all goes as I expect, we can leave in a month or six weeks."

"A month or six weeks!" Hetty cried, stunned.

"Yes. By the early part of January at the latest."

"But what—? You said—! I mean, you've been urging me to go with you to Stonehaven for the past *month*!" She stared at him, dumbfounded.

"I understand your surprise, my dear, but you seemed so reluctant to go at this season that I decided to put my plans off for your sake. Now, I've made other arrangements. Some business meetings in the city, etcetera. A couple of months' delay is not so important, is it?"

"But of *course* it is! I *can't* wait for two months!" she cried, jumping to her feet and staring at him, aghast.

"I don't see why a small delay should upset you so," said her husband, blinking at her in exaggerated innocence.

"Because . . . because I've invited someone to come with us. How can I turn around and tell her we're not going until *January*?"

"Invited someone? Who is it?"

Hetty dropped her eyes guiltily. This was not the way she had planned the evening at all. She did not want to break the news to him like this, but what else was she to do? "I've asked Lady Rowle and her brother to join us," she said in a timid little voice.

"Oh, I see," said Selby mildly. "That *is* awkward, isn't it."

"Awkward!" Hetty exclaimed. "It's much *worse* than awkward—it's impossible!"

"Balderdash! All you need do is tell the woman we can't go right now, and that we'd be glad to have her with us in January."

"But I can't do that! I shall *die* of shame! You don't know what I had to go through to get her to agree! I couldn't *possibly* cry off now!"

"Seems to me, my dear, that you are making too much of this. If you had discussed this with me, however, before going off and extending invitations without so much as a by-your-leave, you wouldn't be in this bumble-bath."

"Oh?" Hetty raised a quizzical eyebrow haughtily. "I didn't realize that it was necessary for me to ask your permission before issuing my invitations."

"Don't get on your high ropes with *me*, my dear. You know very well that you have absolute freedom to invite to our home anyone whom you wish. But taking Gwen Rowle to Suffolk for two weeks or more is quite a different case, is it not? Don't you think you should have discussed such a decision with me first?"

"I don't see why," Hetty said stubbornly.

"Well, suppose, for example, that I had taken it upon myself to invite your brother. A *fine* hank we'd be in then!"

Hetty looked at her husband keenly. "*Did* you invite Drew?"

"Of course not," Selby said with a holier-than-thou smile. "I would have discussed such a course with *you* first."

"What a whisker!" Hetty snapped. "You would have invited him without giving *me* a passing thought, and he would have arrived at our doorstep without my having been in the least prepared for him."

"Be that as it may, I did *not* invite Drew, but you *did* invite Lady Rowle. Now, what do you propose to do about it?"

"There's only one thing I *can* do about it," Hetty said, her face crumbling in despair and very real tears filling up her eyes. "I shall have to g-go without you. And how I'm to g-get all the way to S-Stonehaven, and how I'm to g-go through the whole ordeal w-w-without you, I'm sure I d-don't know!"

"Ordeal? What ordeal?"

Hetty shot him an alarmed glance. "N-nothing. I just m-meant that I've n-never been at the manor house without you, and it will b-be an ordeal."

"You meant nothing of the sort. And you needn't upset yourself, because I don't intend to permit you to go without me."

Hetty's chin shook with a completely sincere quiver. "But, S-Selby, you d-don't understand! I *must* go!"

"Hetty, have you been up to something? Are you concocting some plot involving Lady Rowle?"

At this, the tears spilled over. Hetty dropped her head in her hands. "Oh, S-Selby," she sobbed, "I shall never do so again. N-Never. But I shall be in the m-most dreadful fix if you don't let me go to S-Suffolk with G-Gwen."

Lord Selby, who had frequently bragged about his ability to remain untouched by his wife's artful use of tears, found himself unable to resist her now. To pursue the game he had been playing seemed almost cruel; she made such a pitiable, endearing sight, standing there before him with her face buried in her hands and her shoulders shaking. His heart quite melted. He reached up, drew her back onto his lap, and took her hands from her face. Brushing her tears away, he kissed her tenderly. "There, there, my dear, don't upset yourself. I shall take you to Suffolk whenever you like, and you shall go through with your plans just as you wish, so long as you promise to consult me in the future."

Hetty looked at him in misty bewilderment. "B-But your appointments... in the city...?"

Selby's eyes wavered. "Oh, I'll... cancel them," he said hastily.

Hetty's face brightened and her wet eyelashes flickered over eyes that shone in happy gratitude. "Oh, Selby," she sighed, and nestled in his arms, "you are the best ... the *very* best of husbands!"

Selby grinned as he rubbed his cheek against her curls. The trip to Suffolk would undoubtedly be a disaster, but so long as Hetty remained convinced that he was the very best of husbands, he might manage to make for himself a fairly pleasant time of it.

Chapter Six

OF COURSE, IT WAS RAINING. Wys, already made utterly miserable by the fact that he would have to enact a false and dishonest scene before the day was out in order to trick his closest friend into going to Stonehaven, found that he could fall to even lower depths of despair. He sat at the window of the small sitting room of his stylish hunting-box in Melbourn and looked out at the dismal scene before him. One expected such weather at the end of November or during December, but not on the last day of October. The rain was so cold that it formed little traces of ice on the few remaining leaves, and if one ventured outside, the wind sent the raindrops flying into one's face, cutting like hundreds of little knives. One could neither ride nor shoot nor walk out of doors.

Wys glanced at his friend, sitting near the fire

engrossed in reading a dusty copy of *Rasselas* which he had found on the mantel in his bedroom. Drew had been an ideal guest. Although the weather had been impossible ever since their arrival, he had not complained. He had made easy conversation, played cards by the hour, and had even spent an afternoon repairing a broken chair, all with apparent enjoyment. Most praiseworthy of all, when Wys's chef, the talented Albèrt, had taken ill and a woman from the village had been hired to replace him, Drew had said not one disparaging word about the dreadful meals she had prepared.

The chef's replacement was, in a way, the one lucky stroke Wys had had. Now it would not be hard for Drew to believe that Wys could be made ill as a result of her cooking. But how should he make the pretense? Should he groan? Double over? Quietly take to his bed? Hetty had made it sound so easy, but he didn't know how to play-act. The whole idea was downright deceitful, and how he was to face Drew when the masquerade was over, he did not know.

Wys turned back to the window and sighed.

"That's the longest, most tragic sigh I've heard since I saw Kemble perform *Hamlet*. What's wrong with you, Wys?" Drew asked, putting aside his book and looking quizzically at his friend.

"Nothing's wrong. Only this cursed weather. I'm sorry to have dragged you from London to this siege of rain and boredom."

"You have offered me this unnecessary apology several times already. I have assured you each time that you did not 'drag' me to Melbourn—I came quite willingly. Eagerly, in fact. I've assured you that I do not feel at all besieged, either by weather or by boredom. You must know without my saying it that I'm not bored by your company."

"Yes, I know. You are the best of good fellows, Drew." Wys smiled at his friend weakly and turned back to the window, hoping to see a sign of clearing somewhere in the leaden sky. There was none. He sighed again.

"There you go again. This air of depression is unlike you, Wys. I've suspected that something was wrong ever since we arrived. What *is* troubling you?"

Wys looked up at Drew standing before him and realized that he could not go through with the pretense. He could not repay Drew's thoughtfulness and friendly cheer with lies! Hetty would probably never forgive him, and perhaps he would never forgive himself, but he would tell Drew the truth, and right now. "Drew," he began, "there *is* something troubling me. I—"

But an expression of intense pain suddenly crossed Drew's face and stopped Wys in mid-sentence. Drew blinked and tried to smile. "Yes? What were you saying? Go on, old fellow."

"Is something wrong?" Wys asked in concern.

"No, no. Go on with what you were saying."

Wys eyed him dubiously and proceeded. "Well, what I have to tell you may anger you, I'm afraid. But you must keep in mind that all parties mean well. You see, about a week ago, Hetty sent me a note asking me to wait upon her. She had devised a scheme— Drew! What is it?"

For Drew had clasped his hands against his waist with a gasp of pain. "Sorry," he said in a husky, short-winded voice. "It's really nothing, I expect. A touch of . . . indigestion . . ."

Wys's jaw dropped. "Indigestion!" he breathed, awestruck. Drew took no notice, for he winced and gasped again. Wys helped him into a chair. "You're in pain!" he exclaimed. "How long have you been feeling ill?"

"The past . . . half-hour . . . or so . . ." Drew said tightly.

"Good lord, man, why didn't you say something?"

Drew glanced up at his friend and tried to smile. "I didn't want to push you . . . any further into the dismals. I hoped it . . . would soon pass. It will soon, of course . . ." And noting Wys's expression of shocked anguish, he added, with an effort at a laugh, "Don't look . . . so stupefied. That cook of yours would...give a...a *horse*...indigestion!"

Wys's mind was in a whirl. Drew, sick! *Drew!* It should have been *he*! He, *Wystan Farr*, should be sitting there in Drew's place with *his* brow knotted and *his* hands clenched in pain. Of course, he would have been play-acting, but Drew's suffering was real. Before he could permit himself to dwell further on the strange coincidence, he had to help Drew. He bent solicitously over his friend's chair. "Do you think I should send for a doctor? I know of one in Melbourn who is said to be quite competent."

"I think," said Drew, somewhat white about the lips, "that it would be...a very good idea."

Two hours later, the doctor had come and gone, and Drew was sleeping quietly in his bedroom upstairs. Wys, seated before the fire with his chin in his hand, was trying to decide what to do next. He knew that Hetty was expecting that a carriage would draw up to her door at any moment and that her brother would climb out and help a sick and feeble Wystan Farr into the house. The situation was almost laughable. If he had not spent the last hour watching the doctor force poor Drew to puke out the contents of his stomach, Wys would be enjoying himself hugely.

The doctor had left some very specific instructions. Wys was to see to it that Drew rested quietly for the next few days. His diet during that period was to be most judiciously planned and prepared: he was to eat no meat at all; clear soup was advised for the first day, fresh eggs boiled no more than two minutes might be added the next day, but only if the patient's appetite had begun to improve; the patient would shortly thereafter find the addition of cooked rice, gruel and other such foods to be beneficial, and he should, by the end of a week, feel quite himself again.

Wys explained to the doctor that the chef he had

brought from London had taken ill and had returned there for proper care. Blaming his substitute cook for Drew's illness, he asked the doctor if a two-hour carriage ride into Suffolk would be harmful to Drew in his present condition, requesting the medical man to keep in mind that, at the end of the trip, the patient would be provided with food, nursing and attention vastly superior to that which he would receive here. "Well," the doctor had replied with a shrug, "the shaking up your friend will receive in the carriage will do him no good at all, I can promise you. But if the care he'll receive in Suffolk will be as good as you say, by all means proceed with the plan."

Wys sat imagining what their arrival at Selby Manor would be like, and he couldn't help smiling. If he had followed Hetty's instructions—and Drew had not taken ill—the whole plan would have gone awry. Wys could *never* have performed his part well enough to have been convincingly ill. He was no actor. But Fate had stepped in and dealt Hetty a much better hand with which to play this game of chance. With Drew *truly* ill, Gwen Rowle would never suspect that Hetty had hatched a plot. There was now at least a reasonable possibility that her plot would work. All Wys had to do now was to get Drew to agree to take the trip. And Wys need not really lie to Drew—he need only omit the information that Lady Rowle was in residence at Stonehaven.

Wys waited as long as he could before waking Drew, but by four o'clock it was plain that the rain was not going to stop and that it would soon be dark. He went to Drew's room and shook him awake. Drew groaned and sat up, looking pale and tired.

"Sorry to wake you, old man," Wys said hesitantly, "but I have an idea I must discuss with you. The doctor left instructions that you'll be needing a special diet in the next—"

"Ugh!" Drew grunted. "Oblige me, please, by not talking about food!"

"But I must. You're going to need rest, care and well-prepared food, and I'm afraid you won't get it here."

"Been thinking the same thing myself," Drew said, trying to shake himself awake. "I think we'd best start for London tomorrow."

This took Wys by surprise. "London? Oh, I don't think . . . that is . . . it's much too long a trip for you in your condition!"

Drew peered at his friend through the deepening gloom. "Light a candle, will you, Wys? I can barely see you. What time is it?"

"About four," Wys replied, lighting a candle and carrying it to the bedstand.

"Four, eh? Well, what were you going to suggest?"

"Selby's place. Hetty told me they were spending a few weeks there. I think it's not above a two hour ride. If we left now, we could get you there before they sit down to dinner."

"Now?" Drew's brow knotted and he looked at his friend sharply. "What bobbery are you up to, Wys?"

"Bobbery?" Wys repeated nervously. "I don't know what you mean?"

"You started to tell me something earlier today. What was it? Something about being troubled . . ."

"I don't remember saying anything about being troubled."

"Yes, you do. You were mooning and sighing like a lovesick calf, remember?"

"You must have been dreaming," Wys insisted. "You've been quite sick, you know. I shouldn't wonder if you'd been a little delirious."

Drew's frown deepened, and he eyed his friend with suspicion. "Are you trying to tip me a rise?" he asked.

Wys drew himself up proudly. "Have you ever known me to do so? It seems to me that when a fellow is trying to help a friend—"

"All right, Wys, take a damper! I'll go with you to Selby's place. But don't try to flummery me into believing that there's not more to this than meets the eye."

With Wys's assistance, Drew managed to dress and pack within an hour, but he found himself surprisingly unsteady on his legs and still in a state of considerable queasiness. He said nothing about it, however, and they set out on the journey. The day was already darkening, and the cold and miserable rain was falling unabated. Glancing at Drew's taut face, Wys warned him of the doctor's prediction that the ride would not be comfortable for him. Drew merely nodded and settled himself into a corner of the carriage.

The ride turned out to be an ordeal worse than anything the doctor could have imagined. As night fell, the air became colder, freezing the rain as soon as it fell to the ground. The road and the trees became sheeted with ice. The horses skittered and slithered over the road alarmingly, as did the wheels of the carriage. Inside the carriage, the occupants were tossed about relentlessly. Drew's face grew steadily more pale and tense, and though he made no complaint, his silence told Wys more eloquently than words that he was suffering considerable discomfort. Twice the carriage had to be stopped so that Drew could climb out and retch. His clothes became damp, and when he came back to his seat even the blankets that Wys carefully tucked around him did not prevent his teeth from chattering. The struggle against the elements necessitated slow and careful driving and lengthened the travel time by more than an hour. As the two friends stared moodily out of their respective windows, they both wished fervently that this nightmarish journey would come to an end.

Hetty had been nervously awaiting Wys's arrival all day. Wys was the weak link in her plan, and she knew it. He was not likely to perform his part very well, and if his feigned illness failed to fool Drew, she was very much afraid they would not come. And even if they *did* appear, would Wys's performance fool Gwen? Well, Hetty would bustle Wys off to his room the moment they set foot in the door, thus getting him out of the way as soon as possible.

Otherwise, her plan had been proceeding quite well. It had been her intention to make Gwen's stay so dull that Drew's arrival would be a welcome relief. That part of the plan had succeeded beyond her expectations. No members of the local gentry had been able to pay calls because of the forbidding weather, so they were forced to endure their own company all day long. No outdoor pursuits could be enjoyed, either. Hetty felt quite sorry for Tom, who had not had one morning of riding nor one day of shooting. Fortunately, he had discovered a long-unused billiard table in one of the closed saloons, and had amused himself by improving his technique with a cue.

Gwen had been gracious and ladylike, but Hetty had caught her several times stifling a yawn when Hetty had been prosing on endlessly about the details of a new gown she had ordered or repeating a bit of gossip she had told Gwen twice before. Hetty did not enjoy playing the part of an irritating and boring bibble-babble; she hoped Drew would appreciate the fact that she had sacrificed her usual charm and wit in his behalf.

As the day drew on, Hetty found it more and more difficult to keep her nervous anticipation from becoming noticeable. She several times had been on the verge of jumping up and looking out of the window, but she'd managed to restrain herself. By six, she was in such a state of anxiety that she kept herself closeted in her dressing room to prevent Gwen from seeing her agitation. She calmed herself by imagining the romantic scene which would occur when Drew and Gwen confronted each other.

She had imagined the scene many times before. Drew would be standing in the center of her hallway, lit by the chandelier directly above. His cape would be thrown back from his right shoulder so that he could support the drooping Wys with his right arm. Gwen, her hair drawn back so that a mass of soft curls hung from her crown and her dress clinging in casual folds around her lovely form, would emerge from the drawing room. The two would stare at each other for a moment in delighted surprise. Then, they would greet each other with, naturally, some stiffness. But by the time Drew had explained about his friend's unexpected illness, Gwen would soften and go to his assistance. Their eyes would meet over Wys's lowered head, and they would smile shyly...

When there was no sign of a carriage by seven o'clock, Hetty gave up hope and reluctantly ordered the butler to announce dinner. Heartsick as she was by the apparent failure of her plan, she was by nature a warm and hospitable woman. She made every attempt to make the meal a cheerful one, but while she smiled and made pleasant conversation, her mind was busy trying to think up schemes to end this fiasco of a visit. Therefore, when her butler bent over her, in the midst of the second course, and told her that Lord Jamison and Mr. Farr were awaiting her pleasure in the hallway, she was taken by sincere surprise. "Drew? Here?" she cried, and looked across the table at Gwen in some confusion. "Oh, Gwen, I... Will you excuse me, please?" she asked awkwardly, and ran out of the room.

Selby, who had been watching his wife all day with well-concealed amusement, felt an irresistible curiosity to see the stiff and fastidious Wystan Farr make a cake of himself play-acting the part of a sick man. He glanced across the table at Lady Rowle. Her eyes were beginning to smolder. Selby quickly got to his feet. "Please excuse me, Lady Rowle. You, too, Tom. I think I, too, should see what has brought my brother-in-law to our door. Pray, go on with your dinner." And he turned and hurried after his wife.

Gwen rose in chagrin and looked at her brother. "How *could* Hetty deceive me like this? She told me I'd be perfectly safe from her brother here in Suffolk!" she said furiously. "The deceitful wretch! Come along, Tom, we're going to leave this place!"

"Hang it, Gwen," Tom said irritably, "don't fly off the

handle. You can't be sure your suspicions have any grounds. Give Lady Selby a chance to explain."

"I don't need any explanations. The explanation is as plain as pike-staff. They've tricked me, all of them! But I'm not going to let them succeed in their horrid little hoax. We'll leave here tomorrow morning, and until then I won't speak a *word* to any of them. And I expect you, my own brother, to support me in this. Are you coming with me, or not?"

"But I haven't finished my roast, and it's deli—"

"Tom!"

He sighed and got to his feet. "I'm coming," he muttered reluctantly.

Gwen stalked from the dining room in quick, angry strides, but she stopped at the threshold in astonishment. In the hallway right before her stood Selby and Hetty, frozen into stunned immobility by the spectacle before them. In the center of the hallway, directly under the chandelier, stood Wys, supporting a limp and shivering Drew. Drew, who had always appeared to the world as a pattern-card of Corinthian elegance—his clothes impeccable, his stance gracefully erect, his eyes clear and gleaming with humor, his expression intelligent and alert, and his chin high—now stood before them with his head down, his clothes wrinkled and damp, a blanket hanging from his shoulders, his hair hanging about his face in wet tendrils from which icy droplets trickled down his cheeks, and his eyes clouded and unseeing.

Gwen's hand flew to her mouth. "My God! Drew!" she gasped.

Her cry seemed to rouse the others from their stupor. "Drew! What's happened to you?" Hetty cried, flying to his side.

Selby turned to the butler. "Get the south bedroom ready," he ordered. "Quickly!" And he went to help Wys. "Have you had an accident?" he asked urgently.

"No, no," said Wys calmly. "It's not as bad as it looks. Drew took ill—something he ate at my hunting-box in

Melbourn. I thought it better to bring him here than to take him back to London. He needs rest and care, that's all."

"Oh, my poor Drew," Hetty said soothingly, brushing the hair back from his forehead fondly. Drew shook his head and focused his glazed eyes on her.

"Ah, Hetty," he said thickly. "We got here. Didn't think we'd ... make it."

"Well, you did make it. You're here, and we shall have you snug and warm in a very few minutes," Hetty crooned, as if she were talking to a sick baby.

"Don't ... make a ... fuss ..." Drew mumbled. "I'm just a bit ... dizzy ... There's no need to ... be alarmed. Doctor said I'll ... be ... fi—" At that moment his eyes fell on Gwen. "Good Lord!" he said, and blinked at her in disbelief.

Here was the moment Hetty had been waiting for. She looked across at Gwen, who was standing at the threshold of the dining room, one hand covering her mouth, the other clasping Tom's hand as if she needed support. She was staring wide-eyed at Drew, but Hetty could not read the expression in those lovely dark eyes. Hetty glanced back at Drew, but he was no longer looking at Gwen. His eyes had become unfocused, and his face was turning quite green. "Wys!" he muttered. "My bedroom! Get me to my bedroom! Quickly!"

Wys nodded knowingly and took Drew's arm. Without another word, they went quickly up the stairs, Drew's blanket trailing pathetically behind him. Hetty shook her head in vexation. *This* was the romantic meeting she had gone to such trouble to arrange! If she weren't a well-brought-up, respectable matron, and if she weren't surrounded by her husband, her guests and her servants, she would lie down on the floor, right here and now, and have a kicking, screaming tantrum!

Chapter Seven

THE HOUSEHOLD WAS SILENT by eleven, the turmoil stirred up by Drew's arrival having exhausted everyone, but in opposite wings of the house, the two women were not asleep. Hetty insisted on sitting up at Drew's bedside, and Gwen lay on her bed unable to fall asleep. The feelings that the sight of Drew had stirred up in her had caught her unaware. She had realized from the first—from the moment he had drawn her into his arms at the Selby ball—that she was more strongly attracted to him than to any man she had met in her life. But she had made up her mind that very night that she would not let the attraction develop any further. He had killed Rowle. For that, he could never be forgiven.

She lay on her side, staring at the embers still glowing in the fireplace across the room and remembering the

endearingly-boyish look on Drew's face as he had stood
shivering in the hallway earlier tonight. Her heart had
gone out to him. She had felt an almost overwhelming
urge to run to him, to help him into a chair, and to cradle
him in her arms. She had watched Hetty brush back his
hair with a pang which she could only describe as
jealousy. She had reached out and grasped Tom's hand,
instinctively seeking some physical support to prevent
herself from going to Drew's side. What had come over
her? What was it that she felt for him?

Gwen had never known love—the love that can exist
between a man and a woman. She had married Edward
Rowle to oblige her family. The family, the Spauldings of
Somerset, though well-connected, had never been rich,
and her father suffered from a chronic ailment that had
eroded much of the capital on which they depended.
Rowle had pursued Gwen Spaulding with a youthful
intensity that had been engaging, and when he had offered
her father a generous settlement, Gwen was urged to
accept him. He had seemed charming and vulnerable, and
she had put her girlish dreams of love aside and had
obediently married him.

It was not long before she learned that she had made a
mistake. Edward Rowle could be amusing and likeable
when he wished to put himself out, but more often he was
moody and sullen. He was addicted to gambling, he drank
too much, and his friends seemed to encourage him in his
profligacy. He wasted huge sums of money. Sometimes,
when he came home drunk and offensive, she found
herself forced to lock her bedroom door against him. For
this, she felt a growing guilt and began to blame herself for
the weaknesses in his character which were growing more
and more evident. His mother, Lady Hazel—the one
person to whom Gwen could tell her troubles—tried to
soothe her by blaming Rowle's background, his inherited
nature, even his upbringing, but Gwen could not rid
herself of her growing sense of guilt. In spite of several
brave attempts she made to change things, her relation-

ship with Edward worsened steadily. At last, she determined to coax her husband to abandon London entirely. She hoped that—removed from London, its gambling dens and the dissolute cronies with whom he spent his time—they could rebuild the crumbling foundations of their marriage. It was at just this time that the duel took place. At its conclusion, Rowle was dead, and it was too late for her to make amends.

For this, Drew was to blame. She would have liked to believe Rowle's death was accidental, but she could not. Everyone knew that Drew was a crack shot. There was no excuse for him to have met Rowle at all. It would not have been dishonorable for Drew, universally recognized as the best marksman in London, to withdraw from an encounter with a mere boy who was inexperienced, unsteady from too much drink, and certain to lose. No matter how often she turned over in her mind the circumstances of the duel, she could find no way to exonerate Drew Jamison.

Gwen suddenly became aware that the rain's tapping on her window had stopped. She got up and went to look out. Opening the drapery she had drawn against the howling wind, she saw that the moon had appeared between two silver-edged clouds. The sight of the grounds took her breath away. Ice had covered every twig, every leaf, every shrub and blade of grass with a thin coating of glassy resplendence which the moonlight touched here and there with a diamond sparkle. It was a scene from a fairy story. Gwen leaned against the window frame and let her eyes drink in the sight. But her mind stubbornly dwelt on the problem with which it had been occupied all night. Suddenly it seemed to her that some of the sparkle of the scene outside crept into the darkness of her thoughts and brought with it an illumination—a realization that was, at one and the same time, a flash of joy and a barb of searing pain: she had fallen in love, but with the one man in the world she *had* to hate.

*   *   *

Drew opened his eyes and watched a circle of sparkling sunlight on the ceiling with mindless pleasure. After a moment, he remembered that he had been ill. With a pleased sigh, he realized that the pain was gone. He considered lifting his head, but the effort seemed greater than he was willing to make, so he let his mind do the work for him. Where was he? If he remembered correctly, he had come with Wys to Selby's place in Suffolk. Perhaps, if he turned his head and looked around, he might recognize the room. Closing his eyes and taking a deep breath in preparation for this tremendous feat, he turned his head toward the source of the light he had seen on the ceiling. He found himself looking at a bright window, in front of which sat a woman, her head bent over a book. Her hair, lit by the sunshine behind her head, glowed like a halo of gold-tipped curls. He blinked and tried to see her face, but the light behind her was too bright. "Good morning," he said aloud. The sound of his voice surprised him—it had an unexpectedly shaky croak.

"Oh, are you awake at last?" asked a strangely familiar voice. "It's afternoon, you know."

His heart stopped for a second and then resumed with a rapid pounding. He knew that voice. *"Gwen?"* he croaked, and with a great effort he lifted his head. She rose quickly and came to his side, pressing her hand against his shoulder and gently pushing him back against the pillows. "Don't get up. You're to rest in bed for a few days. I'll go and tell Hetty you're awake. She's having some excellent chicken broth made for you."

"No, don't go," Drew said quickly, and reached out to grasp her skirt. "I don't understand. Where am I?"

"Don't you remember? You're at Stonehaven. You arrived last night, in quite a state."

"Yes, I remember that. I *thought* I saw you, but I . . . told myself it was a delusion . . ."

"It was no delusion," Gwen said with a smile in her voice.

"I can't see you clearly with the light dazzling my eyes,"

Drew said pleadingly. "Come around to the other side of the bed and sit down, won't you?"

"But I promised to tell Hetty as soon as you were awake. We've got to get some broth inside you."

"Please. Never mind Hetty for the moment. And as for the broth, I promise you I intend never to eat again."

Gwen laughed and did as he asked. She pulled a chair to the side of the bed and sat down beside him. "There, now," she said, as if to a petulant child, "what do you want to talk to me about?" He didn't answer. She looked down at him. He was looking up at her as if he didn't quite believe that she was real. It was a look of such astonishing tenderness that her heart seemed to flip over in surprise. She could not meet his eyes, but turned her own away in confusion. It was the moment Hetty had been waiting for, but Hetty wasn't there to see it.

"What...? How did...? How is it that you're here?" Drew asked at last.

"Hetty invited me." Gwen smiled without looking at him. "She assured me that I would be completely safe from you here in Suffolk."

"Oh, she did, did she?" Drew asked thoughtfully. Somewhat absently, he reached out and took Gwen's hand. "Did you *want* to be safe from me?"

"Lord Jamison, you have been ill, and I am a guest in this house. I've decided to call a truce between us while we are both under this roof. But you must remember that it in no way changes the real situation between us. And you must make the truce possible by agreeing not to pass beyond the bounds of polite friendship. Please release my hand."

He held it tighter and looked up at her, his smile a faint counterpart of his old mocking grin. "And if I don't agree?"

"Then my brother and I will leave as soon as I can arrange transportation."

"In that case," he said, kissing her fingers lightly and letting her hand drop, "I give you my word."

"Good," Gwen said briskly, and rose. "Now I'd better call Hetty. If she knew you were awake, she'd be furious with me for not calling her."

"Speaking of my sister, does it occur to you to wonder at the strange coincidence that brings us here together?" Drew asked musingly.

Gwen sat down again. "Well, it *had*. I was furious when I first heard that you'd arrived. But then I saw how ill you were, and all suspicions flew out of my mind. Why do you ask?"

"Hetty and my friend Wystan Farr have been up to something," Drew said, heaving himself to a sitting position. "I'm sure this meeting of ours is the result of one of Hetty's little plots."

"How can you be sure?" Gwen asked. "Please, Lord Jamison, don't sit up. You're supposed to be resting."

"Don't act as though sitting up in bed is equivalent to riding to the hounds," Drew said with a grin.

"You are *not* going to be a difficult patient, are you?" Gwen asked him sternly.

"Oh, no, ma'am. Meek as a lamb, I assure you."

"So I see. Well, Lord Jamison, how can you be so sure it was a plot?"

"I'd be glad to share my suspicions with you, my dear, but I find it difficult when you insist on addressing me in that formal way. Do you think our truce could include your calling me by my Christian name?"

"Oh, very well, I suppose so," said Gwen with a little smile. "But don't push me any further. I don't approve of such encroaching ways."

"Very well, Lady Rowle. I *was* going to encroach further by asking your leave to call you Gwen, but I see I had better not."

"Good, because I will *not* give you leave to do so. You seem to call me 'my dear' quite frequently. That will have to suffice."

Drew nodded obediently. "Yes, I can see why 'my dear' meets with your approval. It makes me seem so . . . avuncular!"

Gwen laughed. "Exactly so. An uncle-niece relationship between us will suit me very well."

Drew grunted. "Well, *my dear,* to return to my theory of the plot against us—"

"I'm rather surprised that you should think of the plot as being against you. I should have thought that you would be a party to it. You *did* threaten, not so long ago, that you would find a way to see me..."

Drew raised his brows in disdain. "If you think I need to devise plots and enlist cohorts to make my case with you, my girl, you have much mistaken your man," he said coldly.

Gwen lowered her eyes. "I...didn't give you leave to call me 'my girl,' you know," she said in a chastened voice.

"Sorry," said Drew, his grin breaking out again. "I forgot myself. Well, let us proceed with our analysis of the plot. It's clear that Wys invited me to Melbourn on Hetty's instruction. Hetty was well aware that Wys's hunting-box is not a very long way from here."

"Good heavens, Drew, you are not suggesting that Mr. Farr had you *poisoned!*"

"No, no. I'm quite certain he did not. Even *Hetty* would not go as far as that! You said it quite nicely, by the way."

"What?" asked Gwen in bewilderment.

"My name. 'Good heavens, Drew.' It sounded quite lovely."

"Never mind that, you idiot," Gwen said with a blush. "If they didn't plan to poison you, what do you think the plan was?"

"I don't know. They had to find *some* way to get me here. Evidently my illness did the job well enough to suit."

"Oh, that Hetty!" said Gwen between clenched teeth. "I could *strangle* her."

"Can't say I blame you. I'm surprised you didn't leave this place the moment you suspected what she was up to."

"I couldn't be sure. You were so terribly sick, you know. Besides, the ice is keeping me prisoner here."

"Ice? What do you mean?"

"Didn't you notice that the rain was turning to ice last night? It has covered the entire countryside. Too bad you can't see it from the bed—it is a magnificent sight."

"Then I'm going to get up and take a look. Is there anything resembling a dressing-gown lying about?"

"Yes, right here. But do you think you should? Mr. Farr said that you must be kept in bed for a few days at least."

"I think my constitution can stand a stroll across the room," Drew assured her. "You would not ask me to miss the magnificent sight, would you?"

Gwen smiled. "Then you must let me help you," she said, and brought over the dressing gown. He stood up carefully, surprised to find himself quite unsteady, but with her support he managed to reach the window without tottering. The scene before them, if not quite the fairy-tale setting it had been by moonlight, was nevertheless a remarkable sight. The sun sparkled dazzlingly on a world which seemed to have been miraculously transformed—as if a divinely gifted sorcerer had waved his wand and changed all matter into crystal. Drew and Gwen stood at the window and stared at the splendor before them. They held their breaths as a gust of wind swept by, filling the air with an unfamiliar, magically tinkling sound. Gwen looked up at Drew and smiled at his look of rapt pleasure. As if he felt her eyes, he turned and looked at her, their eyes holding for a silent moment. "I do love you so," he said softly.

She shut her eyes in pain and held up her hand as if to ward him off. "Drew, don't," she said. "You gave your word."

"I'm sorry. I'm a bit weak today," he said. She glanced up at him worriedly, to find him smiling down at her. "I'll be stronger tomorrow, I promise. There will be no more lapses."

"Then I'll leave you until tomorrow," she said firmly.

"Perhaps you'd better. I'm finding it an overpowering

struggle to keep from taking you in my arms."

She gasped, and with one quick, embarrassed glance, she flew from the room.

For the next few days, Drew proved himself to be a very difficult patient indeed. He felt quite well enough to get out of bed, but neither Selby nor Hetty nor Wys, all of whom kept him almost constant company either singly or in a group, would hear of it. It was only by giving his promise to remain in bed when they were gone that he had any time alone. Gwen did not visit his room for two days. Instead, he was visited by her brother. The boy tapped on his door early on the second day of his recovery. Drew called "Come in," and Tom put his tousled head in the door.

"I'm Gwen's brother. May I come in?" he asked shyly.

"Of course. I'm glad to see a new face. I'm getting deucedly bored with my sister, my brother-in-law, and that other fellow who calls himself my friend. Their solicitude has been quite depressing."

Tom smiled and came to Drew's bedside. He put out his hand awkwardly. "I'm pleased to meet you, Lord Jamison," he said, awestruck.

Drew shook the proffered hand. "My friends call me Drew. You're Tom, I collect, aren't you? Sit down, and tell me about yourself."

Tom took a chair beside the bed and looked admiringly at the man who was the idol of all his friends. "Nothing to tell about me, my lord. I've heard a great deal about you, though. Been wanting to meet you for a long time."

"Have you? I can't imagine why."

"*Why?* Ever since I came to London, I've heard the fellows talk about you. That you beat Onslow in a bruising race, that you're a crack shot, that you stood up with Jackson and have a punishing right—"

"Enough. You'll put me to the blush. You young

fellows make too much of these sporting pursuits. Tell me, what has a young sporting buck like you been doing with himself here in Suffolk?"

"It's been a dashed bore, I can tell you. Rained almost every day. And now the ice. If it hadn't been for the billiard room, I'd have been blue-deviled beyond belief." He gave Drew a quick, shy glance. "That's why I couldn't wait 'til *you* got here. I've been hoping you'd have time to teach me to shoot."

Drew raised his eyebrows. "Oh? Were you *expecting* me?"

Tom gave him a startled look and stiffened. "Well, what I meant was...that is...not exactly," he stammered awkwardly.

"No need to poker up. You didn't spill the beans. I've known for days that my sister was up to her neck in a plot." He looked at Tom speculatively. "I just don't see what *your* part was in all this."

Tom let out his breath in relief. "You've known about it? I'm glad, truly I am. You mustn't be angry at Aunt Hazel, though. She did it with the best of motives, I assure you."

"Aunt Hazel? You don't mean *Lady Hazel Rowle?*"

Tom winced. "Oh, lord, I've spilled the beans again! Hang it all, I'm a regular babble-mouth!"

Drew grinned at him. "You certainly are. So Lady Hazel has something to do with this, has she? How did Hetty draw *her* into this bumble-broth?"

"I've already prattled too much, I suppose, but since you seem to know most of it, you might as well hear the rest—or at least as much as I know about it. From what Hazel told me, I think it was *her* idea, not Lady Selby's. Aunt Hazel was worried about Gwen's burying herself away, and she thought you'd be the one who could pull Gwen out of herself. So Hazel went to Lady Selby, and together they cooked up the plan."

"Well, well, think of that! Lady Hazel! I must buy her

some flowers as soon as we return to London."

"Buy her flowers? I thought you'd be angry..."

"At Lady Hazel? Not at all. I'm delighted to know she holds no bitterness toward me. But I *am* angry at Hetty."

"But why, if you're not at Hazel?"

Drew stared at the boy thoughtfully. "That's a good question. Why, indeed? I shall have to give the answer some thought. But you have not explained how *you* were drawn into all this."

"Well, you see," said Tom, drawing himself up importantly, "*I* had the cough."

"The cough?" asked Drew, completely perplexed.

Tom grinned. "Yes. I coughed a few times at the breakfast table, and my sister was convinced that I was suffering from an inflammation of the lungs. Lady Hazel encouraged her fears and suggested that country air might be the best way to cure me. So, when Hetty arrived at the propitious moment and offered to take us to the country—"

"Ah, I begin to see. How could a devoted sister refuse such an offer? I had no idea that Lady Hazel could be so deliciously devious. I shall buy her a *very large* bouquet and deliver it in person."

"I think Aunt Hazel will like that. She didn't enjoy having to trick you, you know."

"But Lady Selby did, I'll be bound. Tell me, did our lovely country air cure your inflammation?"

Tom laughed. "Completely. I no longer cough at all."

Drew grinned at the boy warmly. "How miraculous! I should have thought the air would have drowned you... or frozen you!"

"Or both!" Tom added, laughing heartily. But soon his expression sobered. "I suppose we'll have to leave now," he said, a shade regretfully.

"I hope not," Drew responded promptly. "I thought you wanted to do a bit of shooting."

Tom brightened. "Oh, do you think we could? It would

be famous to be able to tell the fellows that I'd been taught to shoot by Sure-shot Jamison! But Gwen will want to leave, I think."

"Then we must do what we can to see to it that she stays," Drew said decisively.

By the fourth morning, Drew had had enough of convalescence, and he got out of bed and shaved. By the time he heard the first knock at the door, he had put on his shirt and breeches and was standing before a mirror tying his cravat. "Come in, Hetty," he called.

But it was not Hetty. "Good morning," said Gwen cheerily. "Oh," she said, pausing in the doorway, "you are getting up!"

"I *am* up," he said firmly, putting on his coat. "But do come in. How kind of you to come see me at last. Did you think I needed all this time to become strong enough to behave with—what did you call it?—polite friendliness?"

The color rose in Gwen's cheeks. "I did think something of the sort," she admitted.

"Well, you need not feel troubled any more on that score. I am now strong enough for anything."

"I'm glad of that," she said softly, her head lowered. There was a long moment of embarrassed silence. At last she lifted her head and said, "I've come this morning to thank you for your kindness to my brother. He has spoken of no one but Drew ever since he saw you."

"I gave him no kindness. He is a delightful boy, and I was thankful for his company. I had no *other* visitor I wanted to see."

Gwen blushed and lowered her eyes again. Drew came close to her and lifted her chin. "I waited for you for three long days," he said, his eyes looking down at her with their disconcerting warmth.

"Drew," she said pleadingly, "you must not—"

"Oh. Sorry. I have passed the bounds." He took his hand from her chin and stepped back.

Gwen crossed the room to the window and stood

looking out. "I . . . I'd like to talk to you about Tom," she said hesitantly. "He says that . . . that you agreed to teach him to shoot."

"Yes, I did. Do you object to it?"

She turned slowly and faced him. "Very much," she said defensively. "Does that surprise you?"

"I suppose it should not," Drew said, his voice suddenly bitter. "Is *that* why you've come to see me this morning?"

Gwen glanced at his face and realized that she had hurt him. "Drew," she said, trying to explain herself, "you can understand my concern, can't you? You, of all people, should understand that I prefer that no one in my family handle firearms."

"I understand perfectly," Drew said coldly. "You are afraid I'll turn *him* into a murderer, too."

"That was unfair," Gwen said in a low voice, suddenly finding herself on the verge of tears.

"If it was, I apologize." He turned away from her. "It is difficult to behave with *polite friendliness* to someone who can see me only as a killer."

"I *knew* no good would come of these encounters," Gwen said in a choked voice. She came up behind Drew and put her hand on his arm. "Is there no way we can abide by our truce?" she asked gently.

"Not if I'm the only one of us who must make a sacrifice for it."

"What sacrifice would you have *me* make?"

He turned to her. "Can't you, for a little while at least, forget that cursed duel?"

"Forget—?" Gwen's eyes flew to his face in fear. "You mustn't ask! Oh, Drew, if I forgot the duel I would be—!" She covered her mouth with a trembling hand and stared up at him.

He grasped her shoulders and shook her roughly. "Would be *what*? Say it!"

"Lost," she whispered, not quite realizing the extent to which that simple word revealed the state of her emotions,

emotions she had taken such trouble to hide. "I'd be lost."

He understood fully what she had admitted by those words. He expelled a long breath and pulled her into his arms. So instinctive and natural was the gesture that the tensions between them seemed to relax. She lay against him, sobbing into his shoulder, unaware that her arms had encircled him tightly. He put his face into her hair murmuring, "My darling, my darling," not realizing that he was saying anything at all. They remained locked in each other's arms until the emotions of the moment had spent themselves. Then Gwen lifted her head, looked up at him strangely, and freed herself from his embrace. "But there *was* a duel," she said in an emotionless voice.

"Yes," he said with a feeling of alarm.

"And Edward was shot..."

"Yes."

"By you..."

There was no way around it. "Yes."

She made a sound like a moan. "I must go. Now. Today. And I must not see you, ever again. Do you understand, Drew? Not ever."

"Gwen!" He took a step toward her.

"Don't come near me." She moved backward to the door, her eyes watching him warily. "Edward is dead by your hand," she said in that strange, emotionless voice. "It may be the only cruel thing you ever did. I *can* believe that. But it is the one thing I must never forget. It's a wall between us, more real than a wall of stone." She opened the door. "Forget me, Drew. There's no future for us." And she closed the door behind her.

Drew remained motionless for a moment, then walked slowly to the window. Outside the almost-bare branches of the tall oak brushed against his window in the wind. The ice, which had been slowly melting away in three days of wintry sunshine, was still dripping in little rivulets down the windowpane. The fairyland of ice had almost completely disappeared.

*　　*　　*

He was still standing at the window an hour later when Wys scratched at his door. "Come in," he said absently, not moving.

Wys came in and closed the door carefully behind him. He watched his friend for a long moment. Then he cleared his throat. "She's asked me to take her home," he said hesitantly.

Drew merely nodded.

"Drew, I...I don't know what passed between you, but it must have been...er...painful. I'm sorry."

Drew sighed and turned. "Actually, it was something I should have expected. She merely told me she can never forget that I killed her husband."

"I see," said Wys, his face mirroring his sincere sympathy. "Drew, I certainly don't mean to interfere ever again. God knows how much I regret this whole episode. But I'd like to say one thing more, if I may."

"You're my friend, Wys. Say anything you like."

"Don't you think it's time you told her the *truth* about the duel? Do you think it sensible to let a *scruple* destroy the happiness you both might share?"

"I've thought of that, Wys. I've thought it over very carefully. Do you think it is egotistical of me to expect the girl I love to love me enough to believe, *without being told,* that I am *not* a man who would kill a frightened boy like her husband?"

"No, not egotistical, but..."

"But what?"

"Perhaps you are expecting too much."

"Am I? Answer a question for me, Wys. As truthfully as you can. If someone—a magistrate, perhaps; a reputable and honest magistrate—told you I had murdered someone, what would you say?"

"I'd say it wasn't true."

"But how could you say that? The magistrate would point out to you that you had not been a witness to the act."

"I'd say that I know you. I've known you for years, and

you couldn't have done it."

Drew nodded. "That's it, you see. *You* could not believe me capable of murder. But *she* can."

"But she hasn't known you very long, Drew. Grant her that at least."

Drew smiled bleakly. "I grant her that. But I thought that love was beyond time. Lovers are supposed to understand in an instant what others take years to learn, isn't that so?"

"So the poets say," Wys agreed sadly.

Drew sat down on the bed wearily. "Take her home, Wys. There's nothing else to do."

Wys nodded and turned to the door.

"By the way, does the boy go with her?" Drew asked suddenly.

"I don't know. Why?"

"The poor lad deserves *something* for his pains. He's had a dreadful time. Tell her to leave him with me. I'll give him a few days of riding, at least." He gave a rueful laugh. "Tell her I promise not to teach him to shoot."

After Gwen and Wys had left, the weather cleared. For the next few days, Tom and Drew spent many hours together riding over the downs. Tom, having grown up under the care of an invalid father, and having no brothers, blossomed under Drew's attention. Unconsciously, he copied Drew's walk and his manner of speech. Consciously, he copied Drew's way of sitting a horse and the way he tied his cravats. He kept up with Drew's pace and did whatever he could to win Drew's approval. On his part, Drew was grateful for the boy's company. Keeping busy and active in the brisk autumn air cleared his head of the many misgivings he had felt about letting Gwen go, and cleared his spirit of the doldrums that so often threatened to overcome him.

But Hetty was thoroughly bored, and before long she had coaxed the little party of men to agree to return to London. On their last evening in Suffolk, Tom had excused himself early and had gone wearily to bed. Selby, Drew and Hetty sat comfortably before the drawing-room fire, too somnolent or lazy to push themselves out of their chairs and mount the stairs to their bedrooms. "By the way, Hetty," Drew said suddenly, "I have not yet taken the opportunity to give you a good scold."

"Scold?" asked Hetty, all innocence. "Whatever for?"

Selby snorted. "Minx! You know perfectly well what for!"

"Oh, that!" said Hetty carelessly. "Drew knows I meant it all for the best."

"Nevertheless," Drew said firmly, "I'm very angry with you. A few days ago, Tom told me that Lady Hazel had given you the push, and then he asked me a very interesting question. He asked why I was *pleased* with Lady Hazel and *furious* with you."

"That *is* a good question," Hetty said promptly. "You ought to be fair, after all. If I did no worse than *she* did, why be angry at *me?*"

"I've thought about it since," Drew went on. "Do you want to hear my answer?"

"Will I like it?" Hetty asked.

"No."

"Then don't tell me."

"Shameless wench," said her husband sternly. "You should be on your knees begging his forgiveness instead of giving him pert answers. Tell her, Drew. Whatever it is, I'm sure it will teach her a lesson."

"Shall I, Hetty?" Drew asked kindly.

Hetty glanced up at her husband's stern face and nodded sheepishly. "Yes, please, Drew. I know I deserve whatever you have to say to me."

"Well, then, here it is. Lady Hazel did what she did because her daughter-in-law is blinded by grief, guilt, all sorts of complicated things, and needs someone to help her. Lady Hazel tried to help. I love her for it—"

"But . . . *I* tried to help, didn't I?" Hetty asked plaintively.

"*Whom* did you try to help?"

"Why, *you* of course."

"That's just it. That's what makes me angry. Am *I* making a muddle of my life? Am *I* blind and prejudiced and in an emotional turmoil? Is *that* what you think of me?"

"Oh, Drew! Of course not."

"You admit that I'm capable of conducting my own affairs adequately?"

"Oh, more than adequately," she assured him.

"Then I don't need your help, do I?"

"Well, I . . . I . . . guess not."

"Be *sure,* Hetty. You weren't helping me with this scheme of yours if I didn't need your help. You were *meddling.* If you have any respect for me at all, you must let me handle my own life from now on."

Hetty's eyes filled. "Oh, Drew, I *am* sorry." She got up and ran to his chair, dropping down on the floor in front of him and embracing his knees in humble contrition. "Please, please forgive me. I'm a complete fool, but I promise I'll never, *never* do such a thing again," she said, tears running down her cheeks.

Drew looked across at Selby in dismay, then looked down at his sister. "Hetty, do get up! Please. I didn't mean to make you cry. Of course, I forgive you. Hetty, please! Selby, do something!"

Selby shook his head and laughed. "Don't upset yourself, Drew. You know Hetty's tears. Talented little minx, I've always said so. If she's play-acting, there's no harm in it. And if those tears are real, they'll probably do her a world of good. So let her cry, my boy. Let her cry."

Chapter Eight

IT WAS AFTER TWO in the morning, and Sir Lambert Aylmer was no closer to being repaid than he had been when the evening began. He, Lord Warrenton, and Sir George Pollard sat over their brandies in Pollard's rooms, facing each other in discouragement. Sir George was in debt to Lambie for more than a thousand pounds, and to Richard Warrenton for a sum much larger than that. Even Sir George did not know the full extent of his indebtedness to numerous other creditors throughout London.

"Are you telling us, George," asked Richard Warrenton incredulously, "that you've not a feather to fly with?"

Sir George reached for the brandy bottle and refilled his glass. "I've been punting on tick for months," he said carelessly.

"If that don't beat all," said Lambie in disgust. "I thought we'd come here tonight to settle accounts. Instead, you sit there calm as summer noon and try to bamboozle us out of another role of soft!"

"I hate to admit this, George, but for once I have to agree with Lambie here. You know I stand your friend, but you can't expect me to untie my purse strings for you again without any hope of recouping."

"Or me either," Lambie added, shaking his head vigorously in agreement.

Sir George frowned at them. "You needn't worry. I'll come through in the end. Haven't I always done?"

"Don't know anything about that," said Lambie dubiously. "You ain't ever been this badly dipped before, have you?"

Warrenton helped himself to the brandy absently. "You're counting too heavily on the cards, old boy. I know you often have the devil's own luck, but cards are a fickle mistress. Wouldn't care to advance you *my* blunt with your talent at the card table as my only security. Too chancy by half."

"Well, what security would you care for? My estates are mortgaged to the hilt already. I *do* have a rich uncle, of course . . ."

At this, Lambie and Warrenton perked up and leaned forward. "Ah! A rich uncle!" said Warrenton. "Is he old? Is he sick?"

Sir George favored them with a sardonic smile. "He is old and sick and he despises me."

His friends leaned back, defeated. "I've always suspected you have a fortune hidden in that cane of yours. Diamonds or some such thing," Lambie suggested as a last, desperate hope.

"Whatever made you think that?" asked Warrenton.

"Well, he carries it with him everywhere. Mighty smoky, carrying a thing like that wherever you go."

George laughed mirthlessly. "Would you like to see what's inside it?" His guests watched interestedly as

George unscrewed the handle and pulled the handle from the stick. Attached to the handle was a thin-bladed, deadly-looking sword.

"Good heavens! What an evil-looking thing!" muttered Lambie, crushed.

"But useful from time to time, I imagine, eh, George?" said Warrenton, running his fingers over it in admiration.

"From time to time," George agreed, sheathing the blade with the hollow cane. "So . . . there's my treasure." He placed the cane, as always, well within reach, and the three men lapsed into silence.

"There's nothing for it, then, George. Except one thing," said Warrenton at last.

"And what's that?"

"Marriage. As soon as possible."

"You're out there," said Lambie, speaking with the authority of one whose familiarity with the social scene was beyond dispute. Lambie might be a fop and a court-card, but his disposition was cheerful, his clothes in the latest mode, and his fortune substantial; therefore, he was on every hostess's list of desirable guests. There was not a party or ball given in London to which Lambie was not invited. His foolish prattle irritated some and bored others, but most people were quite entertained by his on-dits and steady flow of gossip. There was very little going on in London that did not come to Lambie's ears or go out on Lambie's tongue.

Richard Warrenton, therefore, turned to Lambie with interest. "Why am I out?" he asked. "I see no reason why marriage is not a good idea. Look at George, now. Not bad looking, is he?"

Lambie regarded George with a professional eye. "If you don't count the scar on his cheek and his heavy eyebrows, yes, I suppose you could say he's not bad looking," Lambie conceded.

"Thank you," said George drily.

"And he has a good leg, hasn't he? Stand up, George, and show us a leg."

"Oh, go to the devil," said George, turning away in disgust.

"I'd say he has a good leg," Lambie said, ignoring George.

"And good address. You've got to admit he has excellent address," Warrenton added.

"Oh, yes," agreed Lambie, "no doubt about that."

"Well then, what else would a lady want?" Warrenton declared, self-satisfied at having made his point so well.

"He has no fortune," Lambie said, unmoved by Warrenton's logic.

"Pooh. Rich young ladies can manage without. Young ladies don't care for that."

"Their *mammas* care for that. And every mamma of every heiress in London knows that George is a loose screw," Lambie said with authority. "Sorry, George, but there it is."

George snorted. "Don't restrain your remarks on my account. You've said nothing that I haven't said myself."

"You see, Dick? He admits he's no prize on the marriage mart. Besides, everyone knows he's been in hot pursuit of Gwen Rowle ever since Rowle was shot."

"Yes," agreed Warrenton. "That's a mistake, George. There's no money *there,* you know."

"I don't need you two to tell me that," growled George. He filled his glass again and passed the bottle down the table. Warrenton filled his and Lambie's, and the three men drank in silence.

"I *will* get married," George said suddenly. His eyes glittered with the effect of brandy and inspiration. "One more loan, gentlemen, and you shall have your money back—every penny I owe you—in less than six months."

"Foxed," said Lambie to Warrenton confidentially. "Not a bit surprised. Feeling a bit well-to-live myself."

"I'm not foxed, you fool!" George snapped.

Lambie blinked at him. "Mus' be. Can't get married. We jus' settled all that."

"Do you think your society heiresses are the only rich

women in the world? I tell you, I'll marry a girl with more blunt than even Bella Arbuthnot."

"Impossible," declared Lambie.

Warrenton regarded George closely. "What are you thinking of, George? You're not thinking of selling yourself to a *cit?*"

"Why not? I'll find some nabob who wants my title for his daughter."

Lambie, on whom the liquor was beginning to have its effects, nodded drunkenly. "Good idea. Marry a cit. 'S done all the time."

"I don't know, George," said Warrenton dubiously. "Your title can't be worth very much, can it? A mere baron—?"

"True enough," agreed George with a sneer, "but I also have some other selling points, have I not? You said so yourself. I've a good leg, excellent address and I'm not bad looking, if one doesn't regard the scar and the eyebrows, isn't that right?"

Lord Richard Warrenton laughed and got to his feet. "Well said, old boy, well said. I suppose I can invest some blunt on your title and ... er ... other assets. What do you say, Lambie? Shall we stake him?"

Lambie looked up at Warrenton with bleary eyes. "Wha'ever you say, ol' f'llow. Jus' get me home to bed."

Warrenton smiled at George. "You have your stake, George. Lambie and I seem to be agreed once more." He turned and helped Lambie to his feet. When they had donned their hats and coats and stood at the door saying their goodnights, Warrenton gave Sir George a last warning. "This is the very last time, George. I hope you realize it. Remember, you have only six months."

Gwen had walked all the way from Hookham's library, and by the time she reached home her nose and fingers were tingling with the cold. She handed her pelisse to Mitching and was about to remove her bonnet when she noticed an enormous vase of fresh flowers on the table near the drawingroom door. "Oh, how lovely!" she exclaimed. "Where did those beautiful flowers come from, Mitching?"

"From Lord Jamison, my lady," the butler said impassively. "He gave them to Lady Hazel."

"Oh, I see," she said shortly. She stared at them, frowning for a moment, and then walked quickly up the stairs. She found Lady Hazel in the small sitting room, seated near the west window, a pair of spectacles perched precariously low on the bridge of her nose. Hazel was trying valiantly to catch the last of the daylight to illuminate the slipper she was crocheting for Tom. Gwen came into the room and almost slammed the door behind her. Lady Hazel looked up over her spectacles. "Oh, Gwen! How was your walk?" she asked cheerily.

"Never mind my walk," Gwen said furiously. "How could you *dare* to permit Lord Jamison into my house? And to accept his flowers! You knew very well that I would *never* have permitted it, had I been here!"

Lady Hazel regarded her with mild surprise. "I believe you are laboring under a misapprehension, my dear..."

"Misapprehension? I think not," Gwen said icily.

"But really—" Lady Hazel began.

"Were those flowers brought by Lord Jamison?"

"Yes, indeed, but—"

"Then I've apprehended the situation perfectly." She threw her bonnet on the sofa with an angry toss and began to pace about the room. "Am I never to be free of that man? I thought I had made it quite clear to him that— But never mind. There's no hope for me at all if my own family connives with him behind my back. Really, Hazel, I would have thought that *you,* of all people—"

"Gwen, don't be a shrew," Lady Hazel said, putting down her crocheting and rising with elaborate dignity. "You're making a cake of yourself."

"Good heavens, Hazel, you sound like Tom. Whatever do you mean?"

"I mean that you have no right to scold me about Lord

Jamison's visit. It had nothing whatever to do with you."

"Nothing to do with *me?*" Gwen asked, baffled.

"Nothing," Lady Hazel responded decisively. "The gentleman came calling on *me,* if you please."

Gwen was at a loss for words. "On you?"

Lady Hazel was enjoying herself hugely, though she was careful not to smile. But her eyes had a decided twinkle as she threw her shawl over her shoulder with an insouciant swing and swept to the door. "Yes, on *me.* And incidentally, my dear, the reason he came was to give me a gift. He wanted to deliver it in person."

"A g-gift?"

"Yes, my dear, a gift. Flowers. The flowers, you see, were for *me!*" And with a saucy toss of her head, she sailed out of the room.

Gwen stared after her, openmouthed. Had Drew truly come to see Hazel? She felt a complete fool. With a little stamp of her foot in irritation, she glared at the door. Hazel had quite enjoyed watching her make a dolt of herself. She ran to the door and down the hall. She caught up with her mother-in-law at the bend of the corridor that led to Lady Hazel's bedroom. "Hazel, wait," she said breathlessly.

Hazel paused and turned. With an eyebrow raised quizzically, she asked demurely, "Yes, dear?"

"How can you be sure?" Gwen asked challengingly. "How do you know that Drew wasn't just using you..."

"Using me?"

"As a ruse to get into the house to see me."

Lady Hazel looked at Gwen with an expression that combined pity with annoyance. "You're becoming quite puffed up with yourself, Gwen," she said shortly, and turned on her heel and marched off down the hall. "I *know* he came to see me because he told me so," she called over her shoulder. Then she disappeared into her room, letting the door close behind her with a decided slam.

Gwen pouted and followed. Without bothering to knock, she opened Hazel's door and poked her head in.

"He *told* you so, did he? Well, what does *that* prove?" she asked in a tone of heavy sarcasm.

"It proves nothing to a suspicious mind," Hazel retorted, motioning Gwen to come in and sit down. "However, since he waited outside our door in his carriage until he saw you leave the house, I am quite convinced that he had no interest whatever in seeing you."

"Oh," said Gwen, crestfallen. "Did he do that?"

Lady Hazel's eyes had held a twinkle throughout the exchange with her daughter-in-law, but now the twinkle faded. "Yes, love," she said kindly, "I'm afraid he did."

"I see." Gwen sat down on the edge of a chair, her eyes thoughtful. "Hazel, has it occurred to you that Drew can accomplish through *you* the goal he could not accomplish through me?" she asked, her tone no longer tinged with accusation but with a weary despondency.

"What goal is that?"

"He had hoped that a ... friendship with me would put an end to the gossip concerning the duel. He could not succeed in that, so ... don't you see ... ?"

Hazel fixed her puzzled eyes on her daughter-in-law's face. "No, I'm afraid I don't quite ..."

Gwen looked up at her mother-in-law earnestly. "A friendship with you—Rowle's *mother*—would accomplish the very same thing." Her eyes wavered and dropped embarrassedly as Hazel's face showed her disdain for what Gwen was suggesting. "Isn't it true that *your* approval of his company would quiet the gossip as effectively as mine?"

"I suppose it would," Hazel answered coldly. "Are you asking me to refrain from receiving him?"

Gwen recognized the coolness in Hazel's voice. She glanced up, her eyes troubled. "I can't ... I know I shouldn't ask such a thing of you—" she began hesitantly.

"Well, you needn't worry," Hazel cut in. "When Lord Jamison brought the flowers to me today, he explained—in the kindest way possible—why he intended never to visit this house again. So you see, you are quite out about his motives."

"Oh," Gwen said in a small voice, edging back in her chair and lowering her eyes. "May I ask what reason he gave you for that intention?"

"He said that he at last realizes that his presence causes you pain. He therefore has decided not to 'inflict' himself upon you again."

Gwen stared at Hazel for a moment, then looked down at her hands folded in her lap like a chastised schoolgirl. "I *have* been quite puffed up with myself, haven't I?" she asked, shamefaced.

"Yes, a bit," Hazel said gently.

"You should be quite cross with me. I've been terribly rude to you."

Lady Hazel came up behind Gwen's chair and put her hand on Gwen's shoulder. "You are my family, as I am yours. If we're rude sometimes, we can easily be forgiven on the grounds of intimacy. Especially if the injured party understands the reasons."

"*Do* you understand the reasons why I was so rude?" Gwen asked, turning to look up at her.

"I think I do."

Gwen looked down at her hands again. "You think I...I...love him...don't you?"

Lady Hazel looked down at Gwen's averted head with a small, tender smile. "I've been suspecting something of the sort."

Gwen got up and walked slowly to the door. "It doesn't make any difference, you know. Not a bit of difference. I'll never marry him," she said in that weary voice. And she left the room.

Hazel looked at the closed door with troubled eyes. "No, I don't suppose you will, poor child," she said with a sigh.

Drew was just finishing a letter to his man of business when Mallow announced Tom. Drew had not seen the boy since they'd returned from Suffolk, and he looked up from his desk with a warm smile. "Tom, old man, it's good to see you," he said. "I had quite convinced myself that, in the press of your various London activities, you'd forgotten me completely."

Tom shook his head in an embarrassed denial. "You know that's not so," he said shyly. "I just didn't want to make a dashed nuisance of myself."

"Cawker!" Drew said affectionately. "You know better than that."

"I hoped you'd come around to our house," Tom suggested tentatively.

Drew turned away from the boy's direct stare. "I'm afraid I won't be stopping at Rowle House in future," he said quietly, fingering his quill pen absently.

Tom, well aware that a serious rift had occurred between his sister and Drew during the stay at Stonehaven, looked down at his shoes in awkward silence.

"However, I hope I don't need to say," Drew said earnestly, "that you are welcome here whenever it pleases you to come. And your visits had better be frequent," he added with a smile, "or you shall have me thinking that my reputation among the young bucks of your acquaintance is slipping badly."

Tom grinned. "No fear of that, at any rate."

"Can you take luncheon with me today? I'm expecting Wys shortly, and I know he'd like to see you."

"Yes, thank you. I'd like to. By the way, Drew, my friends and I stopped in at Jackson's gym last week. I looked for you, but I was told you hadn't come in."

"Circumstances prevented it last week. But I plan to go in next Thursday. Would you like to come along with me?"

Tom looked at him eagerly. "Do you mean it?" he asked, obviously thrilled at the prospect. "I wouldn't be in your way?"

"Don't be a gudgeon. Would I ask you if I thought that?"

Tom blushed with pleasure. "Well, if you're sure..."

"Good," Drew said smiling. "I'll come by for you next Thursday at two—" His expression clouded over. "I mean . . . perhaps you could come by *here* at about two," he finished lamely.

Tom nodded and awkwardly got to his feet. In an obvious attempt to dispel the shadow that Drew's relationship with his sister had cast between them, he looked around the room for a subject to talk about. His eye fell upon a magnificent pair of dueling pistols which were mounted on the wall above the fireplace. "Oh, I say, Drew," he said admiringly, "what fine pis—"

But Drew seemed not to hear. He had risen and walked to the window. He now stood with his back to the room, staring out at nothing in particular. "Did you tell her you were coming here today?" he asked without turning.

"Do you mean Gwen?" Tom asked, feeling stupid and inept.

Drew nodded.

"Well, I . . ." Tom paused. He would have liked to throttle his sister. If she had any sense, she would know that a man like Drew could never have done anything dishonorable. Drew seemed to Tom so honest, so manly, so competent, so strong, so confident! He might have been Tom's brother-in-law, if Gwen were not so blind! Tom, whose father was confined to a sedentary life and who had no older brother to model himself upon, felt that his association with Drew was the most fortunate stroke of fate ever to have befallen him. Would his sister spoil even *this?* "I didn't tell her," he admitted miserably.

Drew heard the shame in his voice and roused himself from the mood of self-pity which had suddenly engulfed him. He had been selfish and thoughtless and had embarrassed and depressed his guest. He turned quickly and crossed the room. Putting his arm across the boy's shoulder, he said in a direct, casual way, "Perhaps it *is* best not to discuss me with her. I don't want you to lie to her about anything, of course. If she should ask you where you've been or where you're going, you must tell her. But I see no harm in avoiding the subject of our friendship, if you can. The knowledge would only upset her, after all."

Tom nodded gratefully. Drew's straightforwardness had cleared the air. "I won't tell her about going to Jackson's next week, then," he said in relief.

"No need to, as far as I can see. I'll get you home early enough to prevent her feeling any concern about your whereabouts. Now, then, what did you ask me a moment ago?"

"Oh, yes. I was wondering about those pistols on the wall. They are *something like!*"

"Aren't they?" Drew smiled and crossed to the fireplace. He took one of the pistols down from the wall and handed it to Tom. "The silver work on the butt is remarkably intricate—a veritable work of art, I'm told."

Tom took the pistol in his hand and turned it over admiringly. "Those stones—they're surely not *real* rubies, are they?" he asked in awe.

"My boy!" said Drew in mock dismay. "It won't do at all to suggest that the Regent would possess anything false!"

Tom goggled at him. "Did these belong to the Prince Regent?"

"Oh, yes. Who else would have ordered a pair of weapons of such grandeur?" Drew laughed.

"How did *you* come by them, Drew?"

"Prinny wagered them in a shooting match. I won."

Tom gaped at him in awe. "What a prize! I'd give an arm to own a gun like this!"

"Nonsense. All that ornamentation would spoil your grip. Those pistols are good only for display."

"You mean you've never used them?" Tom asked thoughtlessly. "Aren't these the guns you used to—?" He stopped, colored to the tips of his ears, and hung his head miserably.

"To fight my infamous duel? No, those were not the guns, have no fear," Drew said drily.

"I... I'm s-sorry..." Tom stammered.

"Look here, Tom," Drew said pleasantly, "you must learn to speak your mind freely, if we're to be friends. It won't do to have to walk on eggs with each other, you know. By the way, if you really like these pistols, I'd be glad to give them to you."

"Give them to me!" Tom said, overwhelmed. "Oh, no, I couldn't take such a gift!"

"Why not? *I* never liked them above half. Prinny's taste has always seemed to me more than a little ostentatious."

"I don't know about that, Drew," Tom said firmly, recovering his equilibrium, "but I know that I can't accept them. However, I'd be more than grateful if I could borrow them for a day or two..."

"Borrow them? Of course you may. But whatever for?"

"Well, you see," said Tom with a mischievous grin. "I'd like to show them to Ferdy and Quent. Ferdy has a watch fob from his father that he shows off constantly, and Quent makes us wild bragging about his brother's thoroughbred. If I could show them *these,* they'd turn positively *green!*"

Drew grinned. "I see. Well, then, take them by all means. We'll have Mallow find the case and pack them up properly. There's nothing more satisfying in the world, I am sure, than making one's friends green."

Wys strolled at a leisurely pace down Jermyn Street, having left his lodgings in plenty of time to arrive at Drew's door at the appointed hour for luncheon. The day was bright and sunny, though the wind had a strong bite in it, forecasting the winter weather that daily threatened to arrive. He was glad he had worn his brown greatcoat. Although it sported only three capes, it afforded him more than adequate protection against the brisk wind.

The street seemed unusually noisy this forenoon: a number of dirty urchins were gathered on the opposite side of the street quarreling loudly over some prize; a number of carts and wagons were trundling along clattering over the cobbles on their way toward St. James Street; vendors were hawking their wares in their timeless, singsong way; and, most irritating to Wys, the driver of a hired hack was shouting curses at a wizened, gnarled old man who was pulling a cart loaded heavily with apples.

Wys watched the machinations of the hack-driver with some amusement, in spite of his irritation. Every time the driver tried to pass the cart, some vehicle appeared to block his way. His curses became louder and more crude, but neither his maneuvers nor his language assisted him in his progress. Suddenly the driver's patience exhausted itself, and—seemingly heedless of the consequences—he urged his horses to move around the cart. There was a horrid, wrenching sound, the rear right wheel of the cart broke off, and the cart tipped over directly in the path of the hack and spilled its russet contents all over the street. The horses, after a moment of nervous shying, calmed down and nosed interestedly through the apples.

The wizened old apple-vendor confronted the hack-driver, amply proving that he was the driver's equal both in the volume of his voice and the crudity of his curses. To Wys's surprise, the door of the hack was thrown open and a young lady, blushing hotly in embarrassment and chagrin, stepped out. Wys could not help staring at her. Wrapped in a rose-colored pelisse and a modest poke bonnet, she made a startling contrast to the drab surroundings, like a blooming rose in a winter landscape. Wys could see that under her bonnet her hair was dark, her eyes, now beginning to brim with tears of frustration, were a soft grey, and her mouth had an expression of unusual sweetness. She tried to say something to her driver, but her voice had no effect in the din of the street and the shouts of the two antagonists.

Wys could not help but go to her aid. He strode into the street and gave her a quick bow. "Your servant, ma'am," he said politely. "May I be of assistance?"

The grey eyes flew to his face in gratitude. "Oh, yes, sir, if only you would," she said in a voice that, Wys noted with pleasure, seemed perfectly to suit her modest demeanor. "I find I am not at all equal to this dreadful situation. No one is paying the least attention to me."

Her words, spoken with a woeful tremor of the voice, were accompanied by the lowering of her eyelids, on which some tears were already clinging. Wys, always susceptible to feminine affliction, was particularly inspired by the young lady now before him. He turned on the disputants with greater fury than his moderate nature had ever before permitted him. "Will you both be still?" he shouted. "Hold your vile tongues!"

The driver and the old man turned to him in surprise, their argument suspended. "Eh?" the driver asked, blinking. "And 'oo the devil might *you* be?"

The wizened old apple-man knew quality when he saw it and touched his cap to Wys respectfully. "Beggin' y'r pardon, sir, but look what this damn' chaffer-mouth 'as done to me cart!"

"That's no excuse for using such execrable, disgusting, and repellent language!" Wys said furiously. "Don't you see there's a lady present?" He wheeled around to the driver. "And as for *you,* you unspeakable cur, have you so forgotten yourself as to ignore your passenger? When a lady hires your hack, she puts herself in your charge! Have you no sense of your own responsibility?"

The driver glanced guiltily at the lady standing alongside the carriage. He dropped his eyes to the ground, and, seeing an apple lying at his feet, kicked it away shamefacedly. "I wuz only tryin' to get 'er to 'er destination. What wuz I to do when this idiot kept blockin' me way!"

"I got a right to the street, same 's you, you bum-squabbled bag-pudding!" the old man burst out, waving a fist in the driver's face.

"Enough of that, I said!" Wys told the old man in a voice that indicated he would not be disobeyed. The old man subsided, muttering under his breath about the ruined cart and the lost apples.

Wys put a hand into his pocket and pulled out five guineas. "Will this cover the price of the apples and the repair to your cart?" he asked.

The man gaped at the gold coins in Wys's hand. "Oh, yes, sir!" he said, licking his lips eagerly. "Yes, indeedy. And much obliged to you I'd be!"

"Very well, then. And here, take this and pay some of those boys to help you pull the cart out of the way."

It was done with a dispatch Wys could scarcely credit. The old man was out of sight before Wys had helped the lady back into the carriage. The driver looked at the mound of apples in the middle of the road and shook his head. "You should've made 'im clean up, you should," he said to Wys accusingly. "Can't leave a pile of apples in the middle of a public thoroughfare."

Wys regarded the apples thoughtfully. "I suppose you're right," he said. He looked at the crowd of passers-by who were watching the little scene delightedly. "Ho, there," he called to them. "You're welcome to these apples—as many as you can carry away." A cheer rose from the crowd, and the pile was set upon with alacrity. Soon every apple was gone. Wys turned to the carriage, where the lady was watching him from the window.

"Oh, sir," she said breathlessly as he came up to the window to take his leave, "I don't know how to thank you. I . . . I know I could not have extricated myself from this muddle without your help."

"Not at all, ma'am," Wys said, feeling suddenly quite tongue-tied and awkward. "It was nothing at all."

The young lady held out her hand to him shyly. "You are too modest, sir. I shall never forget . . . I mean, I am quite in your debt."

Wys took the gloved hand in his and glanced up at her warm grey eyes. He would have liked to say that he wished he could do *more* for her . . . fight a dragon for her . . . win a joust for her . . . buy the *moon* for her. There was something about her that brought out these extravagant emotions in him. He felt quite unlike himself. But a lifetime of restraint is not easily overcome. "It was my pleasure, ma'am," was all he said. He bowed, kissed her fingers, and reluctantly stepped back from the carriage.

The driver flicked the reins, and the horses set off down the street. The carriage was almost out of sight when Wys realized with a blow that he had not learned the young lady's name.

Inside the carriage, Miss Anabel Plumb struggled with herself. Her hand had just been kissed by the most divine gentleman she had ever met, and she wanted to get one more glimpse of him. But if he should see her gawking at him, he would surely think her quite ill-bred. She hesitated for a moment, and then—throwing caution to the winds—she turned around on the seat and pressed her face to the little window behind her. But it was too late. Several carriages and wagons had already come between her and her splendid rescuer. Peering desperately down the crowded street, she managed to get a glimpse of his brown greatcoat and his tall beaver hat, but at that moment the carriage turned a corner and she was carried inexorably away from the most romantic encounter of her life.

Chapter Nine

POLLARD LOOKED AROUND AT the dusty office overlooking Fleet Street in distaste. The sun shone through the smeared windows, making a streak of mottled sunlight through the dusty air, illuminating the piles of notebooks and ledgers which were piled in a seemingly haphazard way on the shelves of the various bookcases ranged along the walls. The walls were completely unadorned, there being no picture or decoration of any kind to enliven their bleak grey-green expanse. Opposite Sir George, on a chair at a large, paper-laden desk, sat the man he had come to see, regarding him closely through a pair of gold-rimmed spectacles.

George shifted uneasily under the directness of the man's stare. Those owl-like eyes, large and protruding to begin with, seemed enormous and disconcerting through the spectacles. The man had a broad, ugly nose mottled by a number of broken blue veins which could be seen quite plainly through the reddened skin. His hair, thin on top, had been permitted to grow unstylishly long at the bottom and blended with his grizzled side-whiskers to give him a rather stern and forbidding appearance. His mouth had a full underlip, his cleft chin was nothing if not decided, and all in all, Sir George had the uncomfortable feeling that this man would make a formidable adversary.

After what seemed an interminable period, the man leaned forward and spoke. "All right," he said brusquely, "fifteen thousand on the wedding day and three thousand a year thereafter."

"I'd rather have forty thousand at once than the yearly stipend you suggest," George said in a tone which did not at all betray his inner tremor at the effrontery of his suggestion.

"Do you take Joshua Plumb for a flat?" the man at the desk asked in disgust. "I didn't amass a fortune single-handed by behavin' like a damn fool. You ain't an earl or a duke, y'know. You come pretty high for a baron, near as I can learn from my friend Harry Atwater, who got a real marquis for his girl for a lot less than I'm offerin' you."

"If, as I believe, you are speaking of the Marquis of Wetherbridge, your friend made himself a bad bargain even at *that* price. The marquis is a fop and a dolt and has cost your friend a fortune on his jewelry alone. I'm told the marchioness complains that her husband does nothing all day but change his clothes," Sir George said with a sneer.

"That may be," Mr. Plumb said. "But it's worth it to Atwater just to hear himself say 'my daughter the marchioness.' Anyways, I'd be a damn fool to give you a sum outright. What'd keep you from runnin' off as soon as the money was in your hands?"

George put up his chin in his haughtiest manner. "My dear Mr. Plumb, you are speaking to a *gentleman!*"

Joshua Plumb snorted. "In matters o' money, I've yet

to see a man behave gentlemanly. I've no wish to quarrel with you, Sir George, seein' as how I'm considerin' makin' you my son-in-law, but Joshua Plumb ain't a man to talk in circles. The straight of it is that you're marryin' for money. On matters of money, Joshua Plumb knows whereof he speaks." He leaned forward, his elbows on the desk, and wagged a pudgy finger at Pollard. "I don't make investments without they have proper security. I make my fifteen-thousand-pound investment in you the day you marry my girl. As long as she keeps tellin' me you're good to her, you'll get your annual payment. If she's happy, you'll find me more than generous. Well, take it or leave it."

Sir George looked at the man balefully. "Very well. Agreed."

"My girl has to see you first, before things can be settled. But if I tell her, she'll have you, so there's nothin' need worry you there. But I ain't got time for a long courtship. I want the thing settled as soon as can be."

"Why is that, may I ask?" George said suspiciously. "You're not trying to...er...pass on to me some *damaged goods,* are you?"

Mr. Plumb ogled at him owlishly for a moment, and then George's meaning burst upon him. He sputtered speechlessly, his neck growing red and his face apoplectic. As soon as he could catch his breath, he rose to his feet and banged his fist furiously on the desk. "Why, you—! You damned make-bait! I'll pull out your brummish tongue for you! My daughter is the sweetest, purest flower in all England, and much too good for a dirty-minded ivory-turner like you. Out of my office, you hear! Out!"

Sir George realized he'd made a serious blunder. The father's shock at his suggestion that the girl might be less than pure was absolutely genuine. He had better find a way to make amends. Men of Joshua Plumb's wealth, men who were eager to buy titles for ready cash, were not easy to come by. It was only through the good offices of Richard Warrenton's man of business that he had learned of Mr. Plumb. This was his only lead, and he must not make a mull of it. He had the reputation of being a man of ready wit and good address. Now was the time to prove it. "Please, Mr. Plumb," he said earnestly, "I beg to be forgiven. It was inexcusable. I see that now."

"Inexcusable! It was . . . *unspeakable!* Just get out, you damned court-card. I won't have anything to do with you."

"But, sir, remember that I have not the advantage of having *met* your daughter. I'm sure if I had, I would have known that such an accusation was unthinkable."

"That at least is the truth," Mr. Plumb said, still furious.

"I see that now, of course. But you must understand my position. You are the one, after all, who put the idea into my head."

"*I*, you jackanapes?" Plumb roared. "How could I even *hint* at such a thing about my girl?"

"Well, you *were* urging a wedding in rather unseemly haste," George suggested carefully.

Joshua Plumb eyed him dubiously. There was some logic in what he'd just said. Joshua sank back in his chair and looked at the younger man. Pollard was good-looking and certainly not a fool. His clothes were up to the mark but not so foolishly foppish as Harry Atwater's son-in-law was wont to wear. Pollard seemed to be the sort of man that women take pleasure in, though Joshua himself did not like him much. Something about the eyes . . . a coldness . . . something he couldn't put his finger on. But his wife was pressing him to marry Anabel off, and there was no doubt that *this* specimen was better than some he'd seen. Well, he thought, I may as well try again. "All right," he said gruffly, "perhaps I *did* put that curst idea in your head. Sit down, sit down, I'll not strike you. I suppose I'd better explain why I said I wanted a short courtship."

"It's not necessary. I have no doubt you have a good and honest reason," George said smoothly.

"Of course it's necessary! I don't want you to have the slightest doubt about my daughter! Not the slightest! She's a good girl. The best! It's my wife, you see, who's the problem."

"Your wife?"

"My second, y'know. Damned nuisances, second marriages, let me tell you. Anabel is the only child of my first wife, and as pretty and sweet a little thing as ever walked. But her mother passed on more'n ten years ago, and a man needs a wife, y'know, especially when he's used to one. So I married the second Mrs. Plumb, without thinkin' that her two daughters from *her* first marriage was goin' to cause such a ruckus in the house. Plain as lemmings they are, poor things, and you can imagine that Mrs. Plumb don't like my Anabel takin' the shine out of her girls."

"Ah," said Pollard, his brow clearing. "I begin to see—"

"Right. Nothin' for it but to get Anabel married and out of the way. But I want to do right by my girl. She's educated proper—like any Lord's daughter, I promise you—and I want her to have a title and mix with the swells and have a town house and a country place and everything money can buy. I'm determined on it. Well, that's the long and the short of it."

"I understand, Mr. Plumb," Pollard said, rising and reaching for his hat and cane. "Now I quite see the need for haste, and I am willing to set a wedding date just as soon as I can put certain of my . . . er . . . *affairs* in order. That is, if your daughter approves of me. I'm sure that, from what you say of her, *I* shall find *her* delightful."

Mr. Plumb stood up and held out his hand. "Then nothin' remains but to come to dinner and see her. Shall we say Friday next?"

Pollard nodded and the two shook hands, each one feeling quite pleased with himself. They had found themselves in rough waters, and each was convinced that his own tact and aplomb had won the day.

* * *

Ferdie Brinsleigh was twenty years old, the only young man in his circle to have his own lodgings. His parents, devoted to country life, had no house in town, but it was worth the expense of permitting Ferdie to have his own London flat to get him out of their way. So Ferdie had rented the largest flat he could afford on a rather generous allowance, furnished it in suitable bachelor style, hired a cook, a valet, and a butler, and had set up housekeeping. The flat became the haven for all his friends, the one place where they could relax, safe from adult supervision.

Late on a November afternoon, Ferdie was playing host to his closest chums, Quentin Cavendish and Tom Spaulding. Too young to be admitted into the various gambling clubs of London, the friends had their own games at Ferdie's table. The wine was plentiful, the company was congenial, and the stakes low enough to be borne by gentlemen whose pockets were far from plump. Today, Ferdie had asked his friends to come early and stay on into the night, for he planned to serve them dinner and, if they wished, a light supper at midnight.

Tom was the first to arrive, carrying under his arm a large case of polished wood with shiny brass fittings. "What have you there?" Ferdie asked when Tom placed it on the table ceremoniously.

"You'll see," Tom answered mysteriously. "Where's Quent?"

"Hasn't arrived yet. Come on, Tom, what's the mystery?"

"No mystery. I just want to wait for Quent, that's all. What have you to eat? I'm starved."

"Dinner is not until six. Meanwhile, you'll have to make do with this port."

"Port? Very well, pour me a glass. But I warn you, I shall probably get tiddly. I always do, if I drink when I'm hungry."

"And you're always hungry," Ferdie said with a snort. "You'd better not drink too much or you'll be completely foxed by the time you go home."

"Don't worry. If you feed me a proper dinner, I shall sober up all right and tight," Tom retorted, and downed the port at a gulp.

By the time Quent arrived, both his host and Tom were feeling giddy. Quent looked at them in disgust. "Couldn't you wait for me?" he asked querulously. "I hate being sober when everyone else is feeling so well-to-live."

"No need to complain. Drink a glass or two and catch up," Ferdie suggested with a foolish smile.

"Besides, we waited for you before we opened the box," Tom said excitedly, his eyes glittering with port-induced brightness.

"What box?" Quent asked.

"This one," Tom said proudly, picking it up from the table and holding it before him. He paraded around the room dramatically, stumbling only once or twice—holding the box high, as if he were carrying the Holy Grail—and humming a martial tune, quite off key.

"Well, open it then," said Ferdie impatiently, "and stop acting as if you're carrying the crown jewels around the room."

"It's almost like the crown jewels," Tom said, grinning. "Closer to the crown jewels than you think!"

"Then open it, man," said Quent, "and let us *see* whatever it is."

Tom looked from one to the other until he was satisfied that they were adequately curious. Then he seated himself at the head of the table and placed the box carefully before him, the clasps facing front. He wiped the fingerprints away with his sleeve and touched the clasps. Then, with a glimmer of mischief, he withdrew his hands. "No," he teased, "I think I'll wait until after we've eaten."

"No, we won't," said Ferdie, and reached over to undo the clasps himself.

"Stop!" cried Tom dramatically. "No one may touch this box but I! On peril of his life!"

Ferdie, just drunk enough to worry about Tom's silly

threat, quickly withdrew his hand. Quent, however, was quite sober and had had enough of Tom's drunken clowning. "Move aside and let me open it," he said impatiently. "I'll take my chances on my life."

Tom pushed him away. "All right, all right, I'll open it now, if you insist."

"I *do* insist, you lobcock," Quent said, and the three heads bent over the box. Tom undid the catches with proper ceremony and lifted the lid. There, nestled in green velvet, lay the two dueling pistols.

"Good Lord!" gasped Ferdie, awed.

"Are they real?" whispered Quent, sufficiently impressed to satisfy Tom.

"Would the Regent order anything false?" Tom said importantly.

"The Regent? Are they *his?*" asked Ferdie.

Quent looked at Tom askance. "I don't believe you. Are you saying all those stones are *real?* There must be *hundreds* of them!"

"They must be worth a fortune! Where did you get them?" Ferdie demanded.

"They're Drew's. He won them from the Regent. Ain't they something like?"

The boys nodded solemnly, Quent passing his hand gently over one of the pistol-butts. "I've never seen anything like them," he breathed.

"Lord Jamison must have windmills in his skull to let you carry these around," Ferdie said jealously.

"Not at all," Tom said proudly. "He offered to *give* them to me."

"*Give* them to you?" Quent asked, astonished. "He *couldn't!*"

"Why not? He don't like them above half. Said they're only good for decoration, anyhow."

"Are you telling us these pistols are *yours?*" Ferdie demanded.

"No. 'Cause I wouldn't take them."

The boys gawked at him. "Why not?" Ferdie asked. "*I*

wouldn't have had the will to say 'no' to a gift like that!"

"I couldn't take such an expensive gift. Wouldn't be at all the thing. Just borrowed them to show to you, that's all," Tom explained.

Quent's eye brightened. "Come on, let's have a duel." He lifted a pistol from the box, and taking the muzzle end in his right hand proffered the butt end over his left arm toward Ferdie. "Here's your weapon, Prince Rhodomontade." Then he repeated the process and offered a gun to Tom. "And yours, Sir Aguecheek. Now, back to back, so. Good. Gentlemen, count your paces, please."

Tom and Ferdie counted ten paces as they walked in opposite directions, the guns held up before them. Quent continued. "When I say 'ready,' you may turn. On my cry 'Aim,' you will cock your pistols, and you may fire any time after I say 'Fire!' Is that clear?"

The adversaries nodded. "Ready...Aim...Fire!" cried Quent. Ferdie shouted "Pow!" and clicked the empty pistol.

"Missed me!" laughed Tom. "Now I have you!"

Ferdie took a courageous pose. "Fire away, you cur!" he said with a stiff upper lip.

"Pow!" shouted Tom. Ferdie clasped his breast and staggered to one knee. "I...I'm done for! Give my fob...to...to the girl I love!" he gasped and fell to the floor. Tom burst into laughter and Quent into applause.

"You belong in Covent Garden," said Quent, helping Ferdie to his feet. "You would have a great career as an actor."

"All my family are superb mummers," Ferdie agreed modestly.

Quent picked up the gun that Ferdie had dropped during his 'dying' scene and fingered it lovingly. "Too bad these pistols are only ornamental and don't really shoot," he said with a sigh.

"Of course they really shoot," Tom said indignantly.

"But you said they were for decoration. I heard you," Quent insisted.

"I said that Drew *uses* them for decoration. He don't like the grip. I never said they won't shoot. Of course they shoot!"

"Easy enough to prove," Ferdie remarked with a shrug. "Let's fire one of them."

"That's using your cock-loft," Quent said eagerly. "Good idea!"

"What's so good about it?" Tom asked in annoyance. "How can we shoot without powder and bullets?"

"That's true," Ferdie was forced to acknowledge. "Where'll we get powder and bullets?"

"Don't you have a pistol?" Quent asked.

Ferdie favored him with a look of pure disgust. "Of course not. Why would I have a pistol?"

"It ain't uncommon for people to have pistols," Quent retorted.

"Is that so?" Ferdie challenged. "Do *you* have one?"

"Well, no, but—"

Ferdie snorted.

Quent knew he had been bested in the argument; nevertheless, he attempted to get the last word by muttering, "But I have a rifle . . . in the country . . ."

Ferdie's sneer deepened. "That's marvelous, that is! A rifle! In the country! That does us a great deal of good *now,* don't it?"

Quent shrugged and turned to the table, fingering the pistol box absently. Tom crossed to the sideboard and helped himself to another glass of port. "I guess you'll have to take my word for it. The guns shoot. They're perfect in every way."

"Wait!" Quent said in an arrested voice. "What's this?" He pointed to a small brass fitting at the bottom of the box.

Tom came up to him and looked closely at it. "I don't know. I thought it was just another ornament. What do *you* think—?"

Quent lifted the box and pushed the brass fitting. The bottom of the box dropped open, and out fell a powder horn, a box of bullets, and a silver ramrod. The boys gaped.

"A storage compartment!" Tom said breathlessly. "It's a storage compartment! Now we have everything we'll need!" The boys' eyes shone with excitement.

"Where'll we shoot?" Quent asked. "Into the fireplace?"

"No, no," Ferdie said quickly. "There must be a better place..." And his eyes roamed about the room.

"I know," said Tom. "We'll put a heavy cushion on the mantelpiece and shoot into it. The only thing we'll damage that way is the cushion."

Quent nodded his approval, although Ferdie looked dubious. Tom ignored his host's doubtful look and went quickly to the sofa. He felt the back cushions and the little pillows Ferdie had scattered about, but rejected them. Lifting the round bolster that was wedged alongside the arm of the sofa, he smiled in satisfaction. "This should do," he said.

Quent was busily loading the gun. "How do you put the powder in?" he asked.

Tom went to the mantelpiece and began clearing the objects that cluttered it. "Pour the powder into the muzzle, I think," he said, "and tamp it down with the ramrod." And he placed the bolster on the mantelpiece.

"I think it's all set," Quent said, pleased with himself.

"Let's see," said Ferdie, and he reached for the pistol.

"No!" Quent cried. "I want to fire first." He clutched the gun tightly to prevent Ferdie from pulling it out of his hand. There was a deafening report.

"Now see what you've done!" Ferdie shouted, half in anger and half in fright.

"Sorry, old man," Quent said in consternation. I didn't mean to pull the trigger. What did I hit?"

"I think," said Tom in a strangely constricted voice, "you hit...*me*...!"

They stared at Tom, aghast. A red stain on his left

shoulder was rapidly growing larger. "Oh, my God!" groaned Quent in agony.

Tom put his hand to his shoulder and then raised it slowly in front of his eyes. His fingers were stained with blood. His face grew ashen, his eyes drooped closed, and he slumped to the ground in a faint.

Quent and Ferdie ran and knelt beside him. Quent lifted his wrist and felt for his pulse. "He's alive..." he said, with a dubious hope in his voice.

"Yes, but..." Ferdie bit his lip nervously. "What do we do *now?*"

Wys and Drew sat in front of the fire in Drew's drawing room. For the past few evenings, Drew had not made the effort to engage in his usual pursuits. He had not been to his clubs, had accepted no invitations, nor had he called on any of his numerous acquaintances. Tonight, Wys had joined him in his self-inflicted withdrawal from the social whirl. Wys, too, was in no mood for gaiety and dissipation. Both men had been monosyllabic at dinner, but after a good number of brandies and a quiet hour before the fire, Wys had mellowed considerably, and before he quite realized it, he had told Drew about the girl in the carriage whom he had rescued three days before, and the strange feelings she had roused in him.

"You say she is quiet, well-bred and lovely? Mr. Farr, if I had to choose a young lady for you, those would be the very qualities I would look for," Drew said with a smile.

"Why so?" Wys asked curiously.

"Because there seems to be nothing extravagant about her. You say she is tall?"

"About average height, I'd say."

"Good. You wouldn't want a young lady to tower over you, or to whom you'd have to bend to speak, isn't that so?"

"Quite so," Wys said after considering the matter carefully.

"And her hair—neither too dark nor too light, I take it?"

"A light brown, I think."

"Quite suitable, I'd say," Drew said, hiding a smile behind his hand.

"And she had the loveliest eyes," Wys sighed. "So direct and honest—not blinking or flitting from side to side as so many ladies' do."

"Direct and honest. I would have surmised as much."

"Really?" asked Wys in surprise. "Why?"

"Direct and honest eyes are the only kind suitable for the direct and honest Wystan Farr," Drew answered.

"You may laugh at me," Wys said without a trace of irritation, "but what good is it all if I've lost her?"

"We can't be sure you've lost her. Perhaps, if you haunt Almack's every night, she may turn up there one evening."

"Are you serious? Do you think I should?"

"I suppose I'm half serious," Drew said with a laugh. "Every young lady of the *ton* must go to Almack's a few times during the season. It's almost *de rigueur*."

"But what if she's not of the *ton?*"

Drew looked at Wys in amused surprise. "What? Not of the *ton?* Wys, you astound me! The proper and respectable Mr. Farr could not be attracted to some . . . girl of the *streets,* could he?"

"Stop joking, Drew. She was well bred . . . a lady in every way, but . . ."

"But. . . ?" Drew asked encouragingly.

"But she *was* in a hired hack. And alone . . ."

"Ah, I see. A hired hack. No abigail in attendance. Very, very strange. The mystery deepens."

"You won't take this seriously, will you?" asked Wys, annoyed at last.

Drew looked across at his friend, saw the pain in his eyes, and was immediately repentant. "I'm sorry, Wys. It's only that it's hard to believe that you've tumbled into love at first sight, like the veriest schoolboy. It's so unlike you."

"I know. I can scarcely credit it myself. But she made

me feel—don't laugh, now!—like a . . ."

"Go ahead, tell me. I promise not to tease."

"Like a knight in armor!" Wys said, a bit shamefaced.

Drew shook his head. "The moderate, self-controlled Wys! It *must* be love. What else could have wrought such a change in you?"

"But what am I to do about it? I can't knock on every door in London asking 'Excuse me, madam, is there a girl living here who wears a rose-colored pelisse?'"

"I can't think of anything," Drew said, shrugging sympathetically. "Except that you might stroll on Jermyn Street at the same hour every day. Perhaps she may pass there on some regular errand."

"I've tried that for the last two days. No sign of her yet. It makes me feel so foolish to peer into carriages, I can tell you. I've received a goodly number of questioning glances from the riders."

"I can well imagine it." Drew sighed a melancholy sigh. "I'm afraid, Wys old boy, that neither one of us has any luck in love."

The two men leaned back in their chairs and gazed into the fire moodily. Their abstraction was soon interrupted by Mallow, who came up to Drew's chair and coughed lightly.

"Yes, Mallow, what is it?"

"A young man, sir, name of Quentin Cavendish. Says he must see you on a matter of urgency."

"Cavendish?" Drew mused. "I've heard that name somewhere. Send him in, Mallow."

A moment later, Drew looked up to see a rumpled-looking young man staring down at him in fright. His lips were white, his eyes wide, and he twisted the brim of his very stylish beaver nervously in his fingers. "Lord J-Jamison?" he stammered.

"Yes," Drew said kindly. "I'm Lord Jamison."

"I'm Quentin Cavendish. You don't know m-me—"

"I'm aware of that," Drew said with a smile, trying to tease the boy into a more relaxed state.

"I'm a friend of Tom's," Quent explained.

"Ah, yes, of course," Drew said warmly, rising and extending his hand. "Tom has spoken to me of you." They shook hands and Drew indicated Wys, deep in a wing chair. "This is my friend, Wystan Farr. Mr. Farr, Mr. Cavendish."

Quent extended a nervous hand to Wys and turned back to Drew. He opened his mouth to speak, lost his courage and closed it again. Drew watched him in some amusement and then said gently, "Is there anything I can do for you, Mr. Cavendish?"

"Yes. You see, we have Tom in the carriage outside . . ." he said lamely.

"Tom? Outside? I don't understand—"

"You see, sir, it was rather difficult to . . . that is, we didn't know where else to take him. His sister would raise a devil of a dust if we took him home, you see . . ."

Drew was beginning to feel a sense of impending disaster. "No, I'm afraid I don't quite—"

"He speaks of you so often, you know . . ." Quent said, trying to explain the situation sensibly but quite unable to do so with his head spinning and his stomach churning fearfully. "We hoped you could help him."

"*Help* him?" Drew asked tensely. "Is there something wrong with Tom?"

"Yes, sir, there's something very wrong," said Quent, quite near hysterics. "You see, I . . . Oh, God, Lord Jamison, I . . . shot him!"

Chapter Ten

GWEN STUDIED HERSELF IN the mirror with troubled eyes. She had dismissed her abigail impatiently, preferring to dress her own hair rather than endure the girl's chatter. She was engaged to attend a small dinner party at the Warrentons under the escort of Sir George, and she had determined to make herself enjoy it. One of her favorite gowns was laid out on the bed. The underdress was of a white Persian silk called belladine and had small, puffed sleeves, a square neckline cut in a low decolletage, and a graceful flounce at the bottom. Over this she would wear a bronze-colored sleeveless coat of Venetian twill which would be laced tightly beneath the breasts but would otherwise hang loose to reveal the silk underdress as she walked. Determined to make this evening as festive as possible, she had spent the last of the pin-money she had allotted herself for this quarter to buy a pair of bronze-colored silk slippers and a new pair of long white gloves. These, still enticingly wrapped in tissue paper, the abigail had also laid out on the bed.

But somehow the pleasure she had expected to feel when dressing for this festive occasion was completely absent. She was not sure what it was that so depressed her spirits. Was it her feeling that the people with whom Sir George surrounded himself all seemed slightly disreputable? Certainly the expectation of being ogled by Lord Warrenton through his quizzing glass was irritating, but could it explain why she was so sunk in the dismals? She had subjected herself to his scrutiny before, and she knew just how to give him his deserved set-down. No, it was more than Lord Warrenton's vulgarity which was troubling her.

If she were to be honest with herself, she would have to admit that the whole circle in which she moved was not to her liking. Sir George was an attractive man who never bored her, but even he had a slightly disreputable air. Certainly his friend Lambert Aylmer was above reproach, but Gwen could not abide Lambie for long. He tended to attach himself to her for interminable periods, breathing down her neck with his whispered revelations of the doings of the *ton*. No wonder he was called Lambie the Leech.

In George's circle, the conversation depended heavily on the latest gossip, cards and gambling, or humor heavily tinged with sexual innuendo. Gwen could not accuse any of them of breaking the rules of etiquette, but there were many times when she felt that the remarks and the quips were beyond what she considered good taste. Of course, her values might be too old-fashioned. Was it possible she had become stiff and old-cattish?

Why didn't Sir George and his friends ever talk intelligently about the trouble the Whigs were facing in Parliament, about the chances of peace with Napoleon, about the enduring value of Lord Byron's exciting poetry—the sort of conversation she had heard at Stonehaven? Why wasn't the dinner conversation at the Warrentons at all like the conversation in Drew's circle?

Drew...there was the crux of it, of course. She couldn't fool herself. Not only could she not banish Drew from her thoughts, but she was beginning to waver in her conviction that he was truly at fault in the duel. Everything she had heard of him from people she respected—people like Hazel and Wystan Farr and even her own brother—proved him to be a man of excellent, even admirable, character. Over and over she had heard him described as kind, generous, and honest. Even the gossip which had spread through all the drawing rooms of London with lightning speed following the scene at the Selby ball seemed not to have adversely affected him. He was still seen at his club in the company of many friends, he was still being invited to grace the best tables, and he had even been seen on the arm of the Prince Regent himself at the home of the Countess Livien. Although the duel and his relationship with her were still favorite subjects of gossip and speculation, his reputation with the polite world was evidently too solid to have suffered greatly from all the talk.

But this was dangerous speculation. She must deal only with facts, for her emotions in regard to Drew were too strong to be relied upon. The laughter in his eyes, the endearing warmth of his smile, the charm of his conversation—these were unreliable qualities that had nothing to do with a man's character, yet they had completely turned her head. They had made her wish— oh, so fervently!—that the facts of the duel were not true. But was it not Mr. Dryden who had written, *'With how much ease believe we what we wish!'*? She must be on her guard against such beliefs.

She sighed mournfully and attacked her hair with the brush. She swept the rebellious waves into smoothness and twisted them into a neat knot at the back of her head. Only a few tendrils around her face were permitted to escape the severe confinement of her coiffure. This done, she dressed quickly, with more efficiency than pleasure. No amount of self-chastisement was capable of giving her a sense of happy anticipation of the evening to come. In fact, if she had to find a word to describe her feelings, it would be "foreboding." She was fearful of the evening, but of what, she had no idea. She knew only that she would be glad when it was over, and she would find relief from these thoughts and this mood in sleep.

George Pollard, on the other hand, was anticipating the evening with more cheerfulness than he had felt for weeks. The business with Mr. Joshua Plumb had proved quite promising, and he felt sure that his financial problems were very soon to be solved. He had determined to marry the Plumb chit no matter how dour or insipid she turned out to be, but from Mr. Plumb's remark that "she took the shine out" of her half-sisters, George felt confident that she was at least passable. Her father's settlement was quite generous, which assured that he would take her. There were many qualities of the female nature which George did not like—talkative women irritated him, those who whined disgusted him, plain ones bored him, plump ones revolted him—but none of those qualities were so repulsive that a fifteen-thousand-pound settlement and three thousand a year couldn't make them endurable.

Yes, he could endure anything, especially if he could also have Gwen. He hungered for her as much as he hungered for the fortune that was almost his. Ever since Rowle had brought her to London from the obscurity in which she had been raised, he had wanted her. He yearned to feel her bronze-gold hair clutched in his fingers, her lithe slimness held tightly against his chest, her full lips pressed against his mouth. To marry her was a luxury he could not afford, but give her up he could not. Tonight, he would take the first step in a plan to bind her to him without marriage. Somehow, before the announcement of his forthcoming marriage to Miss Plumb was made public, he must convince—or trick—Gwen into going away with him. He need compromise her only once. He was sure that he could then convince her of the benefits to both of them of a liaison. She was, after all, a widow—not a green girl.

But he knew he must tread carefully. She was not yet in love with him. Although he could tell that she enjoyed his company and thought well enough of him to consult him occasionally on matters of business or on problems with her brother, at other times she seemed far away, or she would suddenly, inexplicably, turn cool to him. She might easily slip from his grasp if he rushed her or offended her sensibilities. He must handle her like a thoroughbred horse, slowly and carefully playing the rope until, at the proper moment, he could pull it tight. Tonight, he would merely give her something to think about—something to keep himself in her thoughts in his absence.

He whistled jauntily as he tied his cravat in an intricate fold he had learned from his last valet. Poor fellow, he had had to let him go because of lack of funds. But it would not be long before he could afford the services of a valet again. Not long at all.

It had been a difficult two hours. Wys had rushed for a surgeon; Drew, with the help of Mallow, Quent, and Ferdie, had carried the still-unconscious Tom to an upstairs bedroom. Drew thought it best to wait until the bullet had been removed from Tom's shoulder before bringing him round, an idea which the surgeon roundly applauded. But the pain caused by the prying forceps roused him, and for several minutes the poor fellow had to exercise some white-lipped control to keep from screaming. At last the ball was removed, the doctor dressed the wound and departed, and Drew and Wys removed Tom's clothing. Mallow, having collected the softest goosedown pillows he could find in the unoccupied bedrooms, settled Tom as comfortably as possible on the bed. Tom, at last able to look around him with some awareness, discovered that Quent and Ferdie were standing at the foot of his bed regarding him in hang-dog misery.

"Oh, there you are," he said foggily. "I *told* you that those guns would shoot."

Drew let out a shout of laughter. Immediately, the teeth-gritting tension of the past two hours seemed to evaporate. Wys guffawed, Ferdie snorted like a neighing horse, and Quent—who had been suffering untold agonies of remorse—doubled over with mirth.

"What's so funny?" Tom demanded. "Drew, what are you doing here?"

"This is my house, you paperskull. Your friends brought you here. The doctor assures me—if you're at all interested—that the wound is neither very deep nor very damaging. You'll be well enough to get yourself into another muddle in a fortnight or so."

Tom smiled. "Oh, I knew the shot was of no consequence. I wasn't in the least upset."

Ferdie and Quent exchanged looks of disgusted incredulity. Drew came up to the bed with a large glass of brandy. "Never mind, old man. We've had enough heroics and hilarity for one night. Drink this down and go to sleep."

"No, no, take it away. Got to get up and go home," Tom remonstrated. But Drew put the glass to the boy's lips, pried open his mouth, and forced him to drink. By the time the glass was drained, Tom was regarding everyone in the room with a foolishly cheerful grin. Drew gently pressed him back against the pillows, Wys pulled a comforter over him, and in another moment the boy had drifted off into a sound sleep.

The four men tiptoed from the room and Drew closed the door softly. They all let out a prolonged sigh. "I think, gentlemen," said Drew, "that we could *all* do with a drop or two of brandy." And he led the way to the drawing room.

Relaxed in easy chairs grouped around the fire, the four sipped their brandies silently. Finally, Drew spoke up. "I think that one of you should tell us just what happened tonight, and then we can all go to our beds."

"Good idea," said Wys wearily.

Quent, after a look at Ferdie—who merely shrugged as if to say, you got us into this so you can get us out—took a deep breath and began. "Tom had brought the pistols to Ferdie's place to show them off," he explained, "and we were quite impressed with them. We played around with them for a bit, and then I remarked that it was a pity they wouldn't fire."

"I think it was I who said that," Ferdie offered helpfully.

"No, it was I," Quent insisted irritably. "Are you going to let me tell it, or shall I give you the floor?"

"Very well, get on with it," Ferdie said grudgingly.

"Then Tom said, 'Of course they can shoot!'" Quent continued, "but neither of us would believe him—"

"*I* believed him," Ferdie cut in.

"Confound it, Ferdie, cut line! However it was, Lord Jamison, nothing would satisfy us—all right, Ferdie, *me*—nothing would satisfy me but to try the cursed things out," Quent said in self-disgust.

"But the pistols weren't loaded," Drew said, confused. "They couldn't have been. They weren't loaded when I hung them on the wall—I checked them quite carefully— and I've never had occasion to load them since."

"Well, you see . . ." Quent explained diffidently, ". . . *we* loaded them."

"You? But how?"

"We used the powder and a bullet that we found in the storage compartment of the case," Ferdie said.

"Storage compartment? What storage compartment?"

"Didn't you ever notice it?" Quent asked. "There's a

little catch under the center handle that released the bottom of the box. There's a whole compartment underneath."

Drew put his hand to his head. "Hang it, I never noticed that!"

"Well, what happened then?" Wys asked. "Don't tell me you decided to have a duel?"

"Nothing so silly as that," Ferdie said quickly.

"Well, almost as silly," Quent admitted. "We decided to shoot into a pillow. Tom put a bolster up on the mantelpiece, I loaded the gun, and then Ferdie and I struggled with it to see who would shoot." Here he stopped and hung his head, too ashamed to go on.

"I see," Drew said. "The gun, of course, went off in the struggle, and Tom was hit."

"That's how it was, sir," said Quent miserably.

Drew got up, walked to the fireplace and stared into it. "I suppose you think I'm going to say that it could have been worse. But I'm not going to say it, because the worst is yet to come." He turned around and looked first at Ferdie and then at Quent. "Who's going to tell his sister?"

Ferdie and Quent exchanged looks of sheer terror. "Good Lord!" Ferdie croaked. "Not me!"

Quent lowered his eyes and remained silent. Drew sighed. "I guessed as much," he said drily. "Wys, I don't suppose that you—?"

Wys looked up at his friend blandly. "Don't bother to ask," he said promptly. "I am only an innocent bystander. Nothing to do with me, you know. Nothing at all to do with me."

No sooner had Wys spoken than Quent leaped to his feet courageously. "I'll do it," he said with determination. "I'm the one who shot him, after all."

Ferdie gaped at him admiringly. "I say, Quent, that's very deedy!"

Drew smiled at him. "Yes, Quent, that was well done. But you're not the only culprit. *I'm* the one who gave him the pistols in the first place. Besides, you look quite done in. Go on home, both of you. I think you've had punishment enough for one day."

After the boys had taken their leave, Wys looked at his friend with a gleam of amusement. "I say, Drew," he said in a rather good imitation of Ferdie's voice, "that was very deedy."

Drew grinned. "Oh, I don't know," he said modestly. "It shouldn't take much courage to face her. She's only a girl, after all. I'm almost a head taller than she is. And I outweigh her by three stone at least."

"True," said Wys, clapping him on the shoulder, "and spoken like a real champion!" Then the amusement faded from his eyes. "Drew," he asked earnestly. "are you as sanguine about this as you appear to be?"

"Sanguine!" Drew exclaimed with a bitter laugh. "I'm more frightened at this moment than I've ever been in all my life!"

Pollard had instructed the coachman to proceed slowly on the journey back to Rowle House. It was more than an hour past midnight. The streets were deserted and the howling November wind added to the feeling of intimacy inside the carriage. Gwen was snug and comfortable wrapped in a warm pelisse, her hands tucked into a large muff and a blanket draped over her legs by the solicitous Sir George. Although the evening at the Warrentons' had turned out quite as Gwen had expected, with Lambie prosing on about the Regent's marital difficulties, Lord Warrenton ogling her decolletage persistently and Flora Warrenton whooping loudly at every opportunity, as if every remark were an indecent *double entendre,* Sir George had behaved in a most exemplary fashion throughout. His attentions to her were all that she could have wished, his conversation to the group in general and to her in particular was witty and in the best taste, and he several times tried, without obnoxiously forcing the issue, to turn the talk to subjects of greater depth. She was feeling so pleased with him that, even though he had placed his arm along the back of the coach seat, quite close to her shoulders, she didn't mind at all.

"You look so lovely tonight," he said after an almost awkward silence. "It's difficult, when you look so enchanting, to say what I must to you."

Gwen raised an eyebrow. "*What* must you say to me, George?"

He removed her hand from the muff and held it gently. "I...Oh, Gwen, my dear, I ought to stop seeing you!"

"George!" she said in complete surprise. "I don't understand. Why?"

"I've been thinking of the future, my dear. For me it looks...well, unpromising..."

Gwen looked at him with sympathy. "Have you had a business setback? I am so sorry, George."

George laughed mirthlessly. "If only it were *one*. *Everything* seems to go against me all at once. My affairs are...but I don't wish to burden you with my problems. I haven't the right—"

"Friendship gives you the right," Gwen assured him gently. "You certainly have the right to confide in me. I have done so in you many times."

George took her chin in his hand and turned her face to him. "You must know that it is more than friendship I want from you."

Gwen knew that the statement was really a question, and it made her uncomfortable. She was an almost penniless widow and was therefore far from being besieged by suitors. Sir George was an exciting and useful escort as well as a friend of long standing. She did not want to lose him. But neither was she prepared to make their friendship into something deeper. In the past month she had learned what it was to love. Although that love was painful and gave her some of her most unhappy moments, she knew that the feelings she harbored for Pollard were not at all the same sort of thing. She did not love Sir George.

Gwen looked at him with a troubled frown. "Do not despise friendship, George," she said earnestly. "It is something that can last through any crisis. It can sustain us through adversity such as you now endure. Why may we not remain friends?"

George noted the troubled look in her eyes and released her chin. Damnation, he thought, the girl is harder to catch than an eel. He had put himself to great effort this evening, yet she still kept her distance from him. But he must not lose patience, he cautioned himself. She was a fish worth catching. Give her line, he told himself, give her line. "I must be frank with you, Gwen, my dear," he said aloud. "Friendship is a pale substitute for what I want. I love you. You must have seen it. I have never pretended otherwise."

Gwen put up a restraining hand. "George, please don't speak of it. I can't—"

"I know, I know. I have no right. I don't deserve—"

Gwen shook her head. "I didn't say that. I never said you are not deserving, but ..."

"There's no need to be kind," George said abjectly. "I know my value—or lack of it. You deserve the very best. I should not even dream of ..." And he lapsed into silence, his head bowed miserably.

Gwen was touched. She put out her hand and touched his arm gently. "Oh, George," she breathed, her voice trembling in sympathy.

He lifted his head, turned, and grasped her shoulders. "No, don't say anything. I could not bear your pity. I should never have revealed my feelings. Forgive me. There is nothing for it now but to say goodbye."

He turned away from her and sat gazing out of the window. Gwen sincerely felt for him. "Is there no way," she asked at last, "for our friendship to continue?"

He did not turn. "It is better this way," he said in a low voice.

"I don't see why, George. Why can't we just continue as we always have?"

He sighed and seemed to struggle with himself. "Is that what you wish?" he asked, turning to face her again.

"Yes, of course."

"Then I haven't the strength to refuse you," he said with a melancholy smile. He lifted her hand to his lips. "I shall remain your friend . . . for a while at least."

He was rewarded with a warm and, he thought, a relieved smile from Gwen. "I'm so glad," she said.

A short while later he handed her down from the carriage and escorted her to the door. Neither Gwen nor Pollard noticed the phaeton waiting a few yards ahead of them. After Mitching admitted her and closed the door, George returned to the carriage, tapped his cane on the roof to signal the coachman, and settled back against the cushions contentedly. The evening had gone well. He had every reason to be quite satisfied with himself.

Sir George's carriage could be heard clattering away down the street as Gwen handed her pelisse to the butler. It was only then that she noticed that the butler was eyeing her in some consternation. "What is it, Mitching? Is anything amiss?" she asked.

"I don't know, my lady. Lord Jamison is awaiting you in the drawing room."

Gwen paled. "Lord Jamison? Why did you admit him? You have my instructions in this matter."

"Yes, my lady, but he said it was urgent."

"Urgent? Nonsense! It's just an excuse to . . . But at this time of night? Why, the man must be mad!"

"He said it was concerning Master Tom," Mitching explained.

"Tom?" Gwen felt a stab of fear. "Is Tom in bed?"

"No, Lady Rowle," the butler said worriedly. "That's just it. He hasn't come in yet."

Gwen gasped and went quickly to the drawing room. She found Lord Jamison looking out of the window, his back to the door. She closed the door carefully, not moving further into the room, and asked in a tense voice, "What has happened to Tom?"

Drew turned. Gwen noted immediately that his expression was grim and his jaw tense. "What has happened to Tom?" she asked again, her voice more shrill.

"Gwen, don't look like that! He's going to be fine," Drew said quickly, taking a few steps toward her.

"For God's sake, *tell* me!" she cried out.

"Won't you sit down first?" Drew suggested.

"No," she said shortly, her eyes fixed on his face.

Drew's eyes wavered. He had planned carefully how he would explain the accident to her, but he suddenly realized that it would be kinder to her to tell her outright—though it would undoubtedly go harder with him. "He's been shot," he said quickly.

Gwen swayed. In two strides he was at her side. He put an arm around her and led her to the sofa. Sitting down beside her, he spoke to her gently. "It's nothing serious, Gwen, I promise you. A shoulder wound. The doctor says he'll be good as new in a fortnight."

"Where is he? I must go to him," she said dazedly.

"He is at my house, fast asleep. I'm certain he won't wake until tomorrow afternoon at the earliest. There's no need to trouble before then."

She shook her head. "No, I must—" Then she stopped and raised her head. "*Your* house? Why?" she asked, her cheeks whitening.

"It's a rather long story—" Drew began.

"Oh, my God!" Gwen gasped. "It was a duel! Did *you*—?"

Drew stared at her stupidly for a moment. Then, realizing what was in her mind, his expression hardened. He looked at her with a bitter sneer and got to his feet. "No, Lady Rowle," he said, turning his back to her, "*I* did not shoot your brother."

He felt his fingers clench into fists. Damn the woman, he thought, I'd like to hit her! What a monster she must think him. He wanted nothing more than to slam out of her house and cut off all ties with her and her wretched family. He strode furiously to the door, but before he could open it, he heard a small intake of breath. The sound stayed his hand from turning the knob. It was a sound that seemed to combine helplessness and misery. His heart melted. He could not leave her frightened and distressed. He loved her, no matter what she thought of him.

With a resigned sigh, he returned to the sofa and sat down beside her. "Your brother and his friends were examining a pistol," he said quietly. "It went off, hitting Tom in the shoulder. It was nothing more than a silly accident."

"You're sure he'll be all right?" Gwen asked in a small voice.

"Yes. He's lost some blood, of course, and he'll have difficulty in raising his arm for a while, but he'll suffer no permanent damage."

"I see." Gwen sighed in some relief. "How is it, Dr—Lord Jamison, that his friends brought him to you?"

"They were reluctant to frighten you, and, being quite frightened themselves and knowing that Tom and I were acquainted, they chose to bring him to me."

Gwen raised her eyes to his face. "May I go to him?"

"But I've told you there's no need—"

She lowered her eyes again. "I realize that this is quite awkward, but I would like to sit with him. Please. I know it is an intrusion on you—"

"Not at all, ma'am," Drew said politely. "My house is at your disposal."

"Thank you. I'm very grateful. I . . . Lord Jamison, I must apologize for suggesting that you had . . . shot my brother. It was inexcusable of me."

Drew got up and turned away from her, so she did not see the mocking sneer on his face, but she could not miss it in his voice. "Don't apologize, ma'am, for I have no doubt you will regret having done so in a very short time."

"Will I?" Gwen asked in bewilderment. "Why?"

"Because, my dear," Drew answered drily, "there are details of this matter you have yet to learn. When you

learn them, I'm certain you will—how shall I put this?—
you will *resume hostilities* with a vengeance."

"Indeed? What are these details I have yet to learn?"

"Let us not discuss them now. This is not the time for
our personal animosity. You have already endured much
tonight. The rest can wait."

"I take it this has nothing to do with my brother's
condition."

"Nothing at all."

"Am I right in assuming, then, that you had some part
in this accident, other than taking my brother in and
helping to see to his wound?"

"Gwen, let us not discuss this now. You are coming to
stay at my house. Hostilities between us had best be
postponed for the present."

"But I must know! If you didn't want to tell me, you
should not have opened up the subject."

"Yes, you're right. Hang my blasted tongue! I was too
angry to think."

"No matter what it is you have to tell me, it cannot be
worse than what I will imagine if I'm left in ignorance. I
will agree to a temporary truce while Tom is in your
house, no matter what it is you have done. So you may as
well tell me now."

"Very well. It has to do with the pistols the boys were
using. They were dueling pistols."

"Is that all?" Gwen asked in relief. "I had surmised as
much."

"That's *not* all," Drew said bluntly. "You see, ma'am,
the pistols . . . they belong to *me*." And he met the look of
dismay in her eyes with an expression of defiance in his
own.

Chapter Eleven

Mr. Plumb surveyed his dining room dubiously.
Perhaps he should not have left the arrangements for
tonight's dinner for Sir George Pollard in his wife's hands.
Martha Plumb was a spirited woman and a satisfactory
wife, but she had had a hand-to-mouth existence before
she hooked him, and now she seemed to want to make up
for her years of deprivation by spending his blunt on every
possible female frippery and household embellishment
that money could buy. The table was a perfect
illustration. All day long she had had the servants
frantically fetching and carrying and polishing to get it
ready. It was covered with the finest figured damask and
set with gold plate. At its center the table was adorned
with an enormous silver epergne overflowing with fruit
and flowers. The epergne was flanked by two candelabra,

each bearing six candles. Arranged around the center-piece were a number of decanters, salt cellars, pickle dishes and relish trays, all either crystal or silver. And at each place—in addition to the gold utensils, the gilt-edged serving plates, the crystal stemware, and the serviettes in their little gold rings decorated with multi-colored stones—the ostentatious Mrs. Plumb had placed a china figurine, each one glazed in bright colors and each completely distinctive.

Mr. Plumb shook his head. "Good heavens, Martha," he said disgustedly to the chubby woman who stood behind him in the doorway, "it's only a family dinner. The five of us and him is all. This fancy stuff on the table will do nothin' but make us all nervous."

"Family dinner indeed!" Martha Plumb retorted. "I suppose we 'ave a peer of the realm to dinner every night! I only want to make a good impression on 'im. Y' wouldn't want us to use the every-day, now would ye?"

"I dunno," Mr. Plumb said grumpily. "It's good enough for me, ain't it?"

"You ain't no baron," his wife said flatly. "Take a look at y'r wife, Mr. Plumb. Do y'think I look right?"

He looked at her as she turned slowly so that he could see her from all sides. Her dress of red-and-white cherryderry was cut low over her ample bosom, and to Joshua Plumb's way of thinking it was plain indecent. But he knew too well what the result of saying that would be— a half hour at least of recriminations and water-works, and he had not time for that. "Looks right enough to me," he muttered, "though I ain't no judge of women's fripperies."

"Don't know why I bothered to ask ye," Martha said crossly, and flounced off to harass the cook.

Joshua made his way to his daughter's bedroom and knocked at the door. Anabel opened the door warily. When she saw who it was, she uttered a cry and cast herself into her father's arms, bursting into long-suppressed tears.

"Anabel, love, don't take on so," said her father awkwardly. He was perfectly comfortable handling a business crisis—he could usually solve it with logic or bluster—but when the women turned on the water-works, shouting or reason were equally ineffective. "You haven't even seen the fellow! You'll be real taken with him, see if you ain't."

"I won't, papa," she sobbed. "I know I won't."

"See here, Anabel," her father blustered uncomfortably, "I won't have a scene. I promised the man a look at you, and a look he'll have. And if he likes what he sees, you'll take him, hear? You'll take him. You'll be a fine lady and live in a fine house and have fine friends, and you'll be pleased as punch you listened to your old dad."

"But, papa, I d-don't want to be m-married. I w-want to stay here with you."

He patted her shoulder fondly, but his jaw was set. "Can't be done, girl, as you well know. You can't live with your dad all your life."

"But I don't l-love this man!"

"It'll come in time, you'll see. Many's the girl who has cried on her wedding day and come back from her bride-trip all smiles."

"I won't! I couldn't! Not when I've already..."

Her father looked at her sharply. "Already what?" he barked. "Has some sly skirter been nosin' round you behind my back?"

"Oh, no, papa, no one. Only..."

"Only what?"

"Nothing. Nothing. But I know I can never love this person you're forcing on me."

"Don't tell yourself I'm an ogre, girl. You're almost twenty. It's more 'n time you had a life of your own. Now, go and dry your eyes and make yourself pretty for Sir George. You'll be glad one day, see if you ain't." And he made a hasty retreat.

Anabel threw herself on her bed in despair. There was no budging her father. And certainly it would be completely useless to appeal to her stepmother. She was doomed. She closed her eyes and tried to remember the face of a heroic gentleman in a brown greatcoat and a beaver hat. Oh, where was her rescuer now?

After George's arrival, Anabel's father had to shout for her three times, to no avail. Finally, a servant was dispatched to fetch Anabel to the table. Sir George was looking decidedly irritated by the time the girl made her appearance. He had been subjected to effusive toadying by the talkative Mrs. Plumb, and was forced to make conversation with her two simpering, giggling offspring. They had inherited their mother's plump figure, but not her lively spirit. They had nothing to say for themselves, and covered the emptiness of their conversation with much high-pitched, embarrassed laughter. All three women had dressed their hair with crimped curls hanging over their ears, and wore brightly-colored dresses and a profusion of bracelets, brooches and necklaces. The effect on Sir George was of such overpowering vulgarity that he had almost decided to extricate himself from the entire situation.

When Anabel appeared, he quickly changed his mind. She was as quietly lovely as her half-sisters were ostentatiously plain. Her hair was simply dressed in neat braids twisted into a knot at the back of her head, her complexion (except for some redness around her eyes) was smooth and creamy, and her expression calm and intelligent. She was slim, well-formed, and her dove-grey dress trimmed with white lace was modest and tasteful. Sir George leaned back in his chair and picked up his wine goblet, scrutinizing her carefully over the rim. Her looks were too unobtrusive, perhaps, for his taste, and her manner too demure, but she would do. She was no Gwen Rowle, whose spectacular beauty turned every head when she walked into a room, but Miss Plumb was certainly lovelier than he had any right to expect. When he considered that she brought with her a large fortune, he had to admit that he was indeed a lucky dog.

Anabel, on the other hand, sat opposite Sir George at the table convinced that she was the unluckiest girl in the world. One foolish little dream had sustained her during the past week—the dream that somehow, through some divine intervention, a miracle might occur and the man her father had chosen for her would turn out to be the man in the brown greatcoat. She knew the dream was preposterous, but, like someone drowning, she had grasped at the only twig she could find. Now the dream was over. The face across the table was not the face she had prayed to see. But she was neither dramatic nor rebellious. She might *think* of running away or killing herself, but she knew she would not. She also knew that her stepmother was delighted and her father adamant. There was no way out. With a heartbroken sigh, so quiet that no one at the table heard, she let her dream die and surrendered to the inevitable.

After dinner, the ladies excused themselves and left the men to their port. George picked up his glass and sipped contentedly. "An excellent dinner, Mr. Plumb," he said graciously.

"I thank you. My wife put herself out a bit in your honor," was Mr. Plumb's artless reply.

"I must certainly thank her for that."

"Well, sir, tell me," Plumb inquired eagerly, "what did you think of my girl? Did I not tell you the truth of it?"

"She is even more lovely than you said. I'm completely taken with her. As far as I'm concerned, you have a bargain!"

Joshua chortled. "I told you Joshua Plumb's word's as good as his bond. Let's shake and have a drink on it."

"Just one small matter before we seal the pact," George said. "You'll want me to clear up my more pressing obligations and to make certain preparations before the marriage, like renting a town house and furnishing it. I'll need some ready cash."

Joshua indicated by a flippant wave of his hand that

the request was a mere detail. "Will a few monkeys do?"

"Quite nicely," said George, smiling. "You're a generous man, Mr. Plumb."

"Until a man crosses me, Sir George. You'd best remember that."

George was silent. Then he looked across the table at his host. "There's one other request I must make," he began diffidently. "I must ask that our...arrangement...be kept secret for six weeks. After that, you may make the announcement public."

Joshua lowered his glass. "May I ask why?" he asked belligerently.

"For two reasons. One, I would like your daughter to get to know me a little. Two, I would like to break the news to...certain persons...in my own time and my own way. I would not like them to see an announcement before I had had a chance to break the news."

"Certain *persons?*" Joshua eyed him shrewdly. "Certain *ladies,* you mean!"

"Mr. Plumb," George said in a tone of intimacy, "you and I are men of the world. I did not live in a glass bottle before I met you and your daughter. I only ask for a little time to clean the slate. To come to her completely unencumbered."

Mr. Plumb rubbed his chin thoughtfully. "That's honestly admitted, at any rate," he said. "I suppose I can go along with you. As long as you deal straight with my girl and don't cause her grief, I'll not hold your past against you. Very well, six weeks. I'll tell the family to keep mum til then."

Gwen had come to Drew's house intending to sit with her brother through the night and return to Rowle House in the morning. But Tom, exhausted by the loss of blood, slept the clock round. When she emerged from the sickroom at ten the following morning, he was still asleep. She found Mallow waiting for her with a message that Drew had removed to his club and that she was to use the house

as her own. She wanted to remonstrate. She could not put
Drew out of his own home. But her head felt so heavy she
could not hold it up, and she yearned for an hour or two of
sleep. So she held her tongue and followed Mallow down
the hall to the lovely bedroom that had thoughtfully been
prepared for her. When the butler withdrew, she pulled
aside the curtains of an elegant four-poster and, without
taking off her dress, she fell down upon it and was
instantly asleep.

When she awoke, it was dark. She learned that Tom
had awakened during the afternoon, that Drew and the
doctor had called on him, and that the doctor had found
his condition good. Drew had played backgammon with
Tom for more than two hours and, before he returned to
his club, had left instructions that Lady Rowle's dinner
was to be served at her convenience. Lady Hazel had also
paid a call on Tom and had left various items—
nightclothes and fresh linen—for both Tom and Gwen.

Gwen went to see her brother, and when she saw him
sitting up in bed smiling at her sheepishly, she burst into
tears. "Oh, Tom, you idiot, you've given me the devil of a
scare! How could you behave so stupidly!" she said,
hugging him. But after those first words, she did not refer
again to the shooting. She merely sat beside him reading
aloud or conversing on unexceptional topics. She had
made up her mind that she would not dwell on the
incident. He had been punished enough. She hoped that
he had learned a lesson concerning the danger of using
firearms, a lesson far more dramatic than any words of
hers would be.

By the second day of Tom's convalescence, her days at
Drew's house had settled into a routine. She sat at Tom's
bedside all night and supervised his care throughout most
of the day. During the afternoons, however, when the
maids and Mallow could be relied upon to do what was
necessary, she retired to her room and slept. At that time,
Tom received visitors, and they filled the afternoon quite
pleasantly for him. Quent and Ferdie showed up every
day and entertained him hugely with their boyish

jocularity. Drew also visited every afternoon and could be counted on to bring in the backgammon board or a deck of cards. Hazel and Hetty were also frequent visitors, each of them supplying him with generous quantities of bonbons and sweetmeats.

Gwen noted that Drew was very careful to absent himself from his house during the hours he knew that she would be awake. She ran into him only once, two days before they planned to take Tom home. She had, by that time, been living at Drew's house for almost a week. She usually slept until dinner time, but that day she had awakened early. She had emerged from her bedroom while still pinning up her hair in a neat bun at the back of her head, and there were three hairpins in her mouth. She and Drew almost charged into each other in the hallway. "Oh!" she'd said, taking the pins from her mouth embarrassedly.

"I beg your pardon," he'd said stiffly, and stepped aside to let her pass.

She had dropped an awkward little curtsey and walked on, but then had stopped and looked back. He was still standing there, looking after her. This time he'd bowed stiffly and was about to turn and proceed down the hall when she'd called out, "Lord Jamison, I . . ."

"Yes?" he'd asked, encouragingly.

"I must thank you for your kindness to my brother and me," she began.

"Your thanks are not at all necessary, ma'am," he'd said curtly.

"But I'm putting you out of your house," she insisted. He remained silent. "There's no need for you to leave your house on my account," she went on. "Now, for instance, I know that dinner is ready, and there is no reason why you should not sit down at your own table . . ."

He raised his eyebrows. "Would you not object to my company?"

"I . . . I . . ." she stammered, "am not at all hungry this evening."

He gave her a bitter smile. "I quite understand. But I

am engaged for dinner with some friends, so you may feel free to have dinner...any time you feel hungry enough. Good evening, ma'am." And he had turned and walked off down the hall.

By the end of the week, the doctor was so pleased with Tom's progress that he gave his permission for Gwen to take him home. Tom could, by then, walk about quite steadily, his color had returned, and danger of infection had passed. If he had not had to wear an interesting-looking sling to keep his arm immobile, no one would have been able to guess that there was anything wrong with him.

On the very day that the doctor gave them the good news, Gwen decided to talk to Tom about something that had been on her mind ever since she had learned the details of the accident. The result of that talk left Tom sullen and angry, and Gwen had felt it expedient to withdraw to her bedroom to avoid any further argument. He sat at the window and sulked until Mallow entered to announce that Lady Hazel was waiting to see him.

He jumped from his chair and, as soon as Hazel had stepped into the room, he shut the door behind her and grasped her arm with his free hand. "Has she told you what she intends to do?" he asked without preamble.

Hazel looked at him with a calming smile. "When I was young, I was taught to greet my guests with a how-de-do, to bow to my elders and to offer them a chair."

"Guest! You ain't a guest!" Tom said impatiently. "And as for being my elder, you know perfectly well that if I started to treat you as if you were an old lady you'd box my ears."

"Never mind, jackanapes. Let me sit down and catch my breath. The stairs are getting too much for me these days."

As soon as she had seated herself, Tom began again. "But has Gwen told you what she intends to do about Drew?"

"Yes, she has."

"Are you going to do as she asks?" Tom demanded.

"Of course. She is my daughter-in-law, and as dear to me as if she were my own daughter. Fond as I am of Lord Jamison, I cannot consider him more than a mere acquaintance. I have no choice."

"Well, he's more than an acquaintance of *mine!* And I'll not let Gwen dictate to me whom to take as a friend!"

"Don't be childish, Tom. She's your sister. If your friendship with Lord Jamison causes her pain—and I know that it does—you too have no choice but to do as she asks."

Tom groaned. "But she's so wrong about him! And it's so unfair to me!"

"I know, dear," Hazel said with a sigh. "I had hoped . . ." She looked up at Tom questioningly. "Tell me, Tom, have Gwen and Lord Jamison been getting on while she's been here?"

Tom frowned and shook his head. "Getting on! They never even *speak* to one another. He stays at his club when he knows she's about. He only comes to see me when she's in bed. My stupid accident has made things worse."

"Yes, that's what I was afraid of."

"But how can she blame *him* for my accident? It's the outside of enough, especially when he's been so good to me."

"I know, dear. But she needs us more than he does. If you remember that, you'll find it easier to do as she asks."

Tom's departure from Drew's house was to take place before noon on Friday, and Drew went to some lengths to arrange to be absent from the house that morning. He had said his goodbyes to Lady Hazel on Thursday afternoon and had then gone in to bid farewell to his young protégé. Tom had been somewhat melodramatic and incoherent in his gratitude, but certainly no plans were made for him to repeat the performance on the day of his departure. Thus Drew was quite perplexed to see the Rowle laudalet in front of his door when he drove his phaeton up at one o'clock on Friday afternoon.

His first reaction was to turn around and go back to the

club. He had been almost completely successful in avoiding Gwen all week and he did not want to face her now. She had an uncanny way of cutting up his peace. Every time they met he came away from the encounter profoundly disturbed. An encounter with her invariably led to indigestion, discontent and sleeplessness. There was no doubt in his mind that he loved her. He loved her spirit, her fire, her sudden shynesses, her flashes of anger, her inconsistencies, her voice, her speaking eyes, the living glow of her hair. What he could *not* abide was her view of *him*. She had a way of making him feel like a brutish beast, and although one part of him was deeply drawn to her, another part wanted very much to wring her neck.

On the verge of turning the phaeton around, it occurred to him that Tom may have suffered a setback. Perhaps that was why the laudalet still stood waiting in front of the house. With a worried frown, he jumped out of his carriage and hurried into the house.

To his intense relief, he was informed that Tom had already left, accompanied by Lady Hazel, and, said Mallow, quite fit for the journey. It was Lady Rowle who still remained. The laudalet was waiting for her. The impassive butler gave his lordship a barely-perceptible sidelong glance as he informed him that Lady Rowle was awaiting him in the library. Lord Jamison raised an eyebrow in surprise, but after meeting his butler's interested eye he nodded casually and went up the stairs with an easy stride. He was quite aware that his pulse had started to race rather alarmingly, and, to add to his intense annoyance with himself, his breath was quite irregular. The library doors were right at the top of the stairway, and although he could feel Mallow's eyes upon him, he had to stop outside the doors to compose himself. Damn the woman, she certainly had a knack of upsetting his composure!

He found her seated on the sofa, looking not quite composed herself. She was wearing her pelisse, her bonnet was resting on her lap, and her fingers were twisting its ribbons nervously. As usual, the sight of her gave him a pang. The light from the library windows behind her lit her hair and reminded him of the morning he had opened his eyes at Stonehaven and seen her sitting in his bedroom. But then he could not see her eyes. This time they were clearly visible and were staring up at him, clearly troubled.

"Lady Rowle," he said quickly, "I'm sorry if I've kept you waiting. I had no idea you wanted to see me."

"It was not a long wait," she said, sounding somewhat timid. "I could not go without telling you how grateful I am—"

"Please," he interrupted, "don't say polite nothings to me. I'd give anything if the accident had not occurred. But it did. Giving the boy—and you—the use of the house for a few days was not at all important. There's no need to mention it—or think of it—again."

"You are very kind," she said, looking up at him with those troubled eyes. "You are making it very difficult for me to say something else. I find it quite awkward to bring it up at all, especially when you've been so good to us throughout Tom's convalescence..." She paused uneasily.

Drew looked at her shrewdly. Here it comes, he thought. They had seldom had an encounter when she didn't cut him with a little knife-blow. His lips twisted into a sardonic smile. "Ah, I begin to see. You are leaving, and our 'truce' is about to end. We will now speak with the gloves off, is that it?"

"The gloves off? That is a boxing expression, isn't it? I'm not sure what it means."

"It means that the hands are bared, that the punches are not pulled, that the blows are sharp, clean, and honest."

"Yes," she said, meeting his eyes squarely, "that is how I mean to speak to you."

"I should have known," he said ruefully. "Well, my dear, when the gloves are off, the punches can be painful.

Perhaps I'd better...Have I your permission to sit down?"

"Of course. Please do."

He pulled a chair from across the room, set it facing her and—he thought with an inward laugh—close enough to touch her, should the occasion arise. She appeared not to notice anything extraordinary in his closeness, so absorbed was she in the problem of telling him what was on her mind. "You are quite fond of prizefighting, aren't you?" she asked, somewhat irrelevantly.

He was surprised by the question. "Yes, I am. Boxing is a sport I enjoy both as a spectator and a participant."

"I thought so. *I* hate it," she said with a shudder.

"Many women of refinement seem to find it not to their liking," he said with a careless shrug. "I suppose," he added dubiously, "that this has *something* to do with the subject you wish to discuss?"

"Yes, it has. It helps me to explain to you why I must ask you to..." Here she stopped and looked up at him helplessly, unable to go on.

"Please go ahead," he urged. "I'll be glad to perform for you any service that I can."

Something she saw in his face seemed to disconcert her. She tore her eyes away and lowered her head. "You are not making this any easier for me," she said, twisting her fingers through the ribbons of her bonnet apprehensively.

He looked at her bent head, her trembling fingers and, as always, he melted. Pulling the bonnet from her lap, he tossed it away and grasped her hands. "Gwen, how can I make it any easier? Don't you know that there's nothing—nothing!—you could ask of me that I'd refuse you?"

Her head came up abruptly, the look of dismay in her eyes startling him. She snatched her hands away and jumped to her feet. "Good God, Drew, stop being so damnably...*benevolent!* All I want to ask of you is that you...leave us *alone!*"

Drew could only stare at her, dumbfounded. What was she talking about? Gwen, seeing the look of blankness in his eyes, felt a wave of remorse rush over her. This man who had murdered her husband and caused her brother to be wounded . . . this man was vulnerable to *her*. She could hurt him! But she didn't want to hurt him; she didn't want revenge. She wanted only to be free of him, of the violence, the masculine barbarity that lay hidden beneath his surface kindness. She sat down again and leaned toward him, determined to explain herself. "Listen to me, please," she said, trying to keep her voice low and controlled. "I only meant that it would be better for all of us if we didn't see each other any more."

"But there's no need to ask me this," Drew said coldly. "I've not come near you since Stonehaven. Even this week here in my own home—"

"I know. I don't mean only me. I mean all of us—Hazel and Tom, too."

He couldn't believe what he was hearing. "Lady Rowle," he said furiously, "not only have I scrupulously avoided you, but I've explained to Lady Hazel that I would not call on her either. However, I have invited Tom to visit me whenever he likes, and I don't care to rescind that invitation. I trust you have a sensible reason for asking me to do so."

"Drew, please understand that I . . . that it is difficult for me to say this when you've been so considerate all this week—"

"Come now," he said bitterly, "don't weaken. The gloves are off, remember?"

"Yes, you're right." She took a deep breath and went on. "Well, then, I think you are *dangerous* for us. I don't think you realize yourself that you seem to generate— well, how else can I put it?—violence. You *like* fighting and shooting and . . . dueling . . ."

"Gwen!" he said incredulously. "You can't *mean* this! I like sport, yes, but as for *generating* violence, aren't you being ridiculous—?"

"Am I? Edward is dead, and Tom wounded. What else can I believe?"

"Good God! Are you blaming *me* for Tom's wound?" He stood up in disgust.

"You yourself admitted to the blame the night you came to tell me about Tom, don't you remember?"

"I admitted to giving him the pistols, nothing more."

"That was enough, wasn't it? They are *boys*. Loaded pistols to boys are like catnip to kittens. How could they resist firing them? I suppose you didn't *mean* to—"

"You *suppose?* Good God, woman, do you think I'd have given him the pistols if I'd known the powder was—?" He suddenly stopped and slapped his brow with the palm of his hand. "Confound it, why am I *defending* myself?" he asked himself angrily.

"It is only natural to defend yourself," she said in a kindly, almost patronizing voice. "One wants to think of one's self as blameless. I don't imagine that you see yourself in the same way I do..."

Drew stared at her and then threw back his head and laughed. As if a dam had burst in him, his laugh poured out in a torrent, loud and long and hearty. His shoulders shook with it, and he gasped for breath. When he finally could speak, he said with his mocking grin, "You're quite right, my dear, I don't think of myself in the same way you do. One doesn't usually see one's self as a *brutish beast.*"

Gwen regarded him in confusion. His laughter had been in some way humiliating to her. She felt that he'd made her seem ridiculous, that somehow he'd turned her carefully-thought-out scruples into farce. She rose and put her head up proudly. "I did not say you're a beast," she said haughtily. "And I don't see what has made you so amused."

"I was amused, ma'am, because you thought I wished to defend myself to you, and my wishes are in reality quite different. So very, very different that I suddenly realized how ludicrous they were."

Some instinct told her she should not ask, but she couldn't resist. "And what were they, these *wishes* of yours?"

"Do you really want to know?" he asked, taking her by the arms and pulling her to her feet. "I wished . . . that you could love me so much . . . so much that even if I came to you with hands dripping with blood you would believe me innocent, and run to me and take my bloodstained hands to your face . . . like this . . . and offer your lips for me to kiss . . ." And putting his hands lightly against her cheeks, he tilted her face up to his and kissed her softly.

As if in a dream, she stood immobile, her eyes closed, her lips pressed lightly on his. But a few heartbroken tears dripped from beneath her lids, and when he felt them he let her go. She walked to where he had tossed her bonnet and stooped to pick it up. Then she turned to him. "You ask too much of me, Drew," she said sadly.

"I know."

"You will respect *my* wishes, then?"

He bowed a low, mocking bow. "Your servant, ma'am. In future, you and yours shall see nothing whatever of me. You may be assured of that."

Chapter Twelve

GWEN HAD MADE HER BED, and everyone seemed to be conspiring to ensure that she lie in it. No one in the household ever mentioned Drew's name. Tom's anger at being forced to keep away from his idol smoldered in his eyes every time he looked at his sister, but he never discussed the subject. Lady Hazel avoided Drew's name with a sympathetic delicacy which Gwen found every bit as irritating as Tom's sullen silences. The strain of side-stepping the subject that lay in the foreground of everyone's thoughts made other conversation awkward and forced, leaving Gwen feeling like a stranger in her own home. And for this, she honestly admitted to herself, she had no one else to blame.

To make matters worse, she found herself listening for the door knocker. Every time she heard it, her heart stopped, and she felt the blood leave her face. She knew she was being utterly ridiculous, but some secret part of her seemed to expect Drew to break down her door and carry her off like Lochinvar—the character in *Marmion*, a book of poems by Mr. Scott which had recently been published and had taken the *ton* by storm. But, unlike the romantic Lochinvar, Drew did not come. The only time she heard his name mentioned was one afternoon early in January. The day had been unexpectedly mild, and she had decided to take her horse for a canter in the park. She had no sooner set out when she was seen by Sir Lambert, who begged so insistently that he be permitted to stroll with her that she dismounted and walked along with him for a while. Among the juicy tidbits of gossip he fed into her ear was the information that Lord Jamison had been seen squiring Trixie Calisher about town on at least two occasions, and that Trixie's mother was said to be in transports.

This news interested her not at all, she told herself repeatedly. But her attitude toward George Pollard seemed to change after she'd heard it. She became warmer to him, more eager to be seen with him in public, more flirtatious in private. It was as if she had to prove to herself that her life was full and happy. It wasn't long before Sir George became confident that her heart was his, and he decided that the time had come to put the final phase of his plan into action. She had only to agree to go away with him. One night alone with her was all he needed. Once a woman was compromised, she was more ready to accept a *carte blanche*. He had succeeded at that game before.

Returning one evening from a concert at St. Peter's, their heads ringing with Handel's music, Gwen and George sat side by side in George's new carriage. Suddenly, he grasped her hand dramatically. "I can bear it no longer," he said in a voice that quivered with emotion. "You must marry me!"

"George!" Gwen said, startled.

"I know I don't deserve you. I know that everything you've heard said of me is true—I'm a gambler, a profligate, a ne'er-do-well. But not when I'm with you. Never with you. With you I am truly a better man. You've made a new man of me! And my prospects have improved, too. I've learned only recently that I shall inherit a large fortune one day soon. If only you'd consent to my plan... we could be so happy..."

The words, spilled out so incoherently, were bewildering to Gwen. She was staggered by the passion in his voice and flattered by his sentiments. But she knew quite well that she did not want to marry George Pollard. "Please, George," she began, holding out her free hand in remonstrance, "I don't—"

"No, wait, love. Let me explain. I've been doing a great deal of thinking about this. My income, as you know, is not great, but lately I've made an accounting of my assets and have discovered that I might manage with a wife in tolerable comfort. In addition, I've learned that an uncle of mine has named me his heir. He is known to be quite wealthy and is old and infirm. Of course, I could not wish for his end for selfish reasons—I pray he lives as long a life as God wills. But he is a bachelor and, for some eccentric reason, wants me to remain a bachelor, too. As much as I would want to remain in his good graces, I can no longer acquiesce to such a ridiculous demand. I can no longer bear to be without you. I know it is an extraordinary request to make of you, my dear, but could you consider a secret marriage? We could go to Gretna—"

"George, I can't consider marriage at all. Not yet."

"You are thinking of Rowle, aren't you? Gwen darling, you must not. You are too vital, too alive to hide yourself away from life. And I need you so! We mustn't let these years go by, you and I."

Gwen tried to withdraw her hand from his clasp. "Forgive me, George, but I cannot—"

He refused to release her. He pretended not to understand why she withdrew. "If it is convention which prevents you, I beg you not to consider what wagging tongues might say. Besides, our marriage can be secret for as long as you wish. We would have each other's love without offending either my uncle or the *ton* of London. Please, Gwen," he pleaded, taking her hand to his lips and kissing her fingers fervently.

Without wishing to hurt him, Gwen felt that she must end this scene. He was a pleasing companion, but she was not ready for marriage. She must make him understand. "George, it is impossible," she said firmly, pulling her hand from his grasp.

"But why?" he asked. "Does the idea of a secret marriage offend you?"

"No, it is not that. It is more essential than that."

George knew what she wanted to say, but he knew that he must not let her say it. If she didn't actually love him, he must make her wonder about her feelings. He must somehow keep her in doubt. His time was running out. If he were to convince her to run off with him, he must at the very least keep her confused. If ever his famous 'address' could aid him, he hoped it would do so now. Assuming a look of passionate agony, he grasped her in his arms. "Gwen, my darling," he whispered urgently, "what is more essential than the feelings we have for each other? I love you to the point of desperation. I need you more than I can say. And you care for me, I know. I've seen it in your eyes when you've laughed with me when no one else in the room understood. I've felt it in your hand when your fingers trembled at my touch. My beautiful, my lovely girl, don't...don't say that you don't care for me!"

Few women would be immune to so passionate an appeal, and Gwen—feeling lonely and a stranger in her own home—was particularly vulnerable. Breathless and confused by his outburst, she wavered in her resistance. Feeling her weaken in his arms, he drew her close. He was artful in the handling of women. He did not attempt to kiss her but let her head rest on his chest, merely putting his cheek gently against her hair. "Oh, George," she sighed, "I don't know what I feel. I don't know what to say to you."

"Just say yes, my darling," he said into her hair.

She lifted her head. "No, I can't do that. I'm too confused to think at this moment. Let me go, George, please."

George gritted his teeth. She was damnably hard to land. "Very well, my dear," he said, allowing his voice to reveal a deep hurt. "I won't press you. Only promise that you'll think about what I've asked. Only think about it."

Relieved, Gwen nodded in agreement. "I will," she said.

He took her hand again. "I know you'll say yes to me. Too much has passed between us. Say that you'll come to me—to tell me—the moment you realize that you want me as I want you . . ." And he pressed a kiss into her palm.

Gwen went to bed that night with much to think about. Bruised and lonely, she had felt a wave of satisfaction to learn that there was a man who loved and needed her. He was a man who, like Edward, had succumbed to the indulgences of the times—the gambling, the drinking, the waste of youth and health. Perhaps with him she could accomplish what she had not been able to accomplish with Edward Rowle. Perhaps she could make a good and useful man of George. Was it fate stepping in to give her a second chance?

On the other hand, she knew that she could never love Pollard. She knew now the true meaning of love. And though she had had to lock it up inside her, she had to admit it was there. Was it possible to be a good wife to one man while secretly loving another? She had married once without love, and the marriage had failed. Could she bear taking a chance on another failure?

The questions repeated themselves over and over in her mind until at last she fell into a troubled sleep and dreamed that George Pollard was beckoning to her from across a wide field. As she ran toward him, her feet heavy and slow as they always are in dreams, he held his arms out to her in mute appeal. With great effort she ran faster, but as she came closer, the face became Drew's, and the hands he held out to her were covered with blood.

The next morning, she climbed out of bed and examined herself in her mirror. Her eyes were shadowed and her mouth seemed to have hardened into what could become a perpetual frown. "Enough of this," she told the mirror severely. "You spend too much time in this fruitless soul-searching. Hazel was right. You think too much about yourself. Get busy and think about other things. You needn't marry anyone yet. Or ever." And as soon as she said it, she felt much better.

Wys had quite given up hope of seeing his young lady drive up Jermyn Street, but he had grown accustomed to walking along that busy thoroughfare every day at noon. In the few weeks of his vigil, his brown greatcoat and tall hat had become a familiar sight to the regular vendors who passed by. They had taken to greeting him, passing the time of day, and making him feel quite at home. Even the noises had lost their ability to irritate him. He almost enjoyed his daily stroll now. At first, the sound of a carriage would fill him with hope which was promptly dashed, and the melancholy that resulted would be enough to cut up his day. Now, however, he glanced at the passing carriages almost out of habit—the hope of seeing the lady again flickered only faintly—and his naturally cheerful disposition was not adversely affected in any great measure.

Thus it was that he almost missed recognizing the young lady when at last her carriage passed him by. The glimpse of a rose-colored pelisse shocked him into action, and he ran down the street shouting, "Ho there! Stop!" His friends took up the cry, one of the vendors going so far as to catch hold of the reins as the horses trotted by.

"What's amiss there?" asked the irritated coachman, pulling the horses to a halt.

"Nothing's . . . amiss," Wys said breathlessly as he

caught up with the carriage. "I merely recognized your passenger as an old acquaintance." He gave a coin to the vendor who had so promptly assisted him and then turned to face the girl who had lowered the window in consternation.

"Good day, ma'am," he said, lowering his voice in an urgent whisper. "Do you remember me?"

The girl gave him a delighted smile. "Of course I remember. I could never forget your kindness to me."

Wys sighed in relief. "I've looked for you all over London. I never dreamed I'd find you after all this ti—"

"Beggin' y'r pardon, guv'nor," the driver interrupted, "but I can't keep the 'orses standin' like this in the middle o' the street!"

Desperately, Wys looked around to find some way to delay the hack. He had dreamed of finding the girl in just this way, but the impracticalities of stopping the hack in the middle of a busy street had not occurred to him in his reveries. "Are you in a great hurry, ma'am?" he asked. "I hope I am not keeping you from an urgent engagement."

"Oh, no," she assured him earnestly.

"This is most presumptuous of me, but may I ride with you a little way? I want so much to talk to you."

She smiled and nodded, and Wys jumped into the carriage promptly. He stuck his head out the window, told the driver to ride on and sat back in relief. Then he turned and looked at the girl beside him. She was as lovely as he remembered, her eyes regarding him with the same direct and honest gaze he had described to Drew, her lips smiling at him with the same sweetness. He shook his head, staring at her as if she had materialized from the air. "I can't believe my incredible luck!" he said, half to himself.

The young lady, not knowing how to respond to this, merely looked down at her hands. After a moment, she looked up shyly. "Did you say you had been looking for me, sir?"

"Yes. Every day! I kept hoping you'd pass this way

again, so I've been haunting Jermyn Street for the past three weeks. Do you come this way often?"

"Oh, yes, quite often. I return this way after visiting my maternal grandmother. I go to see her every week."

"Every week? How is it I've missed you, then? I've peered into every hired hack that passes at this hour."

"I don't pass at this hour all the time. And I often travel in the family carriage," she explained. "It's only when my stepmother or my half-sisters need it that I hire the hack."

"Stepmother? Half-sisters?" Wys asked, laughing suddenly. "*Two* half-sisters, I'll wager."

"Why, yes! How did you guess that?"

"It's so appropriate, don't you see? You are Cinderella! You should have left me a glass slipper when you ran off that day!" he said delightedly.

The girl smiled and blushed. "I'm not at all like Cinderella, I'm afraid," she said wistfully. "My stepmother isn't at all cruel. And our meeting—at noon, not midnight—among all those apples wasn't quite like a grand ball."

"And a good thing too," Wys agreed. "I'm no Prince Charming, and my dancing is atrocious."

There was a silence between them as the fairy-tale atmosphere seemed to evaporate. "Why were you looking for me, sir?" the girl asked suddenly.

Wys was taken by surprise. Surely she must *know* why he'd been looking for her. But suddenly his heart fell. How stupid he was! Just because *he* had dreamed of nothing but her since the day they'd met was no reason to think that she had felt the same. She'd probably not given him a second thought. How could he have assumed that she was as glad to see him as he was to see her? He'd been behaving like a prize fool.

How should he answer her question? With the loss of his confidence, he became awkward and self-conscious. "I . . . I hadn't asked you your name, you see . . ." he said lamely.

"Yes, I know," she said softly. "I remembered that

afterwards. I hadn't asked your name either."

Wys perked up. "*Did* you think of me afterwards?" he asked eagerly.

"Of course. I told you I would never forget your kindness."

Wys didn't know what to make of that. "I'm Wystan Farr," he said.

"How do you do, Mr. Farr," she responded politely. "My name is Anabel Plumb."

"*Miss* Anabel Plumb?" he asked.

"Yes. Is there any special reason why you wanted to know my name?"

"Well, yes, Miss Plumb. I wanted your permission to...call on you."

Miss Plumb seemed to catch her breath. "You wanted to c-call on me?"

"Yes. Very much."

"Oh," said Miss Plumb in a small voice.

"*May* I call on you one day soon?" he asked pointedly.

She looked at him, her honest eyes shining. "Oh, yes, I'd like that very—" But suddenly the shine faded from her eyes, and she gasped in consternation. "Oh, I'd forgotten..." she said miserably.

"Forgotten what, Miss Plumb?" Wys asked in alarm.

"I have just recently...been betrothed..." she said, agonized.

Wys stared at her for a moment, not understanding what she'd said. Then he said quietly, "Oh, I see." He had thought, when he couldn't find her, that he had reached the nadir of despair, but now he realized that there were depths he hadn't plumbed. "Under the circumstances, then, it seems I've intruded on you to no purpose," he said, his tone perfectly polite and matter-of-fact. "I'm sorry to have troubled you."

She hung her head. He turned away abruptly and lowered the window. "Driver!" he called, sticking his head out. "You may put me down at the next corner."

Pulling his head back in, he made an awkward

obeisance to Miss Plumb. "I must bid you good day, ma'am. Please accept my good wishes for your future happiness."

"Thank you, M-Mr. Farr," she said, her lips trembling. The carriage stopped, and Wys opened the door and jumped down. "Drive on," he told the coachman. The carriage started to move. Suddenly, Miss Plumb's head appeared at the window. "Mr. Farr?" she called back to him, a pathetic little smile on her lips. "You...you'll always be P-Prince Charming to m-me."

Why had she said that? he wondered. He watched the carriage disappear down the street, feeling not at all like Prince Charming. If truth were told, he felt more like a frog.

After wandering about the streets for more than an hour, he found himself at Drew's door. Mallow informed him that Lord Jamison had gone out but was expected back for dinner. Wys waited, sitting in the library staring moodily at the fire. So deep had he sunk in despond by the time Drew arrived that he could barely lift his head to greet his friend. "Where have you been?" he asked in a lifeless voice.

"At the F.H.C. They want me to race my chestnuts. I told them that I was in no mood to race—" He became aware of the deep gloom of Wys's face and stopped in mid-sentence. "If I didn't know you better," he said in surprise, "I'd say you were desolate. Of course, I know that desolation is not an emotion indulged in by a moderate man, so I know you cannot feel as wretched as you look."

"Don't roast me, Drew. I'm as desolate as a man can be."

Drew poured two glasses of Madeira from the decanter that Mallow had left on the table for them and thrust one into Wys's hand. Dropping into an easy chair opposite, Drew ordered him to drink up. "I won't have you disdaining my best Madeira, no matter how deep into the dismals you've fallen," he said firmly. "Now, tell me what's troubling you."

"I found her," Wys said shortly.

"What? The girl in the rose pelisse? However did you manage it?" Drew asked curiously.

"She passed along Jermyn Street again."

"Did she indeed! What a bit of luck!"

Wys regarded his friend balefully. "Yes, that's what I thought. It all seemed like ... well, like a fairy tale." He lapsed back into gloomy silence.

"I take it you found the girl not quite up to the mark ... a bit less than your first impression of her led you to expect?"

"Not at all," Wys said with a show of spirit. "She was even lovelier than I remembered."

"Then, what's ...? Oh, I see. Married, is she?"

"Betrothed."

Drew sighed and leaned back against the cushions of his chair. There was nothing he could think of to say to his friend that would in any way cheer him. Wys was inherently a sober, serious young man, not given to light or frivolous emotions. This was the first time that Drew had known him to be taken with a girl. Hetty had tried to interest him in several available females—almost as many as she had foisted on her brother—but Wys had withstood them all. Somewhere deep within him, Wys had a romantic streak, Drew surmised, and the first encounter with this girl had many elements of romance: he had rescued a damsel in distress, there was an intriguing mystery surrounding her identity, she had disappeared completely from his life, and he had spent the last few weeks daydreaming about her. Finding her today must have seemed to him a stroke of luck just short of miraculous. But Drew realized it was not lucky at all. Wys would have been more content to go on dreaming of her than to learn, so abruptly, that he must end the dream altogether.

The old saying that misery loves company was not true

at all, Drew discovered as he looked across at his unhappy friend. Whatever made the old wives who originated the saying believe such nonsense? His misery over Gwen was not making Wys's pain any easier, just as Wys's tale of woe had not soothed him in the least. The truth about misery was that one must shake one's self out of it. And the sooner the better. "Wys," he said thoughtfully, "do you remember the day early last fall when we drove up to Langley Abbey?"

"You mean the day when the phaeton lost a wheel, and we had to put up at that verminous inn?" Wys recalled with a ghost of a smile.

"Yes, and we engaged in a charming adventure with the innkeeper's daughter and her pink-cheeked cousin from the farm behind the stable?"

"Of course I remember. Why?"

"That was less than four months ago. Since then I went to my sister's cursed ball, and you rescued a girl on Jermyn Street. *Love* came into our lives, and in four months two cheerful, high-spirited adventurers have been turned into a couple of mumpish, dreary moon-calves. If this is what love does to men, I'd prefer to spend the rest of my life without it."

"So would I. But we seem to have no choice."

"There may be more of a choice than you think. We needn't surrender to this—what shall I call it?— *onslaught.*"

"Perhaps 'incursion' would be more apt," Wys suggested in his sober way.

"Very well, incursion. We needn't surrender to it. We can fight back."

"How?"

"By going back to the state of mind we had in the fall. We were busy and active, game for any sport, ready for any light flirtation, ripe for any adventure..."

Wys sighed with a noticeable lack of enthusiasm. "Did you have a particular adventure in mind?"

"How about the F.H.C. race, for a start?"

"I thought you'd already turned them down."

"It's not too late to change my mind."

"I don't see why *I* should. I'm not a noted whip. What chance would I have against a nonpareil like you?" Wys asked in the glum tone he'd used all evening.

"What about riding with me?"

Wys looked up with a flicker of interest. "With you? You've never taken *anyone* up with you on a curricle race."

"I'd like to try it this time."

"Do you mean it?" he asked, a real smile appearing on his face at last.

"Of course. More of a challenge. What do you say?"

"I say done!" Wys said, jumping up and holding out his hand to his friend. "What do you say we walk over to the stables right now and see how the chestnuts do?"

The two men, with Drew's arm draped companiably over Wys's shoulder, walked briskly from the room, leaving the gloomy lassitude that had enveloped them behind—for the time being at least.

Interest in the race had been high to begin with. The idea had started with an argument between Lord Sommerfield and Richard Warrenton over the relative merits of their matched pairs, Sommerfield claiming that his geldings could outrace Warrenton's greys over any course at any distance. Before the air had cleared a race had been arranged, and five more contenders had put in claims for their pairs. The Four-in-Hand Club had taken on the chore of organizing the details. Sporting events were infrequent in the winter season, and soon the race was the talk of the *ton*. Bets were being laid at all the clubs, but the feeling prevailed that unless Drew Jamison were a contender, the results would be unsatisfactory. Therefore, when the word spread that Jamison had entered the lists, interest zoomed, and the betting became serious.

The race would begin ten miles up on the Great North

Road, ending at the green at Islington. There would be four starts, ten minutes apart, the winner being the curricle which made the best time. Two curricles would start off together, to be followed by two more ten minutes later, four starts in all. The winner of each start would receive a prize, but the top winner would be the driver of the curricle which made the best time of the eight. All plans, however, were contingent upon the weather, snow and ice being a particular threat in January. But the day agreed upon dawned cold and clear, and an impressive number of carriages started out from London that morning and made their way up the Great North Road. Most people, however, chose to go to Islington and take places at the finish line. By noon a gay crowd had gathered at the Islington green, the watchers well-wrapped in mufflers and mittens and filling the winter air with the sound of laughter and excited voices.

Gwen had heard of the race but did not feel any particular interest in it. Tom, however, was looking forward to it in a fever of excitement. He carefully avoided mentioning it at home, but on the morning of the race his eagerness to be out of the house was so great that it was apparent to everyone. "Where are you off to so impatiently?" Gwen asked him.

Tom hesitated before answering. True to his word, he had not seen Drew since the day he'd left Drew's house, but his interest in his hero remained high. His sister could not expect him to turn a deaf ear every time someone mentioned Lord Jamison's name. He saw nothing wrong in listening to news of Drew's activities, or in attending a sporting event in which Drew was a participant. Although he had every intention of cheering for Drew at the top of his lungs, he did not consider that he would be in any way breaking his word to his sister. "I'm going to Islington," he said offhandedly. "The fellows and I want to see a . . . a curricle race."

Gwen raised her eyebrow. "The race Lord Jamison rides in?" she asked coldly.

Tom stuck out his chin belligerently. "Yes," he said, daring her to oppose him.

Gwen said nothing. Lady Hazel had been watching the exchange with interest. "I'd like to see that race myself," she ventured. "Why don't we drive out there this afternoon, Gwen?"

Gwen flicked a dagger look at her mother-in-law. "No, thank you," she said curtly.

"Why don't you come with *us,* Aunt Hazel," Tom offered magnanimously. "I'm sure there'll be room for one more in Ferdie's phaeton."

"Heavens, dear boy," Hazel laughed, "three young bucks would be too much for me to handle at my age."

"Tut, tut, Aunt. You're becoming chicken-hearted," Tom teased.

"Rather chicken-hearted than bird-witted," Hazel retorted. "And birdwitted I'd be to gad about with three young scamps. But run along quickly, before I change my mind."

Tom made a quick escape, and Gwen thought the subject of the race was closed. But a little before noon, Pollard presented himself at her door and insisted that she join him on his outing to Islington. "I didn't know *you* were interested in the race," Gwen remarked.

"I certainly am. I've backed Richard Warrenton rather heavily to win."

"Oh, George, no!" she said dismayed.

"Don't worry, my dear," George said, smiling at her indulgently, in the fatuous way men have of patronizing women when they speak of sporting matters or other 'masculine' pursuits. "I won't lose. Warrenton has the most magnificent pair of greys you've ever seen. Prime steppers, each one, and no one but I has yet seen them in action. I received very good odds."

"Does that mean that Lord Warrenton is not the favorite?"

"Yes. That is how I received the good odds."

"Who *is* the favorite?" Gwen asked, quite casually.

George sneered. "Jamison, as usual. I'd love to see Warrenton take the shine out of him!"

Gwen lowered her eyes. "I don't think I'd care to go, George. Please excuse me today."

Pollard looked crestfallen. "Are you sure, Gwen? It will be quite exciting, I promise you. And I won't enjoy it half as well without you."

"Nonsense, George," she said, but she was pleased at his words. "Once the race began you'd take no notice of me."

"There would *never* come a time when I'd take no notice of you."

She met his eye and blushed. "Well, I know Hazel would like to go," she said, weakening.

"By all means, ask her to join us. And hurry, both of you. I don't want to miss the first arrivals."

They arrived in plenty of time, but the area around the finish line was already crowded with carriages. George found a place some distance away, at the side of the road on which the curricles would pass. George jumped out of the carriage, talked to some gentlemen and came back with the news that Warrenton had drawn number four, Sommerfield number five, and Jamison number seven. The others were considered by most of those in the know as also-rans.

As soon as Number One and Two appeared down the road, Number Two leading by a length and a half, a cheer went up from the waiting crowd. Though their time was unremarkable, the crowd was delighted to see some action. All necks were craned to the north, for—although Numbers Three and Four had started ten minutes later than the curricles which had just arrived—it was hoped that Warrenton had bettered their time by a considerable margin. The crowd's vigilance was rewarded three minutes later when the curricle carrying a large Four appeared, bearing down on them at breakneck speed. Number Three was not yet in sight. As Warrenton's greys thundered by Pollard's carriage, Pollard stood up and shouted, "Ho, Dick! You're seven minutes ahead!"

Number Three came in five minutes later, followed by Sommerton, Number Five, whose time was less than a minute slower than Warrenton's. After a cheer for Sommerton's arrival, the sound of hooves turned all heads north again, looking for the arrival of Number Six. But a voice, sounding to Gwen very much like Tom's, shouted, "It's Number *Seven!*" and Drew's curricle appeared, having gained on Number Six which had set out ten minutes before him. He had made the course in twelve minutes less than the first arrival, and had bested Warrenton's time by a full five minutes.

The crowd was cheering wildly, and Gwen found herself watching the approaching curricle breathlessly. The chestnuts, heads high and manes flying, obscured her view of the driver, but as the horses galloped by, she had one brief glimpse of Drew, and Wys just behind him. In what seemed to her a frozen moment, she saw their faces clearly in every detail. Wys was smiling broadly, his face radiating pride in his friend's accomplishment. But it was Drew's expression that arrested her. With eyes narrowed and glittering brightly, nostrils flaring, and lips slightly smiling, his look was strange—combining both profound concentration and cool confidence. The look filled her with a feeling of intense terror. Was this how he'd looked when he'd lifted his pistol and pointed it at Edward? She shuddered, imagining herself in Rowle's place. How could anyone have faced those cool, glinting eyes, that almost contemptuous smile, without cringing in fear?

She found Hazel's eyes on her, and she became aware that her hands were trembling and her breathing tumultuous. She clenched her hands and forced herself to breathe steadily. Drew's curricle had crossed the finish line, and he and Wys had jumped down. Wys was pounding on Drew's back, and a number of people were surrounding them. Gwen got a glimpse of Hetty and Selby in the crowd. A girl ran forward and threw her arms around Drew's neck. Gwen saw that it was Trixie Calisher.

At that moment, Drew looked up and saw her. The shock of recognition in his eyes was unmistakable. But he neither smiled nor bowed. With cool deliberation, he turned his back on her and looked down at the girl whose arms still clung around his neck. Gwen's cheeks burned. An anger, stronger and more unreasonable than any she had ever felt before, welled up in her. The man who had taught her to feel love now had shown her what it was to hate.

The drive home was rather silent. Lady Hazel attempted some pleasantries, but, getting little response, she soon subsided. Pollard's disappointment in the outcome of the race kept him glum and taciturn, while Gwen's thoughts dwelt agitatedly on the subject of Drew and his startling ability to discompose her emotions. If only she could find some way to be free of him!

When the carriage arrived at Rowle House, Pollard helped the ladies to alight and bid them good evening. But Gwen unexpectedly asked him to come inside for a moment. Lady Hazel excused herself and retired to her room. As soon as George and Gwen were alone, she turned to face him, an unsteady smile hovering on her lips. "I've been thinking about . . . what you asked me the other night."

"Gwen!" George stared at her, an arrested look in his eyes.

"I've decided that . . . that I'll marry you, George," she said, trying to keep her voice steady and holding out a hand she could not keep from trembling. "I'll marry you just as soon as you care to arrange it."

Chapter Thirteen

THREE DAYS AFTER THE RACE, Lady Hazel and Tom sat down to breakfast wondering why Gwen had not come down. Lady Hazel was about to suggest that Tom run upstairs to rouse her, when Gwen's abigail came timidly into the breakfast room. "Yes, Tilda, what is it?" Hazel asked.

"Excuse me, my lady," the girl said with a quick curtsey, "but there's somethin' troublesome 'ere. Lady Rowle's not anywheres, and this 'ere note was on 'er dressin' table. For you, ma'am."

"You mean she's gone out so early?" Tom asked the girl.

"Yes, sir. And she's took some of 'er clothes with 'er."

"Her clothes!" Tom looked at Hazel with a troubled frown. Hazel was reading the note, her face growing pale.

"What is it, Aunt Hazel? What's wrong?"

Hazel glanced at him briefly, then turned to the abigail. "Thank you, Tilda, you may go."

The girl dropped a curtsey and left the room. Hazel put a distressed hand to her forehead while she wordlessly handed the note to Tom. *Dearest Hazel,* Gwen had written, *it pains me to have to embark on my present course without your presence or even your blessing, but George and I are agreed that secrecy is necessary. Yes, love, we are going to be married. As you read this, we will be riding to Gretna Green. We will not be gone for many days, but I leave it to you to invent some excuse to anyone who notices my absence. Say that I've gone to visit my parents, or anything else that suits your fancy. You may tell Tom the truth, of course, but urge him to be discreet. I know this will shock and disturb you at first, but please believe that I have given the matter much thought before taking this step, and am convinced that a marriage to George is the best thing for me. I sincerely hope you will not despair but will wish me to be happy. Your most affectionate, Gwen.*

"She must be mad!" Tom said in alarm. "Everyone knows that Pollard is a loose screw!"

Hazel dropped her head in her hands. "Good God, what has the poor girl done?" She got up and paced the room in an agony of impotence. "How could I not have seen—? If only I had told her what I really thought of that man!"

"Is there nothing we can do? Perhaps if I ride after them..."

Hazel looked at him helplessly. "Even if you could catch them, do you think she would listen to you?"

Tom's face fell. "No, I don't suppose she would. She'd more likely give me a box on my ears for my pains."

Hazel turned to the window and looked out despairingly at the grey winter day. "How could she do this to herself... twice?" she asked, in a voice so low that Tom didn't hear. But Tom was not attending anyway. He was trying to think of a way to stop his sister. He should go to Drew, of course. Drew would know how to stop her from this ridiculous course. But Gwen would be furious. Had he, her brother, the right to interfere in her life this way? He looked at Hazel and asked hesitantly, "Do you think I would be stepping beyond the bounds if I went to Drew?"

Hazel pressed her hands together, rubbing them nervously. It was an unconscious gesture she often used in times of indecision. "I don't know, love," she said. "I've been wondering about the very same thing. But, Tom, I believe he is our only hope."

Tom jumped up quickly. "I'll go to him, then. We can't let her do this without at least *trying* to prevent it." He kissed Hazel's cheek fondly. "Try not to worry so, my dear," he said as reassuringly as he could. "Drew will know what to do."

Hazel clutched at his lapels, her eyes showing a gleam of hope. "Hurry back to me as soon as you can. I shall be in such agitation, not knowing what is happening."

"As soon as I can. I promise," he said, and ran from the room.

Tom's reception at Drew's residence was not quite what he'd expected. Mallow had received clear instructions on the manner of handling just this contingency. Should Master Spaulding show himself at the door, Mallow was to tell him Lord Jamison was not at home. So when a tense and dishevelled Tom appeared at the door, Mallow followed his orders, albeit regretfully, for he had grown quite fond of the boy during the week he had spent under Mallow's care.

"Not at home?" Tom groaned. "What am I to do now?"

"Is something amiss, sir?" Mallow asked, well aware that he was exceeding his authority.

"Yes," Tom said, "I'm in a devil of a hobble. Can you tell me where I may find him? It's most urgent that I track him down."

Mallow, conscious of the fact that Lord Jamison was at that very moment only a few steps down the hall, found himself at a loss. Young Master Tom was obviously quite upset. Should he send the boy away as instructed, or should he inform his lordship of the boy's distress? "Urgent, you say, sir?" he asked.

"Very urgent, Mallow. As urgent as could be!"

"Very well, sir, I'll inquire. Come inside, if you please, and wait here." Mallow admitted Tom, closed the door behind him, and permitted himself to smile at the lad. "If I may say so, Master Spaulding, I'm glad to see that you no longer need the sling."

"What?" asked the abstracted Tom. "Oh, yes. The shoulder is much better, thank you, Mallow."

Mallow bowed and went down the hall to the study. He emerged a moment later with Drew at his heels. "Tom, old man, how are you?" Drew said politely. "Come into the drawing room, won't you?"

Mallow held the door open for them and closed it discreetly as soon as they had passed into the room. Then, with a relieved sigh that Lord Jamison had not combed his hair for his indiscretion, he went back to his duties.

In the drawing room, Drew faced Tom uneasily. Before he could speak, however, Tom broached the subject head on. "You told Mallow to tell me you were not at home to me, didn't you?" he asked, facing Drew with a bold front that did not hide his wounded feelings.

Drew responded just as directly. "Sorry, Tom. I promised your sister that I would not— Dash it, Tom, you're placing me in a deucedly awkward position."

"Hang my sister, and hang your promise!" the boy burst out. "We're as deep in the basket as can be, and I've no one to turn to but you."

"In that case, I'm glad you've come. Sit down and tell me what's upset you so."

"No, thank you, I'm too churned up to sit. Gwen's run off with George Pollard."

Drew whitened. "What! I don't believe—! Gwen?"

Tom nodded glumly. "I can scarcely credit it myself. But she left a note."

Drew sat down abruptly. "But . . . *George Pollard?* Are you sure?"

"Yes, of course. Would you like to read her note for yourself?" He held it out to Drew.

Drew reached for it, froze for a moment and stared at it, and then shook his head. "No," he said, dropping his arm, "it . . . has nothing to do with me."

"Drew!" cried Tom, "you can't mean that! Surely you won't let her throw herself away on that rackety flat-catcher!"

Drew got to his feet wearily. "I have no authority to concern myself in your sister's affairs. If she prefers George Pollard to—! If she wishes to marry him, what have *I* to say to it?"

"But you . . . you l—"

"What I feel for her has nothing whatever to do with it," Drew said implacably and coldly.

Tom felt as if the earth had been cut away beneath his feet. Drew was letting him down. Drew, who could outrace and outshoot anybody, who could master any situation, find a way out of any hobble, solve any riddle, whom he idolized over any man living—this man was not going to lift a finger to help him out of the worst fix of his life! He stared at Drew, blinking his eyes to keep back the tears that were stinging his lids.

Drew could read in Tom's face every thought that went racing through his mind. He knew he had destroyed the boy's adoration of him. The realization smote him painfully, but perhaps it was just as well, he told himself. No one should be idolized. He was a man, a mere man, not a hero to be set up on a pedestal. He grasped Tom by the shoulders and said in a choked voice, "Let it be, Tom. She's chosen her road, and whether we like it or not we have no choice but to let her follow it."

Tom shook himself free. "*I* have no choice, because she wouldn't listen to me. But she might have listened to *you!* You just don't c-care! N-Not enough to trouble yourself!" he said angrily, turning away so that Drew would not see how close he was to tears.

"Try to understand," Drew said, trying to keep his voice steady. "I am not related—either by blood or my marriage—to your family. Even the bonds of friendship cannot be claimed, since she made me promise to cut them. There is nothing I can do in this matter. Nothing."

"I don't want to hear any more about that damned promise!" Tom burst out, wheeling around to face Drew once more. "What does a promise matter when it's a question of keeping someone from throwing away her life? You just don't care, that's the long and short of it! You just don't care! I'm sorry I ever came here to ask for your help! You can be sure I won't do so again!" With that the boy ran from the room.

"Tom!" Drew called after him, but he could hear the boy's footsteps racing down the hall without a pause. Then the front door slammed and Tom was gone.

Tom stumbled down the stone steps of Drew's residence, blinded by tears, and charged into Wys who was just starting up. Without a word of apology or explanation, Tom made as if to run away, but Wys—seeing his look of agitation—caught him by both arms. "I say, there, Tom," he said, "don't rush off like that without so much as a how-de-do. I want to talk to you."

Tom struggled to free himself. "L-Let me g-go, Mr. Farr. I'm in no mood for t-talking."

"I can see that. But I can also see that something's wrong. If you don't want to talk to me, let's go inside and talk to Drew."

"I don't want to talk to him. N-Not ever!"

"Nonsense, Tom. I've found no one better to talk to when *I'm* in trouble."

The boy turned a tear-stained face to Wys. "That's what I thought. B-But now, when I really n-need him, he's no help at all!"

"I can't believe that Drew—"

"Can't you? Well, Gwen's run off with George Pollard—yes, you may well gape! They are on their way to Gretna Green and your friend won't lift a finger to stop them! I never want to t-talk to him again!"

The shock of his words caused Wys to slacken his hold. Tom shook his arms free and ran off down the street, leaving Wys to stare after him openmouthed. Gwen and George Pollard? It couldn't be! He ran up the stairs and raised his hand to the knocker, but something made him pause. There must have been a dreadful scene between Tom and Drew to have upset the boy so, Wys thought. Drew must be in a terrible state. Perhaps he should wait a bit before inflicting his presence on his friend. This situation required careful thought. What should he say if Drew asked for advice?

He turned and walked back down the steps. His head lowered in deep thought, he proceeded down the street, bumping rather often into passers-by and causing at least one to curse him loudly. When he had walked like this for a considerable distance, he stumbled on a curbstone and wrenched his ankle painfully. At this, he looked about him to see where he was, hoping he could find a place to go where he could sit and think undisturbed. He found that he was on Pall Mall where, just a step away, was the Smyrna Coffee House. Although he was certain they served nothing much better than the dark bohea tea he abhorred, he went inside.

The tables were crowded and noisy, but he spied an empty place in the far corner and made for it purposefully. Before he reached it, however, his arm was tugged, and a cheerful voice said in his ear, "Good day, Farr. This is a bit of luck. I've been meaning to wait on you these past two days." Wys looked around to find Lambie Aylmer at his elbow.

"Good morning, Aylmer," he said in a tone he hoped would indicate his lack of desire for company.

But Lambie was not called 'the leech' for nothing. "I want to congratulate you on the race," he went on, ignoring Wys's apparent disinterest and hanging on to his sleeve. "You and Drew cost me a large roll of soft."

"Serves you right for betting against us," Wys said unsympathetically. "But if you'll excuse me, I see a seat—"

"Come to *my* table, old boy. I'm expecting Sir George. He promised to meet me here."

"You're expecting *Pollard?*" Wys asked, looking at Lambie closely.

"Yes. He's kept me waiting for almost half an hour."

Wys made a wry face. "I wouldn't bother waiting any longer, if I were you. He won't be here."

Aylmer drew himself up in offended dignity. "Of course he'll be here. We made the arrangements most specifically."

Wys could not resist the temptation to squelch Aylmer's pretensions. If he were in a mood to laugh, he would roar at the irony of having in his possession a piece of gossip that Lambie knew nothing of. Lambie's entire social standing rested on his claim to be, always, the very first to know the goings-on. "I tell you he won't be here," Wys repeated. "He is not in London this morning."

Lambie's confidence remained unshaken. "Sorry to contradict you, Farr," he said in his obnoxiously superior way, "but you can't be thinking of Pollard. Pollard is very definitely in London. Very definitely."

"I dislike to be the one to shake your certainty," Wys insisted, "but I have it on very good authority that he is, at this very moment, on his way to Gretna Green."

Lambie stared. "Pollard? Never Pollard, old man. It's not possible. You must be thinking of someone else."

Wys studied Aylmer's face carefully. "Why is it not possible? Tell me, Aylmer, what makes you so certain I'm in error?"

Lambie tried to answer, but the two were pushed aside

by a noisy group of gentlemen who were making their way to a nearby table. "This is no place to talk," he said to Wys as soon as he was able to rejoin him. "Come to my table where we can be more private."

They seated themselves, and both men looked around to see if anyone nearby could overhear. Satisfied that the men around them were strangers and preoccupied with their own concerns, Lambie leaned across to Wys. "What makes you think that George Pollard is on the way to Gretna?"

"I'm not at liberty to say anything else," Wys said primly. He already felt troubled that he had revealed too much to the most notorious gabble-monger in London. "But what makes *you* so sure I'm wrong?"

Lambie delighted in spreading information—always in the greatest confidence, of course!—and needed only to be asked. "Because," he said eagerly, "going to Gretna can only mean an elopement, isn't that so? George would not elope. Not now."

"Why not?"

"Listen, Farr, I'll tell you why not, but only if you promise to keep the information secret. The fact is that George Pollard has been betrothed these three weeks past!"

It gave Lambie the greatest satisfaction to see Wys's face. Mr. Farr actually *gaped*. "Pollard?" he said incredulously. "He can't be! I've seen no notice, heard no word of it. Surely someone would have mentioned such news in my hearing by this time."

"The announcement will be made three weeks from now. You see, the girl's a cit."

"A cit! I don't believe it. Pollard is too high in the instep for—"

"He ain't too high to feather his nest with a fifteen-thousand-pound settlement and a generous annuity." And Lambie sat back, smiling with glee to see the effect his display of knowledge had made on Wystan Farr.

Wys's head was swimming. Lambie's story had the ring

of truth. A man like Pollard, whose income depended on the turn of the cards, would do much for a fortune like that. And it would not be the first time that a wealthy merchant found it worthwhile to buy a title for his daughter. But if Lambie were right, what did this betrothal mean to Gwen? He couldn't concentrate on the possible ramifications of this news, not here in all this noise and hubbub. Besides, Lambie could be wrong. Gossip-mongers often were. He fixed a suspicious eye on Lambie's face. "How do you know all this, Aylmer? Where did you learn these 'facts'?"

"From no less a person than the party most concerned," Lambie answered in his irritatingly omniscient way. "George told me."

"If it is not to be announced for three weeks, why would he tell *you?* Everyone knows you're not to be trusted with a secret."

Again, Lambie drew himself up in offended dignity. "That's a calumny!" he declared. "If you weren't such a particular friend of mine, I'd call you out!"

"Oh, come down off your high ropes!" Wys said in disgust. "Just answer my question."

"I always keep a secret if I think it's necessary. I have more information up here," he insisted, tapping his forehead, "than I ever reveal. But as to your question, I know about George because I gave him the idea. He was indebted to me for a large sum, and I suggested that he marry a cit so that he could pay it off."

Wys was not convinced. "And he took your advice, did he?"

Lambie smiled proudly. "Paid off his debt already," he said.

Wys leaned back and let the information sink in. If George *were* betrothed to a young lady of wealth, it was unlikely that he would cry off to marry a penniless woman like Gwen. What then was his object in carrying Gwen off? The answer, when it presented itself, made him turn cold. He must get to Drew at once and tell him this fantastic story. But should he do it on only Lambie's word? It would be wiser to have some proof. He looked across the table speculatively. "Aylmer, what is the name of the girl to whom Pollard is betrothed?"

"Her name?" Lambie shrugged. "Can't say as I remember. Only a cit, you know. No one important."

"But he must have mentioned it to you. *Think,* man!"

It was Lambie's turn to be suspicious. "Why are you so interested? What's all this to you?"

"Never mind. Just tell me."

"I really can't recall. I think her name is Anabel." He wrinkled his brow in concentration. "Anabel...something that sounded like a fruit...Pear? Anabel Pear...no, that's not it..."

Wys felt the blood drain from his face. "Do you mean Plumb?" he asked in a strangely hollow voice. "Anabel *Plumb?*"

Lambie's face brightened, and he looked at Wys with a dawning respect. "Yes, that's it! How did you kn—?" But the words froze on his tongue. Wystan Farr was glaring at him with a look of such burning fury that Lambie took fright. "Wh—Wh—What's wrong?" he managed to ask.

"Nothing, you toad! Just give me her direction!" Wys said hoarsely.

"But I...I don't kn-know her direction!" Lambie stammered.

Wys stood up and grasped Lambie by his lapels and pulled him halfway across the table. "Tell me!"

"But I don't kn-know! Truly! Wait...I think...Yes. Warrenton knows. He gave Pollard the lead. Ask Warrenton."

Wys thrust Lambie back into his chair but grasped his neckcloth firmly and twisted it. "Very well. I'll go to Warrenton. But I'm going to see how well you can keep a secret, Aylmer. If one word of this conversation gets abroad, I'll pull out your tongue! Do you hear? I'll pull out your gossiping tongue!"

He pushed his way out of the coffee house and strode

down the street. When he'd calmed down somewhat, he looked at his hands. They were still trembling. He smiled at them ruefully. He had been such a moderate man. What was happening to him?

When at last he could think calmly, he knew he had two things to do. He had to warn Drew of Gwen's danger, and he had to find Miss Plumb. He could not let her marry a scoundrel like Pollard. But realizing that Gwen's problem was the more pressing, he set out for Drew's house.

Mallow tried to restrain him from entering. "His lordship is not wishful for company today, Mr. Farr," he said firmly.

"I must see him nevertheless," Wys said, brushing by the butler absently. Where is he?"

Mallow shrugged. Lord Jamison would not expect him to wrestle with Mr. Farr and eject him forcibly. "In the drawing room, sir," he said, resigned.

Wys found Drew sunk in a wing-backed chair gazing gloomily into the middle distance. He broached the subject without preamble. "You've got to go after her, Drew. She's in deeper trouble than you realize."

Drew focused his eyes on Wys and regarded him reproachfully. "I'd rather not talk about this, Wys."

"He doesn't plan to marry her!" Wys went on, ignoring Drew's remark. "I've just heard the most disturbing bit of news. Pollard is betrothed to *my Miss Plumb!*"

Drew shut his eyes and shook his head, as if his mind were rejecting what his ears had heard. "Either you're looney, or you've shot the cat," he muttered. "Go put your head under the pump!"

"Sober as a judge," Wys declared. "I'm persuaded that what I've told you is the truth." He pulled up a chair and recounted every detail of his talk with Lambie. After a few moments, Drew leaned forward and listened carefully to every word. When Wys had finished, he sat back and stared up at the ceiling wordlessly. "Well?" Wys asked. "What do you propose to do?"

"Nothing," Drew said flatly. "If she's jingle-brained enough to run off with that . . . that ivory-turner, let her have joy of him!"

"Drew! You don't understand! He means to force her—or trick her—into accepting a . . . a *carte blanche!*"

Drew winced. He got up wearily and went to the fireplace. Leaning both arms on the mantelpiece, he stared moodily into the fire. "There's nothing I can do. She doesn't want my help. She doesn't want me *near* her. She thinks of me as some sort of uncivilized brute."

Wys made a sound of protest. "I'm sure she never—!"

"Oh, yes. That's how she sees me. She told me so— right here in this very room. Under my pleasing veneer, she said, I'm a barbaric beast. Or words to that effect."

Wys looked stricken. "Oh, Drew!" he said sadly.

Drew laughed mirthlessly. "Lord, isn't it laughable? She thinks *I'm* the brute, and she runs off with that blackguard Pollard!"

"Nevertheless, you can't stand by and—"

"That's just what I *am* going to do. Every time I've crossed that woman's path I've regretted it. Last time, I swore I'd stay away from her. I swore it to her and to myself. I'm not going to break that pledge. Let her get *herself* out of this fix!" He looked up from the fire and smiled ruefully at Wys. "Get out of here, Wys, and take care of *your* problem. At least you can save Miss Plumb from the wiles of George Pollard."

Wys sighed and went to the door. There he paused. "Drew, won't you reconsider?" he pleaded. But Drew didn't turn his head from the fire, and Wys went out.

Drew remained staring at the fire, unable to keep from imagining Gwen in Pollard's arms. Or Gwen's face when she discovered Pollard's plot. The pair had probably been on the road three hours by this time. What route had they taken? he wondered. If *he* had planned it, he would probably head toward Wolverhampton and then straight north. Pollard would not be expecting to be followed— Gwen having no grown man to protect her—so his pace would not be overly hasty. With hard riding, he could probably catch up with them by nightfall. How he would love to throttle Pollard—his fingers fairly itched with eagerness to grasp his wretched throat. A laugh escaped him. Maybe Gwen was right about him; underneath the skin, perhaps he *was* a barbarian—he certainly felt murderous right now!

She had no one to protect her . . . the thought repeated itself over and over in his mind. He had no right to take on that role—no right at all. And she certainly would give him no thanks for his interference. She would probably find some way to blame him for the whole affair. But he *was* going. He'd known all morning that he would go.

He went swiftly to the door. "Mallow," he shouted, "go to the stables and tell them to harness the bays. I want them at the door as soon as I've changed my clothes." As he took the stairs three at a time, he noticed with surprise that he felt almost happy.

Chapter Fourteen

THE HOUSE OF JOSHUA PLUMB was the grandest on the street, standing out among the neat, modest edifices in vulgar pretension. The door was massive and the brass knocker ornate, the iron grille fence was tipped with gold on every curlicue, and every window boasted a little ledge with a wrought-iron railing. Wys banged the knocker with some misgiving. What was he doing here, presuming to give advice to strangers whose way of life he did not know and whose needs and goals were completely mysterious to him?

Only the thought of Anabel kept him from fleeing. He could still see her face as it had looked when she had poked her head out of the carriage window to say those last words to him. Her eyes had been full of tears and her chin had been trembling. Was he a coxcomb to believe that her expression was not that of a girl who was happily betrothed to someone else? With that picture of her woebegone face before him, he determined to do what he could to save her from Pollard.

A neatly dressed serving maid answered his knock. He stepped into a dark entryway which was not made brighter by the large number of paintings and ornaments that covered the panelled walls. "I'd like to see Miss Plumb, please," he told the maid.

"The fam'ly's all at luncheon, sir," the girl said dubiously.

"I see. But I've come on a matter of some urgency. Will you present my card to Miss Plumb and ask if she might spare me a few minutes?"

The maid bowed and disappeared into a room down the hall. There the whole family was indeed taking luncheon. It pleased Mr. Plumb to stroll down from the city every day at noon to join his family for a substantial mid-day meal, consisting of both a cold and a hot course. The five of them sat round an enormous table. They had already dispensed with generous servings of cold roast chicken, ham, and pickled salmon, and were now embarked on the second course of river trout, potatoes, greens, toast, and poached eggs. Gooseberry tarts and custard pudding were still waiting to be served.

The maid brought the card directly to Anabel, who looked at it, gasped, and paled. Since every eye was on her, her consternation was immediately noted and remarked upon. "What is *that?*" Mr. Plumb asked the maid.

"Gentleman to see Miss Anabel, sir," she said.

"*Gentleman?* What gentleman?" asked Mrs. Plumb in a flurry, leaning over to her younger daughter and fluffing her curls while kicking the leg of her elder to remind her to sit up straight.

"It's only...a gentleman who did me a service the other day on my way home from grandmama's," Anabel said, her face now as red as it was pale a moment ago.

"May I be excused to see him for a moment, papa?"

"Just a minute, Miss, just a minute. *What* service did he do you?"

"Well, I . . . He . . . Oh, it would take too long to explain now. I'll tell you all about it after I've seen him," Anabel said, rising hopefully.

"Sit down I say! What's this all about?"

"It's nothing to make a to-do over, Papa. The hack driver got into an argument with an apple vendor and neither would budge. And Mr. Farr settled the whole matter and bought all the apples and gave them to everyone in the street," Anabel said rapidly.

"Well, well! A regular gallant knight, eh? I suppose he's come to claim a reward. Must have cost him a bit of blunt to buy them apples, so now he's hopin' the pennies he threw away'll come back a pony."

"Well, I never!" Mrs. Plumb declared, outraged. "You ain't goin' to give 'im no twenty-five pounds!"

"It was only a manner of speakin', Martha, only a manner of speakin'," Joshua assured her. "I'm not a man to be throwin' my blunt about."

"I'm certain that Mr. Farr hasn't come here for a reward!" Anabel said, jumping to her feet indignantly. "Please, Papa, let me go out to him. It's terribly rude to keep him standing at the door."

"No, my dear, let's have him in here. I'd like to have a look at your Good Samaritan."

"So would I," giggled one of the sisters.

Anabel resumed her seat in a quake. She watched the door with eager expectation, at the same time suffering greatly from the frustration of facing him with all her family as witnesses. More than anything else, she wondered why he had come. After she had last seen him and had realized that her simple honesty in admitting her betrothal had completely cut off any chance she had of seeing him again, she could have cut out her tongue. Now by some good fortune, she had been given a third chance. If only her family were not in her way!

Mr. Farr was shown in. He looked around and bowed to Martha. "I sincerely apologize for my ill-timed visit, ma'am," he said politely. "I had no intention of interrupting you at your luncheon."

Mr. and Mrs. Plumb and Martha's daughters stared at him openmouthed. They had thought Sir George Pollard had been very grand, but something about this gentleman was more awe-inspiring. His coat of dark-blue superfine, cut to perfection; his pale blue breeches fitting over his legs without a crease or bulge; the neat watch-chain hanging from his striped waistcoat with its single fob; his impeccable neckcloth folded in a perfect "Oriental"; and his modest but not shy demeanor, made him stand out in the over-decorated room—among these overdressed, crimped, and jewelry-bedecked people—like a diamond in a pile of glass beads.

Joshua Plumb looked him over in approval. "No interruption at all, I say. No need to stand on ceremony with Joshua Plumb." And he stood up and wrung Wys's hand. "Didn't get your name, sir," he said in an aside.

"I'm Wystan Farr."

"How d'ye do? Sit you down, Mr. Farr, and break some bread with us," Plumb urged heartily. "Nothin' here's too good for the man who rescued my girl."

"Do that, Mr. Farr, sir," echoed Martha eagerly. "There's always plenty at our table, as ye can see. And anything ye don't see that ye've a mind to, we're sure to 'ave in the kitchen."

Martha's daughters giggled in agreement.

"Thank you, ma'am, but, if you'll excuse me, I have a matter of some urgency to discuss with Miss Plumb. Do you think you could permit me to speak to her alone?"

Martha's daughters giggled again. Joshua Plumb frowned at the visitor suspiciously. "What would you have to talk to my girl about? You hardly know each other, from what I've heard, unless..." He turned and glared at his daughter. "... unless she's been pokin' bogey!"

"Papa! It was no *tale!* I've only seen Mr. Farr twice in my life!" Anabel declared.

"*Twice* is it? *Twice?* Seems to me your story covered only *one* meeting. Did he rescue you a second time?" he asked with heavy sarcasm.

"Seems to me there's something 'avey-cavey going on," Martha put in.

Anabel looked at Wys with an expression of such embarrassment and shame that all his gallant instincts were again aroused. If ever a maiden needed rescuing from a houseful of dragons, it was she! He caught her eye and smiled at her, a smile of such understanding and encouragement that her agitation dissolved. Here was an ally, neither intimidated by her father's bluster nor revolted by her stepmother's excesses. She smiled timidly back at him.

"Perhaps, Mr. Plumb, if I could talk to *you* alone, I could explain," Wys suggested.

"Very well," Joshua Plumb said, getting up from his chair with an effort. "Come into the sittin' room."

Wys's imperturbability had given Anabel the courage she had lacked before. "Papa, please let me come, too," she asked, ignoring the obvious disapproval of her stepmother. "Mr. Farr came to see *me,* you know."

"I don't see why 'e can't say what he come for in front of us all," Martha said querulously.

"Can't expect the fellow to talk about private matters with a roomful of strangers listenin' in," Joshua said, dismissing his wife and her girls with a wave of his hand. "You ladies go on with your luncheon. Don't disturb yourselves." And he nodded to Wys and Anabel and led them from the room.

Once settled in the sitting room, Joshua faced this elegant young stranger aggressively. "So, here we are. Say your say without roundaboutation."

"I must ask you a personal question first, Mr. Plumb. Please believe that I do not mean to pry into matters that are not rightfully my concern, but I have some information which may be of use to you and Miss Plumb, and I could not, in good conscience, withhold it."

"Well then, ask your question, sir, ask your question. I ain't sayin' that I'll necessarily answer it, for that depends on the question, now, don't it? But there's no harm in your askin'."

"Is your daughter affianced to a gentleman by the name of Sir George Pollard, Mr. Plumb?"

Anabel started, colored, and fixed her eyes on Wys with an anxious intensity. Her father gave a surprised grunt. "Yes, that she is, though how you've come to hear it is a mystery to me. Nothin' was to be said for three weeks yet to come. *You* didn't tell him, did you, girl?"

"No, Papa, not his name."

"Not his *name?* What does *that* mean?" Joshua said in disgust. "I gave Pollard my word we'd say nothin' at *all!* Just what *did* you say to this here chap?"

"I only told him I was betrothed," Anabel admitted.

"What did you say that for? Couldn't you wait for a few weeks before you spilled the news to every passin' stranger?"

"Hang it, Mr. Plumb, she *had* to tell me," Wys cut in, annoyed at the manner in which Mr. Plumb was castigating his daughter.

"*Had* to? Why?" Plumb demanded.

Wys looked at Anabel for guidance. She met his glance and courageously took over the struggle. "Mr. Farr asked permission to... to call on me," she explained to her father with becoming modesty. "I told him my situation to explain why I had to refuse him."

"She gave me no name, however. I learned the name of her... betrothed... quite by accident," Wys added in support.

"Oh, ho!" Joshua snorted in amusement. "Wanted to call on her, did you? Now things are startin' to become plain. Why didn't you say so before? Of course, I can't give you permission to call on her, y'know, even if the announcement ain't to be made for three weeks. Wouldn't be right, y'see."

"I understand that, Mr. Plumb. That's not why I've come today."

"Well then, what *did* you come for? Can't you speak out straight?"

"No, sir, I'm afraid I can't. This is a delicate matter, and there's a question I should ask your daughter in private before I proceed."

"Private? There's nothin' you can say to her that you can't say before her father."

"Oh, Papa, please—?" Anabel pleaded.

"Quiet, Miss! He can speak up before me, or he can take himself off. Well, sir, what's it to be?"

Wys looked at Anabel questioningly. She hesitated, looking from Wys to her father and back again. "I know this is a most awkward situation, Mr. Farr, but if you can manage to ask your question in front of my father, I will try to be equally brave and answer it."

Wys got up and crossed the room, taking the chair nearest to her. "I hope you will not think this impertinent, Miss Plumb," he said in a low voice, "but trust me that it is important. Is ... Is your *heart* completely engaged in this match with Pollard?"

"What? What was that you said?" said Plumb, almost choking in irritation. "How dare you, a perfect stranger, ask such a thing of my girl? And why *wouldn't* her heart be engaged, eh?"

"Oh, Papa, be still!" cried the sorely-tried Anabel. "I *want* Mr. Farr to know the truth. My father meant it for the best, Mr. Farr, but the fact is that he arranged the match entirely without my consent and ... and very much against my wishes."

This brave declaration was met with choleric fury from her father and a look of glowing gratitude from Wystan Farr. While Joshua Plumb fumed and blustered, completely ignored, Wys and Anabel smiled at each other in happy relief. Plumb at last stopped sputtering long enough to notice the looks passing between them. "Can't see what you're smilin' for!" he blustered. "The girl is promised, no matter what she says, and Joshua Plumb does not go back on his word! Won't do a bit of good to grin at each other like it's roses and midsummer moon with you both! I gave Pollard my word she'd wed him, and wed him she will!"

"Even if the man's a blackguard?" Wys asked calmly.

"Eh? What's this? What do you mean?"

"At this very moment, Mr. Plumb, the man you've chosen for your daughter is eloping to Gretna Green with . . . with someone else."

"*Eloping?* Are you tellin' me he's jiltin' my Anabel?"

"No. It's my belief that it's the other lady he's playing false."

Plumb stared at Wys for a long moment. "Mmmmm. So that's his game. Thinks to run sly with us, does he?" He narrowed his eyes and looked at Wys suspiciously. "Are you sure about all this?"

"Yes, sir. Quite sure."

The suspicious look did not leave Plumb's face. "And I'm supposed to take your word for all this? It seems a havey-cavey rig to me. What do you expect to get for your pains, eh? Want to take Pollard's place with my girl, do you?"

Wys colored. "I didn't think . . . Look here, Plumb, my only purpose in coming here today was to warn you of the character of the man. Of course, if Miss Plumb should decide to terminate her engagement, I hope she will permit me to call on her," he said, stung by the antagonistic and suspicious reaction Mr. Plumb had shown to his news.

"Papa, I—" Anabel began.

"Be still, Anabel, and let me handle this!" her father commanded. He leaned back in his chair and rubbed his side-whiskers thoughtfully. "I will admit that, if your information is correct, I cannot like Pollard's doin's. Still, you say you think he intends to keep his word and wed my Anabel as we agreed..."

Wys jumped to his feet furiously. "You cannot still consider permitting your daughter to marry him, knowing the sort of... I mean, she deserves better than that!"

Joshua leaned forward in his chair. "Oh, she does, does she? Meanin' *you*, I suppose."

"At least *I* would never—!" Wys snapped. He stopped himself immediately, appalled at himself for what he considered a lapse of taste. Returning to his chair, he said quietly, "Excuse me. That is not for me to say."

Joshua Plumb regarded Wys with a softened expression. This chap was more to his taste than that fish-eyed Pollard. This one had spirit and talked to a man straight and eye-to-eye. And it was plain as pikestaff that Anabel was taken with him. But it was a sticky business. He and Pollard had made a bargain. Pollard had asked for six weeks to end his affairs, and he had agreed to it. But this business Farr told him of sounded rather more like the *beginning* of an affair than the *end* of one. If true, the information could well be a reason to break the agreement. "Tell me, Mr. Farr," he asked, "can you give me proof of your accusations against Sir George?"

"Proof? I hadn't given that any thought. I have none now, sir, but I suppose I could find some way to—"

"Good. Get me some proof of your story, and I'll end the alliance between Pollard and my daughter."

"Oh, *Papa!*" cried the overjoyed Anabel.

Wys rose again. "And will I then have your permission to call on your daughter, sir?"

"Now, that's another question, ain't it? I know nothin' about you, y'know. Might you be a duke or a marquis?" he asked hopefully.

"No, sir, I have no title."

"None at all? You ain't even a baron?"

"No, sir."

Mr. Plumb was crestfallen. "I hope you don't think,

Mr. Farr, that if you was to wed Anabel, you'd be entitled to the sum of blunt I'd promised to Sir George. After all, without even a Sir attached to your monniker—"

"Confound it, Plumb," Wys said sharply, "I'd take not a penny from you! If you think I'm at all interested in your 'blunt' you're out in your reckoning! I'm sorry that your daughter has to hear this . . . this discussion . . . but I must tell you, sir, that to think your daughter needs a dowry to make her eligible is not only an insult to her but completely ridiculous. You need only to *look* at her to know that she'd enrich any man she chose, even if she hadn't a penny in the world!"

Plumb's eyes twinkled, although his face did not betray his amusement by the movement of a single muscle. "Very fine talkin', my boy, but it don't put no mutton on the table nor clothes on the back. I didn't raise my girl to be a lady just to throw her away on any here-and-therian who comes along."

"As to that, Mr. Plumb, if and when your *daughter* decides that I am worthy of her hand, I can assure you that I shall provide her with every luxury to which she is accustomed." He looked down at Anabel with a sudden grin. "I may not be a *Sir,* but I can support a wife very well without the help of her father."

Wys found that Anabel was regarding him with a look of such radiance that he forgot her father's presence entirely. Without another word, he pulled his chair close to hers and took her hand. A chuckle escaped Mr. Plumb, but the two did not hear. Plumb pulled himself up from his chair, smiled at them in satisfaction, and went to the door. "I suppose you'll do," he said to the unheeding Wys. He paused at the door, expecting the young man to take his hint and say his goodbyes, but Wys and Anabel did not move. Plumb shrugged. "I suppose I can leave you to be private with each other for a minute or two, eh?"

"Oh. Yes. Thank you, sir," Wys answered absently, so engrossed that he did not stand or turn around but continued to gaze at Anabel, enraptured.

Joshua Plumb, looking at his daughter's face, permitted himself to beam. "Too bad he ain't at least a baron," he murmured as he left the room and discreetly closed the door behind him.

Chapter Fifteen

THERE WAS A DEFINITE scent of snow in the air when Wys emerged from his blissful *rapprochement* with his Anabel. He pulled up his collar and headed straight for the Selby house. Waiting for the door to be answered, he consulted his watch and found, to his astonishment, that it was not yet two in the afternoon. He had been through so much today that it was hard to believe that only a few hours had elapsed since he had met Tom on Drew's doorstep. To his even greater astonishment, the butler informed him that Lady Selby had not yet risen from her bed. "Is she ill?" Wys inquired.

"I don't believe so, sir," the butler said. "Merely a late party last night. But *Lord* Selby has been up for several hours."

"Very well, I'll see him instead. Where is he?"

"In the library. I'll take you to him, sir."

"Don't bother. I'll find my way."

Selby looked up from his newspaper with a cheerful greeting on his lips, but one look at Wys's face told him that Wys had more than a social purpose for his visit. He put a shaking hand to his forehead. "Wystan, old fellow, I'm glad to see you, but if you've come to suggest some activity for me, I beg you to excuse me. My wife dragged me to the Ogilvies' last night, and a duller evening I've never endured. As a consequence, I drank too much port and I'm fit for nothing today but to lounge in my chair."

Wys eyed him askance. "A likely tale! When have I ever found you fit for anything else?"

"A base canard, my boy," Selby replied affably, "but I haven't the energy to refute you. Pour yourself some of that Madeira and sit down."

Wys complied, but after a sip or two of Selby's excellent wine, he lost no time in coming to the point of his visit. "Much as I dislike to disturb your lethargy, Selby, I have a wolf by the ear and need your help. Gwen Rowle has run off with George Pollard, and I learned by chance from Lambie Aylmer that the blackguard has no intention of marrying her."

Selby's owlish eyes grew even larger as he tried to grasp the import of the confusing statement Wys had just thrown at him. After several questions, which Wys answered too impatiently to clarify Selby's confusion, Selby insisted that Wys begin at the beginning and tell him the events of the day step by step. Before this request could be granted, the library door opened, and a heavy-eyed, tousled Hetty—dressed in a loose morning dress and house slippers—padded in. "Heard you were here, Wystan," she said, yawning. "What are you doing, calling so early?"

"Early!" cried the aggrieved Wys. "It's almost two!"

"Oh. In that case, make yourself at home. I'm going to get myself some breakfast."

"Breakfast! At two in the afternoon? That is positively sinful, Hetty. Besides, I need your support with Selby, so sit down, please, and listen to what has happened this morning."

"Wystan," warned Selby, "unless you want the story spread all over London, don't tell her a thing!"

Hetty drew herself up to her full height, an action which—since it brought her up only to her full five-feet-two-inches—failed to impress the observers. "How can you be so provoking, Selby," she asked with dignity, "when you know that I've gone all these months knowing all the facts about Drew's duel and have not breathed a word to a soul?"

"Good for you, my dear," Selby observed drily. "Since you merely swore an oath on your honor, in front of witnesses, that you would hold your tongue, you are much to be commended for your silence."

"Oh, be quiet, you beast," she retorted, her dignity discarded. Perching on a wing chair from which she could watch both her irritating husband and her guest, she tucked her legs under her comfortably and said contentedly, "Now, Wys, tell us what happened this morning."

Wys, forcing himself to curb his impatience, recounted the events of the morning in as much detail as he deemed necessary for their understanding. The account took several minutes, during which he was interrupted by frequent questions and exclamations from the wide-eyed Hetty and by some pungent epithets from Selby. At the conclusion of his tale he looked from one astounded listener to the other and said, "So you can see why we must do *something!* And at *once!*

Selby, whose owlish eyes had grown larger with every detail, now shut them with a wince. "We?" he groaned. "*We?*"

"Well, of course, we!" his wife declared, bouncing out of her chair energetically. "I shall dress at once and be ready before you know it."

"Just a minute, my dear," Selby said quellingly. "Not so fast!"

"But you heard what Wystan said. There's no time to lose!"

"Hetty, sit down," Selby ordered, and fixed his eye on her until she'd obeyed. "Now, then, have you thought to ask yourselves just where we would go, and what we would do when we got there?"

"We'll go after that...dastard, Pollard, tell Gwen what he's up to, and take her back with us," Hetty answered promptly.

"Do you think it's as simple as that?" Selby asked bluntly. "First, we don't know what route he's taken. Second, we can't travel much faster than they can, so that if we ever *do* catch up with them, we may well be too late. Third, I think there's snow in the air. And, last, we have no right to interfere at all. We are not related to her any more than Drew is!"

"Oh, Selby," Hetty said in disgust, "must you always be so deucedly *logical?* We *must* go, in spite of your so-reasonable objections."

"Not all of your objections are valid, Selby," Wys pointed out in his own reasonable way. "First, we can make a good guess at Pollard's route. Second, he doesn't own a horse much better than a slug, so the chances are he won't make good time. Don't tell me your greys aren't a match for anything Pollard may have picked up."

"*My* greys, eh? What about the nags *you've* been bragging about for months? Won't they do as well?"

"Why take the time to stop at my stables when we can much more easily start from here?" Wys answered ingenuously.

Selby growled. He was getting deeper and deeper into a situation in which he had no wish to involve himself. "But I still don't think we have a right to take this on. If *Drew* wouldn't, why should we?"

Wys frowned. "Drew's been badly hurt. I've thought of

asking him again, but, in truth, I'd like to spare him. It's for his sake more than anyone's that I think we must bring Gwen back."

"There's that *we* again. *We!* Why can't *you* do it and leave us out of it?" he demanded, feeling much put-upon.

Hetty got up and went to Selby's chair. Perching on the arm, she rubbed one hand against his cheek and with the other curled a wisp of his greying hair around her finger. "Don't be such an old bear, my love," she said in his ear. "We can't let Wys do this all alone. It's for Drew's sake, after all. And it's too dreadful to think of Gwen in the clutches of that scoundrel. What if it were *me,* and you sat here being logical, and nobody lifted a finger—?"

"*You?*" Selby gave an involuntary shudder. "As if you would ever think of running off like that!"

She bent and planted a light kiss on his forehead. "That's because I have the best—the very best—of husbands," she said fondly.

Wys watched in amusement as Selby visibly wilted under Hetty's quite obvious wiles. Strange that even a clever fellow like Selby could be turned from his intentions by female stratagems that the veriest fool could see through. And Wys smiled to realize that he himself would no doubt behave in the very same way. How pleasant it will be, he thought, when Anabel perches on the arm of *my* chair and makes a dupe of me in the very same way!

"It's a fool's errand, I tell you," Selby grumbled, making his last gasp of independence. "We'll doubtless make a mull of the business and get nothing for our pains but a good trouncing from Pollard and the everlasting enmity of your precious brother."

"Nonsense," said his wife decisively. "We shall do very well, and it will be a perfectly grand adventure."

Selby regarded her as he would a creature from Bedlam. "Adventure!" he muttered, casting a helpless glance at Wys. "*Women!* If you had any sense at all, Wystan, my boy, you'd stay away from 'em. Even that paragon you've discovered this morning."

Hetty, knowing she had won, ignored the affront and bounced up happily from her perch. "Well, I'm going to change. I shan't be a moment."

"Take your time, you troublesome minx," her husband said shortly. "I'm going to have my luncheon, and I won't be hurried."

"Luncheon?" asked his scandalized wife. *"Now?"*

"If you think I'm going to set out on a race to Scotland without a good meal to sustain me," he declared roundly, "you've much mistaken your man! And if you don't like it, you both can jolly well set off without me!" And with that he trotted out the door, slamming it behind him with a satisfying bang.

The snow had started to fall by the time Pollard's coach had reached Stamford at mid-afternoon, and he knew that they would not get much further by nightfall. While Gwen viewed the advent of snow with alarm, George was not at all troubled. The longer they were delayed on the road, the more opportunities he would have to compromise her reputation, and the more difficult it would be for her to find reasons to refuse the offer he would make. He pretended to a concern he was far from feeling about the weather, and tried to console her by drawing her to him to keep her warm.

Gwen's misgivings had grown as the day had progressed. Try as she would to convince herself that she could learn to love the man sitting beside her, she found herself unable to respond to the advances he made with irritating regularity. At one point, she had feigned sleep, sliding away as far as she could from him and letting her head rest on the coach window. That she had resorted to a subterfuge troubled her. She feared that it augured greater dishonesty in their married life to come. As the day wore on, the ceaseless rocking of the carriage made her feel ill. Her head ached and her stomach churned and she couldn't tell if the misery of her spirit was due to the abominable ride or to the decision she had made to marry the man who was now sitting beside her.

It was an immense relief when, at about three in the afternoon, George decided to find the nearest inn and put up for the night. The sky had darkened alarmingly, and the snow was falling thickly enough to make visibility difficult for the driver. "Do you know of any suitable inns in the vicinity?" George called to the coachman.

"Yes, sir!" shouted the driver through the wind, relieved to learn that a warm, dry room and a tankard of ale were not far off. "There's the Rose and Crown, not more'n three miles north o' Grantham."

The Rose and Crown turned out to be a rather modest establishment with a large tap room and two small private parlors on its main floor, and a number of small bedrooms on the upper floor under the thatched eaves. Gwen asked to be shown to her bedroom immediately, leaving George to invent, for the benefit of the innkeeper, whatever tale he felt was suitable to explain their need for two bedrooms. When she reappeared, feeling warmer, less queasy and somewhat refreshed, she was able to greet George with a ready smile. "I've taken a private parlor, *sister* dear," he said with a wink, "so let us go into it and warm ourselves. I've ordered tea and mulled wine."

It was the larger parlor of the two private rooms available, a cheerful room with a wide fireplace in which an enormous log was blazing. She held her hands to the fire, comforted by the cosy atmosphere, although the sound of the angry wind outside the windows told her that her fear of a real storm was rapidly becoming a reality. "Do you think we are in danger of being snowed in?" she asked George in concern.

"I don't think so," he said contentedly. "It will all probably blow away by morning. Come here, love, and sit near me on this settee."

"Do you think that would be quite *sisterly,* brother dear?" she teased. "I'll do quite well here near the fire."

A serving maid appeared soon after with a heavily

laden tray holding tea things, sandwiches, and two mugs of steaming wine. The tea soothed Gwen's spirit as well as her stomach, and a pleasant half-hour passed at the table. When the maid had removed the dishes, however, and George closed the door carefully and looked at Gwen with an amorous gleam, she began to realize the awkwardness of her position. Something that she would not recognize as fear clutched at her chest. Not wishing an embarrassing struggle, she smiled at George wanly and said that the journey had tired her and she would rest in her room until dinner time. George could not object. As he watched her go, he told himself that there was plenty of time. The snow would not soon abate, and a whole lovely evening lay ahead.

In her room, Gwen found that she could not remain lying down. Restlessly she paced back and forth from the doorway to the window, only five paces from one side of the room to the other. Every once in a while she paused to stare out of the window. It was almost dark, but she could see the snow falling thickly and swirling wildly in the wind. What am I doing here? she asked herself over and over. Finally she sat down at the edge of the bed and tried to think clearly. She had come here to marry George Pollard. But she was not happy about a Gretna Green wedding. When it became known, it would sound sordid. Was *that* what troubled her? If so, all she need do is tell George that she would prefer to be wed in London—if he wished, just as secretly—by special license. They could return to town as soon as the snow stopped.

But that was not it. The truth of the matter was that she did not want to marry George at all. What had made her take so rash a step? She must have known, deep inside, that she was making a second marital mistake. She tried to remember the reasoning that had brought her to accept a proposal she had never before even considered seriously. It had something to do with Drew, she remembered. The look on his face at the end of the race. Was she foolish enough to have let her reaction to Drew drive her into the arms of the first available man? No, it was more. It was something about George. George had reminded her of Edward. She had failed with Edward, so she wanted to make up for that failure by being the kind of wife to George she had not been before.

How silly that idea seemed now. George was not like Edward at all. Edward was a *boy,* and because of his youth, Gwen might have been able to change him—though Hazel insisted that she could not have done so. But George was a man. There was something in his eyes that told her he could not easily be manipulated. She could never change him, not without love. If she'd learned anything in her first marriage, it should have been that. She had failed Edward because she did not love him.

She raised her head, the words she had just thought repeating themselves in her ears as if she had spoken them. "I failed Edward because I did not love him." Suddenly it all seemed so clear. She had expected more of herself than was humanly possible. Pushed into a youthful marriage by unthinking parents, she had found herself in a situation *not of her making* and beyond her capabilities to correct. Drew had not killed all hope when he'd pulled that trigger—hope had been dead long before.

She got up and went to the window under the low dormer and sank down on the cushioned window seat. Leaning her forehead against the cold window-glass, she shut her eyes and saw Rowle's face—the petulant underlip, the dark eyes so wild and stormy, the hair that hung in careless curls about his pale face. Poor, poor Edward, she thought, and the tears flowed from under her closed lids and dripped unheeded down her cheeks. When she finally stopped crying, after how many minutes she didn't know, she discovered that she'd come to a decision. To marry George would be a mistake worse than she had made before. She had married Edward Rowle in ignorance. She knew better now.

Gwen lay down on the bed and closed her eyes. She knew just what she had to do. She would rest for a while.

Then, when she was calmer, she would go down and tell George the truth—that she did not love him, and that a marriage without love would be a disaster for them both. This resolved, she sighed in relief and turned on her side. Before she realized it, she had dropped off into a sound sleep.

George had played solitaire for over an hour, had dozed by the fire, had gone up to his room to change into evening clothes, and had ordered dinner, but Gwen had not yet appeared. It was close to seven o'clock. Night had come without any diminution of the wind that howled outside the windows or the snow that fell heavily and was quickly accumulating in high drifts. George was just about to send the serving wench to wake Gwen, when he heard a commotion in the hall outside his door. Voices and the stamp of boots gave evidence that the innkeeper was receiving some new arrivals. He wondered who could be abroad in such weather, but before he had a chance to investigate, the door to the parlor opened, and on the threshold stood Drew Jamison, still in his greatcoat and hat and carrying his riding whip, regarding him with smoldering eyes.

"Good Lord! Jamison!" George said, too surprised to read Drew's expression with any accuracy.

"Where is she?" Drew asked.

"What?" asked George stupidly, not seeing any connection between his elopement and Drew's unexpected arrival.

"Where's Gwen?" Drew said, taking a step into the room.

George began to feel distinctly uneasy. Was Jamison here to scotch his plans? The idea was ridiculous, but what else would explain his question? "Gwen?" he asked innocently, playing for time.

Drew strode into the room and grasped George's neckerchief in one gloved hand. "Where is she?" he asked between clenched teeth.

"Upstairs in her bedroom, asleep," George said, trying to keep his voice matter-of-fact, "though I don't know what business it is of yours."

Drew released him and turned to the door. "If I learn that you've so much as laid a finger on her," he said in a voice that boded no good, "you'll learn what business it is of mine!"

"She was exhausted from the journey," George said quickly. "She'll not thank you for waking her."

Drew hesitated. George used the hesitation to his advantage. "She said she'd be down for dinner. I expect she'll appear quite shortly. Why don't you take off your coat, Jamison, and have a drink?"

Drew gave George a long look, turned, and locked the door to the passageway. He pocketed the key, threw his hat and whip on a chair, and peeled off his gloves. Dropping them beside his hat, he took off the greatcoat and threw it over the chair. "Why on earth did you lock the door?" George asked, holding out a glass of wine.

Deliberately disdaining the wine and the question, Drew went to the fire and warmed his hands. "I suggest, Pollard, that you avoid an ugly scene and take yourself off before she comes down."

"Take myself off? Listen here, Jamison, I don't know what your game is, but you're not going to give *me* orders!"

Drew turned from the fire. "But I know what *your* game is, you see," he said, dangerously quiet.

"If you mean that Gwen and I are on our way to be married, you must also know that she is of age, that she is going willingly, and that I don't care for your interference in something that in no way concerns you," George said with a sneer.

"You'll shortly care for my interference a great deal less, you damned lying blackguard," Drew snarled. He crossed to George in two strides and swung fiercely at his jaw. The blow connected with a sharp crack, and George went crashing to the floor. He blinked up dazedly at Drew who stood over him rubbing the knuckles of his right hand. "So you're going to marry her, are you?" Drew asked coldly. "And what about Miss Plumb?"

"Miss Pl—?" George muttered, confounded. The guilt on his face was all the evidence Drew needed. Turning his back on George, he returned to the fire. "Yes, we guessed your little game. Now, oblige me, please, by getting out of here before I give in to temptation and choke you to death."

A wave of hatred and fury swept over George, so strong that the pain in his jaw was forgotten. He got to his feet and leapt at Drew like a tiger. The two men fell to the floor, knocking over the fireplace pokers as they went down. The pokers clanged loudly on the hearth. George gripped Drew's throat fiercely, and as they rolled on the floor, Drew pulled at those clutching fingers with all his strength. At last he pulled them loose, kicked Pollard away from him, and managed to get up on one knee. He knelt there a moment to catch his breath, suddenly aware of the banging on the door and the shouting in the passageway. Meanwhile, Pollard reached for the nearest chair and, getting clumsily to his knees, he flung it at Drew with all his strength. It struck Drew on his back, and he fell heavily and lay still.

On the wooden settee set against the wall opposite the fireplace, Pollard had laid his coat, hat, and cane. He got up unsteadily and stumbled over to the bench. He picked up the cane, quickly unscrewed the handle, and pulled out the sword.

Drew lifted his head dizzily, but he could see Pollard's boots coming toward him. He reached for the table leg nearest him and pulled himself up in time to see Pollard lunging at him with an evil-looking sword. At the last moment, Drew swung aside, and caught Pollard around the waist with one arm, then grappled for the sword with his free hand. The two men struggled desperately— Drew's hand clenched on George's wrist, forcing the

sword into inactivity, the other arm holding Pollard
firmly at the waist, pinioning him to Drew's side and
preventing him from moving freely. They lurched
dangerously around the room, knocking over chairs and
grunting for breath.

The shouting in the hall and the banging on the door
became louder but went completely unheeded. At last,
Drew managed to place his leg behind Pollard and shoved
him backward. Pollard stumbled over Drew's extended
leg. At that moment, Drew took his arm from Pollard's
waist and reached up for the sword, pulling at the blade
with all his strength. He felt the sharp edge of the blade cut
into his palm, but there was no pain. The tug, coming at
the moment when Pollard had lost his balance, caused
Pollard to release the sword. Drew flung it aside and
smashed his right fist into Pollard's face, a crushing blow.
Drew felt—with satisfaction—the crunch of broken teeth
and the blood that gushed from Pollard's nose as he went
crashing to the wall and slid to the floor unconscious.

Drew stood for a moment trying to catch his breath.
Then, seeing the sword on the floor near the fireplace, he
bent to pick it up. He looked at it interestedly until he
became aware of a tingle in the palm of his left hand. He
looked at it in surprise. A deep gash had been cut
diagonally from the first finger to the heel of the hand,
and the blood was flowing profusely. He looked around
for something with which to bind it, but at that moment a
key was turned in the lock and the door of the parlor was
flung open. There in the doorway stood the innkeeper, the
ostler, and a veritable crowd of strangers, staring at him
with mouths agape. But in front of the crowd, on the
threshold of the room, stood a wide-eyed Gwen.

Her eyes were fixed on his face, as his were on hers. He
watched as she suddenly swept the room with her glance.
She saw Pollard at last—stretched out on the floor, his
head braced against the wall, the blood from his nose
dripping down onto his neckcloth and forming an ever-

widening stain—and her eyes flew back to Drew. He saw them widen with horror as they flicked down to his hands. Drew looked down. In one hand he held the sword. The other was dripping with blood.

Chapter Sixteen

DREW FLUNG THE SWORD away and strode to the door. Grasping Gwen by the arm, he pulled her over the threshold. Then he glared at the gaping crowd. "Go about your business!" he ordered, and slammed the door in their faces. The smear of blood his hand left on the door and the sting in his palm reminded him of his wound. Involuntarily, he looked down at it, and Gwen pulled out of his grasp. She backed away from him in wide-eyed terror until the door stopped her. Trembling, she leaned against it. "Oh, my God!" she said in an agonized moan. "You've murdered him!"

"Don't be a fool, woman," Drew said shortly. "Go and get your things together!" And with his good hand he fumbled at his neckcloth which he untied and pulled from his neck.

She seemed not to hear. "I wouldn't let myself really believe it," she murmured abstractedly. "All the evidence, everything that's happened, and I didn't... I couldn't ... really believe that you...! But now I see it with my own eyes. You're a... monster! A murdering *monster!*"

Drew wrapped the neckcloth tightly around his cut palm and held it in place by clenching his fist. A throbbing pain had begun to radiate from the wound and his back ached excruciatingly from its contact with the chair. "I'm in no mood to listen to you enact a Cheltenham tragedy, Gwen. Your dear George is not dead. He's suffering, I imagine, from no more than a slight concussion, a bloody nose, and some loose teeth. I have no doubt that in a week or two he'll be quite well enough to go about seducing someone else. Now, please, *go and get your things!*"

Gwen, after peering closely at his face to ascertain that he spoke the truth, ran to George's side. Kneeling, she lifted his head. George groaned, opened his eyes, muttered something incomprehensible in a pathetic whisper, and closed his eyes again. She pulled aside the bloody neckcloth, looking for the sword wound she was sure was there, but there was none. She looked up at Drew in exquisite relief. "Were you telling me the truth?" she asked.

"You've checked it for yourself," he said angrily, "so why bother to ask? Now, leave him to the mercies of the landlord and get your things. If we don't hurry, the snow will be so thick there will be no getting back before morning."

"I have no intention of getting back before morning!" Gwen said. Her feeling of cold terror was subsiding, and her pulse—which had been racing alarmingly—was slowing to normal. She got to her feet and went to the door. When she opened it, she found a number of onlookers still hanging about, and the innkeeper was standing in a position which clearly indicated that he'd been listening at the keyhole. She looked at the eavesdropper in disgust. "Since you've heard everything, don't just stand there gaping like a fish! Get me a basin of water and some clean cloths!" And she closed the door again.

"Gwen, I have travelled at top speed for hours in this blasted weather to restore you to your family before morning. Let the innkeeper take care of him, I beg you."

Gwen swept him with a look of burning disdain. "It's just like you to cause this chaos and leave it to someone else to mend! And who *asked* you to restore me to my family? I've told you that I want none of your interference in my life."

"Well, *somebody* must interfere! You're making a fine mull of it on your own!"

"*I'm* making a mull of it?" she asked furiously. With a sweep of her arm, she waved at the overturned furniture, the blood on the floor, and Pollard lying prostrate. "I suppose this mull is of *my* making!"

"Of course it's of your making!" he said wrathfully. "If you hadn't run off with that lying dog, none of this would have been necessary."

"It is none of your affair whom I choose to marry and under what circumstances I choose to do it! What right had you to—?"

"Right? You talk of *rights?* Did you want me to apply to a solicitor for some sort of legal document declaring that I'm empowered to act on your behalf?" he sneered. "It's the right—or rather, the duty—of any decent man to do what he can to prevent an unprotected woman from being led into calamity. Did you *want* to become his...doxy?"

"*Doxy?* What do you—? How *dare* you say that to me?"

"He had no intention of marrying you, Gwen," Drew told her flatly.

She stared at him. "I don't believe you!"

Drew could stand no more. His back ached and his hand throbbed, and though he didn't admit it to himself, he was devastated by what seemed to him incontrovertible signs that Gwen felt a real attachment to the dastard on the floor. Furiously, he grasped her shoulders, forcing her to face him squarely. "Of *course* you don't believe me," he said, the mocking sneer on his face so pronounced that it frightened her. "Why should you? Your superb judgment of the male character has been unerring in the past, hasn't it? In your assessment of Rowle, of Pollard, of me, you have not been—*could not be*—mistaken, not *you!* Why should you believe *me* when you have the word of the very *honorable* Sir George Pollard to believe! Very well, Lady Rowle, *take him!* There he lies, waiting for your loving hands to minister to his needs. The heiress in London will never have him now, so he's yours. All yours. I wish you well of him." He thrust her from him, snatched his clothes from the chair, and flung open the door.

He froze in his tracks at the sight that met his eyes. There in the corridor stood Wystan Farr, shaking the snow from his beaver hat. Behind him, Hetty was being assisted out of her pelisse by a red-nosed, snow-covered Lord Selby. Drew looked from one to the other in stunned fury. "It wanted only *this!*" he exclaimed wrathfully, and—without waiting for a word of greeting or explanation—he pushed past them and out the door.

"That was *Drew!*" said the stupefied Hetty, turning to Wys. "I thought you said he refused to come!"

"It *was* Drew," Wys said, a smile dawning on his face. "I should have known he'd come! Drew! Drew!" he shouted, and ran to the door. But out in the courtyard, Drew had jumped into his carriage which was now turning toward the road at a speed unpardonably reckless in the confined and snow-covered space provided by the inn. Before Wys had time to shout again, the maneuver was completed with surprising finesse, and the carriage disappeared into the whirling snow.

"He's gone," said Selby, who had come up behind Wys. "And as cross as nine highways. Something's gone amiss, as I told you it would."

The two men turned and went back inside. Hetty had

already entered the parlor and was surveying the chaos, aghast. "Gwen, you poor child!" she cried. "What has happened here?"

Gwen—who had been standing, transfixed, on the spot where Drew had left her—seemed not to see the three friends who were staring at her in concern. But after a moment, she began to shake, and her eyes filled with tears. "He said...he s-said...George wanted to...s-seduce m-me," she said in a pathetic little voice.

Hetty ran to her and hugged her soothingly. "There, there, dear," she crooned, "come and sit down here with me. Everything will be all right now." She led the trembling girl to the settee, where Gwen sank against Hetty wearily and yielded to her tears.

As she sobbed in Hetty's arms and Wys watched in helpless ineptitude, Selby, more immune to tears, surveyed the room. "Take a look at Pollard, will you? Drew's given him his just deserts, I'd say," he said almost gleefully.

Wys, turning from Gwen to the unmoving form on the floor, nodded his head, untouched by the sight before him. "Seems to have done a complete job. Landed him a facer."

"A good right, I expect," Selby surmised.

"Wish he'd left a little work for me," said Wys, rubbing his knuckles. "I was looking forward to a good mill myself."

"I know," Selby agreed. "So was I. Nothing for it now but to clean him up." Selby went purposefully to the door. There in the corridor stood the innkeeper, basin in hand and towels on his arm, hesitant to come in. Selby laughed. "It isn't nearly as bad as it looks, my man," he said. "Come in, come in."

The innkeeper entered and looked around curiously. Then he knelt at Pollard's side and lifted him to a sitting position. Selby unceremoniously poured most of the water in the basin over Pollard's head. George shuddered as his eyes opened, sputtered, and groaned. He recognized

Selby at once. "Oh, no," he said, and shut his eyes again.

"Everyone seems so delighted to see us," Selby muttered sarcastically. "Get him a drink of brandy, Wystan."

"Wait a minute," Wys said in an arrested voice. "What's this?" And he held up the blood-covered sword he had noticed on the floor.

Gwen, who had lifted her head at the sound of Pollard's voice, uttered a strangled cry.

"What is it, my dear?" Hetty asked her in concern.

"That . . . bloody thing . . . is Drew's!"

"Can't be," said Wys positively. "Drew doesn't like swordplay above half. Look at this handle, Selby. I've seen it somewhere before, I believe."

Selby frowned. "It's . . . it looks like Pollard's *cane!*

Gwen blinked at it. "Why . . . I think you're *right!*" she said, puzzled.

A quick look around the room revealed to Wys the hollow cane lying under the settee not far from Hetty's foot. Wys stooped, picked it up, and fitted the sword into it. He screwed the handle tightly into place and held up the familiar cane for Gwen's inspection.

"But what does it mean?" Gwen asked. "Did they duel with swords?"

"Not likely," Wys said thoughtfully. "There is no *other* sword in the room. And Drew had none with him when he left. I've never known Drew to use a sword, have you, Selby?"

"Never. It's plain as a pack-saddle that this *snake* pulled it out and attacked Drew with it."

"And Drew was plainly unarmed!" said Wys, appalled. He looked down at George, who was conscious and blinking about dazedly. "You rotter!" Wys muttered, looking down at him, revolted.

Gwen was completely bewildered. "But . . . but *Drew* was holding the sword when I came in. And it was covered with blood! I thought—"

"You thought *my brother* would attack an unarmed

man with a sword?" Hetty asked, recoiling from Gwen in disgust.

"Drew obviously had to protect himself—he must have wrenched it from Pollard. I wonder how he managed it," Selby said.

Wys looked troubled. "It must have been quite a struggle. I *thought* I saw something white on Drew's left hand. I wonder if he's hurt."

"Worse 'n this 'un," the innkeeper ventured, looking up from his work on George's face. "All that blood on the floor didn't come from this gent 'ere. T'other gentleman wrapped this cove a rum 'un, I'll admit, but a bloody nose never made all that mess there."

"Do you mean to say, my good man, that the only thing wrong with that *creature* you are tending is a bloody nose?" Hetty asked in a tone that revealed a disappointment great enough to be called outrage.

"Well, no, my lady, I ain't sayin' that. 'Is nose is right swole and might be broke, as far as I can tell. And 'e won't be a pretty sight for a few days, I expect," said the innkeeper, scratching his head speculatively. "But I don't see no signs of real damage." He got to his feet and addressed the other gentlemen with a smile. "That ain't to say that your friend what left so sudden-like ain't real 'andy with 'is fives. They must 'ave 'ad a good mill. Wish I could 'ave seen it."

Gwen was staring at George incredulously. "Do you mean he has no sword wound? Didn't Drew use the sword at all?"

"Of course he didn't," Selby said, becoming as impatient with her as he was with Gwen. He turned to Wys. "Let's get Pollard up to his room. Then we can wash our hands of him and decide what to do next."

"The innkeeper and I can handle him," Wys replied. "You stay here with the ladies."

They lifted George to his feet and half led, half carried him out of the room. Gwen sank back on the settee and dropped her head in her hands with a moan.

"Your fine suitor doesn't look so romantic now, does he, Lady Rowle," Selby remarked, looking at Gwen with a marked lack of sympathy.

Gwen shook her head, unable to look up. Hetty's expression softened. "Don't be hard on her, Selby. She's been through a great deal. Go to the tap room and get us some wine. And there's no need to hurry back with it, my dear. Do you understand me? No need to hurry back."

"Eh?" Selby asked, puzzled. "Oh, I see. Very well, I'll leave you for a while. Wys and I will be all the better for a chance to down a few brandies."

"Now, you foolish girl," Hetty said with compassionate affection, "tell me how this came to pass. What made you take such an ill-considered step as to agree to elope with George Pollard?"

"I don't know," Gwen said, her voice quivering in despair. "I can't even explain it to myself." She looked up unseeing, trying to gather her thoughts and make some sense of what had happened. "I told myself that I could do for George what I failed to do for... Edward." She laughed mirthlessly. "Foolish was scarcely the word for it. I see now that I scarcely *knew* George. I know you won't believe me, Hetty, but I decided a while before Drew came in to return home tonight. I realized that I couldn't marry George... not without love. I would have had to face the same problems all over again—perhaps worse ones. I had come down to tell George of my decision when I heard the fighting."

"Of course I believe you," Hetty said earnestly, "but I doubt that he would have permitted you to go back to London."

Gwen faced her friend with a troubled frown. "Tell me, Hetty, what Drew meant when he said... that George meant to make me his... doxy."

"Did Drew say that? It was unkind of him. But you see, Wys learned from Lambie Aylmer that George was about to become betrothed to an heiress—a daughter of a nabob from the city. A rather large financial settlement was involved."

"Are you sure?"

Hetty nodded. "I'm afraid so. You see, the young lady in question is known to Wystan Farr. He went to see her and spoke to the nabob himself."

Gwen was silent. Finally she asked in a small voice, "I don't suppose there is any possibility that George had decided to jilt his heiress and marry me instead?"

Hetty lowered her eyes and shrugged. "I cannot pretend to know what was in Sir George's mind. However, I do know that he has enormous debts. He's already accepted a considerable sum from Mr. Plumb, I'm told. I don't think he'd be likely to—"

"I see," said Gwen bitterly. "Sir George intended to have his cake and eat it too." She shuddered. "What a fool I've been! How ridiculous I must have seemed to... to your brother. He was quite right when he spoke so scornfully of my judgment of men."

She got up and went to the fire, staring at it moodily for several minutes. Then she turned to Hetty. "I am beginning to realize how very much I owe to you and Selby and Wys... and... Lord Jamison. I do not deserve such consideration at your hands. That you have made this journey—in this weather—in my behalf is an act of generosity I find quite overwhelming. I don't know how to thank you."

Hetty smiled. "If this night's work does anything to make you see my brother in his true light, I shall be thanked enough."

Gwen turned back to gaze at the fire. "I have been unforgiveably unfair to your brother tonight. And I'm at a loss as to how to make my apologies to him. He may even be badly hurt...!"

"I feel sure his wound cannot be severe. He looked in adequate health when he came stalking out of here," Hetty said. "And as for apologies, they won't be at all necessary if you'll only tell him that you'll have him."

Gwen swung round. "*Marry* him, you mean?" She smiled ruefully. "I'm quite certain that Lord Jamison discarded *that* idea many weeks ago. I've long since killed any *tendre* he may have had for me."

"I'm not at all sure of that, my dear," Hetty ventured.

"But I am. Besides, nothing has really changed because of this dreadful night. I still could never marry the man who killed Edward Rowle, no matter how I've wronged him since."

Hetty jumped up and stamped her foot in irritation. "Dash it, Gwen, are you still harping on the *duel?* I dislike railing at you when you are so sorely beset, but it makes my blood boil to think that, after all he has done for you, you still believe that my brother is capable of a cold-blooded murder!"

"I don't blame you, Hetty, for saying these things. He is your brother, and loving and devoted to you at all times, I have no doubt, but—"

"Don't talk fustian! Not that it signifies, but he is certainly *not* always loving and devoted. He scolds me quite vigorously when the occasion demands. He has, on occasion, a quick temper and a harsh tongue. But he is never, *never* thoughtless or unkind or cruel! And for you to persist in the belief that he intentionally harmed poor Rowle is the outside of enough!"

"I'm sorry, Hetty. I don't wish to quarrel with you when you've been so very good to me. After tonight, I won't speak to you of the duel ever again. It does you credit to have such faith in your brother's good character."

Hetty pouted. "It's *you* who should have faith in his good character."

"How can I?" Gwen asked sadly, turning back to stare into the flames, "when Sir George told me how—" She gasped and stiffened. Turning quickly, she looked at Hetty with eyes wide with horror. "My God! Do you suppose that George lied to me about the duel, too?" she asked in a hoarse whisper.

"I don't doubt it for a moment," Hetty answered firmly.

Gwen ran to the settee and knelt at Hetty's feet, neither one of them noticing that the door had opened. "Hetty, for God's sake, tell me!" Gwen pleaded, grasping Hetty's hands in hers. "What really happened at that accursed duel?"

"Of course I'll tell you," Hetty said promptly, pulling Gwen up and urging her onto the settee beside her. "It is more than time that you heard the whole story."

"Confound it, Hetty, have you no conscience? No sense of honor?" came an aggrieved voice from the doorway. Selby stood there, a mug of steaming wine in each hand and a stern frown on his face.

"Oh, Selby, why did you have to return so quickly?" Hetty said petulantly.

"A good thing I did," he said, entering the room like a stern schoolmaster. Wys followed, his hesitant step indicating a certain lack of support for Selby's stand.

"Here, Lady Rowle, drink this," Selby said, offering her a mug. Then, handing the other to his wife, he added, "and you drink that. You may as well, for you've done all the *talking* you're going to do."

Gwen looked from one to the other. "I don't understand. Has Hetty done something wrong?"

"She was about to," her husband said grumpily.

"We all gave our words not to talk about the duel," Wys explained.

"To whom?" Gwen asked.

"To Drew, of course," Selby said brusquely.

"I see," said Gwen, lowering her head.

"Then I hope you won't mind if I change the subject," Selby said in his most business-like tone. "Wystan and I have been discussing what to do. The weather is worsening rapidly, and we think it would be foolhardy to attempt to return to London tonight. As much as we all would dislike remaining under the same roof as Sir George, I think, Lady Rowle, it may be necessary."

"He is sure to sleep for many hours, Gwen," Wys added hastily, "and you may be sure that we will see to it that he has no opportunity to cross your path. So, you may rest comfortably and without fear."

"I've taken the liberty, ladies," Selby said, "to order dinner to be served in half an hour. The innkeeper has prepared another parlor down the hall, so that we need not remain here amid all this chaos. Whether you wish to go to your rooms to rest, or to sit at the fire in the other room, this would seem to be the time to leave this one."

Gwen rose quickly. "You have been more than kind. I can't find words with which to thank you for all you've done. Your arrangements are quite satisfactory to me. However, if you will all excuse me, I shall retire for the night. I don't feel quite up to eating dinner, and I s- suddenly find that I'm quite w-weary..." Her voice seemed to fail her and, with her head lowered, she walked hurriedly to the door.

"Gwen, wait!" Hetty cried in concern. "You *must* eat something. Please say you'll come down for dinner."

Gwen, her hand poised on the doorknob, her back to the room, tried to speak, but her throat ached with the sobs she was holding back. With a quick, negative shake of her head, she ran from the room.

Hetty, arms akimbo, glared at her husband. "*Now* see what you've done! She's upset all over again."

"I don't know what *I* have to do with that," he said innocently.

"Why couldn't you leave us alone? It's more than time that poor girl learned the truth about the duel."

Selby raised his eyes to the ceiling. "Is there never to be an end to my wife's interfering tricks?" he asked the heavens. "Am I never to have a moment's peace? Am I expected to put up with deceit and lies and dishonor?"

Wys expelled a little snort of laughter. "Doing it a bit

brown, aren't you, Selby? I must admit I'm almost in agreement with Hetty in this."

Selby rolled his eyes toward Wys in dismay. "You can't mean it!"

"But I *do* mean it. Hasn't this gone far enough? What harm can it do to tell Gwen now?"

Hetty nodded with satisfaction. She was delighted to have support from this unexpected quarter. "See?" she said triumphantly to her husband. "Even Wys agrees with me now! Go ahead and answer his question."

"I don't know what harm it can do, just as I don't know what *good* it can do," said the always-logical Lord Selby ponderously. "I only know that we gave our solemn words. Does your word mean nothing to you any more, Mr. Farr?"

"You know it does! That's the devil of it," Wys admitted ruefully.

Hetty threw up her hands in disgust. "Oh, you men and your *honor!* It was your stupid honor that caused the duel in the first place, and it is your stupid honor that now prevents us from curing the ills that resulted from it. Well, I, for one, have had enough of your honor. I'll gladly break my word if it means my brother's happiness. So stand aside, please. I'm going up to Gwen."

"How can you decide for your brother what will make him happy?" her husband asked with asperity. "What makes you think he still wants Gwen Rowle? After the ridiculous way that shatter-brained female has behaved all these weeks, it's my belief that Drew is well rid of her!"

"That's unkind, Selby," Wys remonstrated. "Gwen has had her reasons for what she's done. And one of them is the fact that she's been kept in ignorance about that duel."

"Yes, indeed," Hetty said in vehement agreement. "If I had told her when I first wanted to, they might be happily wed by this time."

Selby snorted. "Ha! Wishful thinking, if you ask me. But be that as it may, the fact remains that I saw Drew storming out of here not over an hour ago with a look on his face that chilled my blood. If that was the look of a man in love, I'm out in my reckoning."

"I don't know, Selby," Wys said thoughtfully. "He swore to me this morning that he'd have nothing to do with her, yet here he came! How would you explain *that,* if it were not due to love?"

"It *could* have been due to decency. Drew has always had a chivalrous streak."

Wys subsided. "You may be right. We have no right to meddle, in any case," he said slowly.

Hetty's face dropped. "You mean you've changed your mind?" she demanded of poor Wys. He looked at her regretfully and shrugged. "Well, *I* haven't. I'm going to Gwen right now." And she walked to the door mutinously.

"Hetty," came her husband's voice, coldly calm, "if you break your sworn word, I will not speak to you again."

Hetty hesitated at the door. She knew that tone in Selby's voice. She knew, too, that her happiness depended on him and his love. Her resolve wavered, but her conviction that she was right and the men wrong was quite strong. "Oh, pooh!" she said bravely, "you'll never stick to a resolve like that!"

"My word of honor," Selby said briefly.

She flashed a questioning, frightened look at him. He met her eye, unmoved. Her hand fell from the doorknob, and she turned to surrender to his demand, when her eye fell on a puddle of blood drying on the floor. Drew's blood. She raised her head defiantly. "Well, you must do what you must," she said quietly, "just as *I* must." And she opened the door.

"Hetty!" her husband said warningly.

She cast him one last glance—a strange combination of boldness and appeal—and fled. Selby remained rooted to the spot, his eyes on the door she had just shut, a wave of perplexed chagrin washing over him. Feeling Wys's eye on him, he turned. Wys was watching him with an unmistakable hint of laughter hovering about his mouth. "What do you find so amusing?" Selby barked.

"Nothing, nothing," Wys said quickly, trying—not too successfully—to keep the grin from widening. "It's just...well, you should not have given your word of honor, you know." He choked back a laugh. "You're going to have to endure a good many years of enforced silence."

"All right, you lobcock," Selby sputtered, "let's have a little silence from *you!* I don't care what the rest of you do now. As for me, *I'm* going down the hall to eat my dinner!"

Up in her bedroom, Gwen sat at the window under the dormer and looked out at the blackness. All she could see were the little white flakes that swirled close enough to the window to catch the faint light from her room and an oblong patch of light which spilled from the window of the taproom onto the snow below. From the look of it, the level of the snow had deepened considerably since she had left the window some two hours ago.

But the snowstorm no longer worried her. Her commitment to marry George no longer worried her. There would be no marriage and no burning necessity to hurry back to London. She was safe, surrounded by friends who were concerned for her welfare and ready to protect her, even from herself. The ache inside her should therefore diminish, the turmoil of the thoughts abate, the pounding in her temples cease, the flush of her cheeks fade. But neither the torment of her spirit nor the restlessness of her body had yet eased. She could not banish from her mind the picture of Drew as she had seen him when the innkeeper had opened the door of the parlor—his hair disheveled, his cheek bruised, his left hand dripping blood. And another picture haunted her— his scornful eyes and mocking sneer as he made a scathing denunciation of her judgment of the character of men. What was it he had said? "Your superb judgment of the male character has been unerring in the past, hasn't it?"

Oh, yes, she had erred. She had mistaken the character of Edward badly enough, and she had gone on to be completely taken in by George. How badly had she been mistaken about Drew? Was it possible that he had not been at fault in shooting Edward? Had she, because of blind prejudice and her own guilt, been more susceptible to Pollard's lies than the truth that everyone else, even Hazel, had been able to see? If so, she had foolishly, wantonly, *unforgivably* thrown away her only chance of happiness.

Because she knew now how much she loved Drew. When she had thrown open the parlor doors and seen what she thought was Pollard's dead body on the floor, it was not for Pollard that her heart had broken. It was for the fate of the murderer who stood before her with the sword in his hand. It was fear that Drew would end on the gallows that had made her blood run cold.

When Hetty came in, Gwen could almost guess what she would say. Once she was able to admit the possibility that she could have been wrong about the duel, she could begin to imagine other circumstances. If Drew had *not* aimed the gun deliberately and cold-bloodedly at the frightened, white-faced and shivering Edward (and how out of character for Drew that action now seemed), then something else must have taken place. The possibilities were many. Why had she not seen that before?

Hetty sat on the bed and told Gwen the story in full detail. At its conclusion, Gwen merely nodded. Hetty could read the agony in her eyes as Gwen relived the moment that Edward, in hysterical relief to see Drew indicate his intention to delope, pointed a shaking pistol at Drew and fired too soon. But Gwen could not say a word. After a while, Hetty rose to go. "I hope I've done the right thing, telling you all this, my dear," Hetty said in deep concern, "but perhaps you will believe me now."

Gwen turned to gaze at Hetty with a look of profound regret. "I should have known it without being told," she said in a voice vibrant with pain. "Oh, Hetty, I *should have known!*"

Chapter Seventeen

DREW, DESPITE THE WOUND in his hand, managed to return to London by morning. The others, however, because of their decision to remain at the inn for the night, found themselves unable to leave. The snow continued unabated for two days, making the roads impassable. Their imprisonment within the confines of the small hostelry was not a particularly pleasant one. For one thing, Selby, keeping his word of honor, would not say one word to his wife despite the fact that they were thrown together much more than they would have been at home. For another, George Pollard had recovered enough in a couple of days to leave his room from time to time, and one or another of the party would come face-to-face with him in the corridor with embarrassing frequency. He was, however, wise enough to avoid Gwen.

Gwen, in gratitude for what her friends had done for her, did everything she could to make things cheerful and companionable in the little parlor where they spent most of their days, and Wys was—as always—pleasant and good-humored. But a prison the Rose and Crown seemed to be, no matter how much they pretended to be cheerful, and they all looked forward with eagerness to a thaw which would permit them to return to their own homes.

Meanwhile, back in London, Drew retired to his bed and slept the clock round. When he awoke, Mallow discovered the bloodstained neckerchief and, clucking with disapproval at Drew's neglect of his wound, covered it with a healing salve of his own concoction and bound it securely. After another day had passed, Drew realized that neither Wys nor his sister and brother-in-law had returned to town, and that they must be snowbound. It occurred to him that Lady Hazel and Tom would have had no word of Gwen's fate or her present whereabouts and must be sick with worry. He wrote a brief, businesslike note, informing them that Lady Rowle was safe and well, that no marriage had taken or would take place between Lady Rowle and Sir George Pollard, and that Lady Rowle had been in the company of Lord and Lady Selby and Wystan Farr ever since the first evening of her departure. The note dispatched, he tried to put the whole business from his mind. That message was the last thing he would ever do to connect himself with Gwen or her family. And, he said to himself, it was a good riddance.

He was therefore somewhat chagrined when Mallow interrupted his reading in the library the following morning to tell him that Tom was at the door. Drew put his book aside with a sigh. "Tell him to come in," he said to Mallow.

"He says he won't stay but a minute and doesn't want to remove his boots," Mallow replied. "He asks if you'd be so kind as to step into the hallway to see him."

Drew shrugged and went to the hall, Mallow at his

heels. Tom stood just inside the door, his cheeks pink
from the invigorating walk through the snow, the flakes
melting on the capes of his greatcoat. "Good morning,"
Drew said, holding out his hand. Tom seized it and shook
it heartily. "I can't thank you enough for sending round
that note," Tom said with a smile that held all his old
adoration. "You've no idea how glad Aunt Hazel and I
were to get the news."

Drew did not intend to let Tom know that he himself
had gone to find Gwen, so he merely nodded and said,
"Save your thanks for Wys and the Selbys. They should
all return as soon as we have a thaw in the weather."

Tom shook his head. "You're trying to make me think
you had nothing to do with this, but I *know* you found
her."

"Really?" Drew asked with a noncommittal lift of his
eyebrow. "And how do you know that?"

"I came back that day," Tom said, looking down at the
floor in shame-faced recollection. "You see, I had said a
lot of things to you that I deeply regretted—"

"You said nothing that a loyal brother should not have
said. I have already forgotten the incident."

Tom looked up at him in gratitude. "That's good of
you, Drew. I've been perfectly miserable ever since that
awful morning. It was dreadful of me to abuse you when
you had been so good to me."

"Look here, Tom, haven't I told you—?"

"Please, Drew, let me say it. I must apologize, or I
won't be able to live with myself."

Drew smiled. "Very well, you've apologized. Very
nicely, too. Now have done."

"You do forgive me, then?"

"Completely."

"Thank you, Drew. But it's important to me that you
understand that I came to apologize *before* I knew that
you had gone after Gwen."

"See here, Tom, you don't *know* anything of the sort."

"Oh, yes, I do, so stop bamming me. Mallow told me."

"Mallow?" asked Drew with an edge to his voice. His eye turned to his omnipresent butler who was discovered assiduously polishing a nearby mirror with intense concentration. "He *did,* did he? How *thoughtful* of him."

"Don't blame him, Drew. I wormed it out of him," Tom insisted. "But I had to come and tell you that I'll never forget what you did. Never." Tom looked at Drew with glowing eyes for a moment. "Look, I'm going. I know that my coming here like this is against the rules you and Gwen have set up, and I won't do so again. I just want to say a proper goodbye."

Drew gripped the boy's shoulders affectionately. "I'm glad you did. Thank you for coming. Kiss Hazel for me. Goodbye, Tom." A quick handshake and the boy was gone.

Drew turned to Mallow, but the butler was already hastening down the hall. "Mallow," Drew called with ominous gentleness.

"Yes, my lord, I'll be with you in a moment," Mallow said hurriedly. "I'm needed in the kitchen with utmost urgency." And he disappeared into the nether regions where he remained until he was convinced that his lordship had forgotten his intended reprimand.

The weather thawed after five days, and before the week was out the party returned from the Rose and Crown. Hetty promptly paid a visit to her brother, only to learn from Mallow that Drew wished to inform her that he was not speaking to her. Ostracized thus by the two most important men in her life, poor Hetty returned home. For the next two weeks, the only satisfaction she found in life was abusing her servants in an unwontedly shrewish manner and spending her afternoons at her favorite shops—buying bonnets and gowns with reckless abandon.

Wys received the same message from Mallow when he paid a call, but, ignoring Mallow's remonstrances, he marched into the library, sat down opposite Drew at the fireplace, and proceeded to tell his friend all manner of gossip, cheerfully ignoring the fact that Drew made no response. He related to Drew the events at the Rose and Crown after he had left: how comical George had looked with a large gap in his upper front teeth and his nose swollen to twice its normal size and gleaming in purple majesty; how Selby had manfully managed not to speak to his wife through an entire game of backgammon; and how badly Selby had handled the ribbons on the icy road back to London. After about half-an-hour of forcing his face to look supercilious and repressive, Drew began to feel foolish and a smile forced its way out. From there it was a short step to laughter, and finally Drew gave up his intention to sulk and surrendered.

"Don't know why you were put out with me at all, old boy," Wys remarked after they'd shaken hands. "How was I to know you'd changed your mind and gone off all alone? You should have come for me. I had a stake in the matter too, you know."

"You're right, Wys. I feel like a fool about the whole business. Let's not talk about it any more. I want to forget the whole thing. Did you go to see your Mr. Plumb since your return?"

"Oh, yes, I went at once. He was so overjoyed that I'd saved his daughter from that bounder that he quite forgave me for lacking a title. I shouldn't wonder if I'm betrothed before the month is out."

"Wys, you're a lucky dog! Let's have some Madeira to drink to your future happiness."

After a few companionable drinks, Wys looked up from his glass and said thoughtfully, "It's not fair of you, Drew, to forgive me and keep Hetty at arm's length. The poor chit is having enough difficulty with Selby."

"No, I don't agree," said Drew. "You, as you pointed out to me a moment ago, had a reason of your own for going to find Pollard. But my sister was meddling, as I'm sure Selby warned her. I've had quite enough of it, I can tell you."

"She came at my insistence, Drew."

"Did she?" Drew said, reconsidering. "Well, I'll think about it. Meanwhile, let her simmer a bit. It'll do her good."

At Rowle House, Hazel soon noticed that Gwen had changed. She was subdued, downcast, and uncomfortably humble. She neither argued nor held very long to an opinion. "If you say so," was always on her lips. It was as if she no longer trusted her own judgment. She wandered about the house aimlessly, and several days passed without Drew's name being mentioned. Hazel felt strongly that Gwen should make an effort to show Drew proper gratitude, and finally brought up the matter. "I've been thinking about what you told me about Lord Jamison, Gwen. Don't you think you owe him some sort of apology?"

"Yes," Gwen said with a sigh. "I was unforgivably insulting to him when he had gone to such lengths to help me. What do you think I should do?"

"Go to him and tell him," Hazel said promptly.

Gwen gave her mother-in-law a frightened glance. "Oh, no, I couldn't! Never! He doesn't want to see me again. He made that clear. Don't ask me to do such a thing, Hazel. I couldn't face him."

Hazel sighed. "Very well, then, write him a note. It's the very least you can do."

That afternoon, Gwen sat down at her graceful little Sheraton writing table and began. *Dear Lord Jamison, how can I ever express . . .* No, that was not the right tone. It was too effusive, too dramatic. She tried again. *My dear Lord Jamison, Although this letter will probably stir up memories of a scene you would prefer to forget . . .* No, that was too negative a way to approach an apology. She tore up the sheet and started a third time. *Dear Drew,* she wrote, letting the words flow unchecked, *Dear, Dearest Drew, I have hurt you so many times, so unjustly, but oh, my darling, each time it hurt me more . . .* This sheet she tore into tiny bits, so tiny that nobody would ever be able to read it.

The note was delivered to Drew the next morning, and he tore it open carelessly. After a quick glance at the signature, he noticed that the hand that held the paper had begun to shake. With a surge of self-disgust, he tossed the letter aside and turned to the other messages that Mallow had placed at his elbow. But he could not make his way through even the first one, and he quickly dropped it and picked up Gwen's note again. *My Dear Lord Jamison,* he read, *For your many kindnesses to me in the past, and in particular for the invaluable service you rendered to me not a fortnight ago, you have been rewarded by abuse and ingratitude. I now realize how mistaken I have been and how I have misjudged you. I cannot ask you to forgive what I myself consider unforgivable, but I wish to assure you that I am now more grateful than words can say for everything you have done in my behalf, and shall always remain so. Most sincerely, Gwen Rowle.*

In spite of the hand that shook as he read the note, Drew's face had a mocking sneer. Oh, no, my girl, he said to himself, you'll not trap me again. Not any more. You've cost me too much and waited too long to expect a few humble words to make it up. And the hand that shook crumpled the note and tossed it aside.

The next day, Gwen received a reply. *My dear Lady Rowle,* she read, *Please be assured that apologies and thanks are not at all necessary. I have already been more than adequately thanked by your brother, and since I am sure that the incidents to which you refer will soon be forgotten, there is no need to dwell on them further. With every good wish for your future happiness, I remain, Yours, etc., Andrew Seymour Viscount Jamison.*

"Lord Jamison has sent a very polite response to my note," Gwen said to Hazel with a strained smile, "so we may now forget the whole affair. The amenities have been attended to." With that, she crushed the letter in her hand, ran to her room, and wept.

"Selby," Hetty said to her husband, who sat before her pretending she did not exist, "since you are not speaking to me and therefore cannot scold, I'm going to make a confession to you. I'm going to interfere again. You needn't get so red in the neck, for it's nothing so very terrible. I'm not going to break my word or do anything *really* dishonorable."

Selby made a strangled sound in his throat.

"I saw Gwen Rowle at the Pantheon Bazaar today, and she looks thinner and paler than she looked after Rowle died. She is pining away for Drew and too proud to do anything about it. And you can't tell me—oh, of course you can't if you're not speaking—but you couldn't even if you *were* speaking, tell me that Drew is happy. I've never seen him look so hagged! Well, it's about time somebody did *something* to bring those two together. And there's nobody else but me to do it. Don't look at me like that, Selby, because I won't be talked out of it! Well, *glared* out of it, if you must be accurate. If *we* only had a friend like me, she would have done something for *us* by now, and we wouldn't be living in this awful silence. Oh, I know *I'm* not silent, but you know what I mean."

Selby choked and shifted in his chair.

"I suppose you're wondering what I mean to do. It's a very simple plan, really. I'm going to send each of them a note and ask them to come here on Thursday at four. Neither will know the other is coming. They will think it a tête-à-tête with me alone. But, *I won't be here!* Well, I really *will* be here, but I'll be hiding in my room. They'll have to face each other, and I know that is all it will take to make them fall into each other's arms. Good heavens, Selby, why are you getting so red? I do believe you're about to suffer a stroke!"

"Hetty," Selby burst out, unable to contain himself any longer, "I absolutely *forbid* it!"

"Selby!" Hetty squealed. "You *spoke!* You broke your word of *honor!*" She flung herself into his lap and wrapped her arms around his neck. "Oh, you darling! Can it be that you care for me more than for your *honor?* Oh, Selby, I've never been so flattered in all my life!"

Poor Selby found himself being smothered with kisses. Since it had been some time since he had estranged himself from his wife, he found the sensation quite enjoyable, and he couldn't resist putting his arms around her and responding to her embraces. He quite forgot *why* he had spoken, so enraptured was he by the enchanting little vixen in his arms. If he had known that dishonor would be so rewarding, he might well have opened his mouth a week or two sooner.

The notes were identical. They read, *I am in most urgent need of your advice. I am in despair. Please spare me an hour on Thursday, about four. I shall make sure we are alone. Don't fail me. Hetty.*

When Drew arrived, Gwen had already been shown into Hetty's Egyptian drawing room. The butler, following Hetty's elaborate instructions, closed the door quickly behind Drew as soon as he'd stepped over the threshold. Gwen saw him first. "Drew!" she gasped, caught unaware.

"Good Lord!" Drew stared at her, too astonished to be angry. He could not help noting that she looked more drawn and tired than she'd ever seemed before. But her hair still glowed with that suppressed vibrancy that had so attracted him when he'd first seen her, and her eyes, so surprisingly dark, still had the power to stir him profoundly. There was something new in her eyes as she stared at him now, he noticed. They were less guarded, more...what was it? he asked himself, and a word popped into his mind...*vulnerable.*

But none of this was of concern to him. He had no intention of remaining in the same room with her. What was his sister thinking of to do such a thing to him? Where *was* Hetty? He quickly scanned the room.

"Your sister hasn't come down yet, Lord Jamison," Gwen told him.

"So I see. Good afternoon, Lady Rowle. Do you really think our Hetty will appear?"

"Well, I— Oh!" Gwen breathed, a blush suffusing her cheeks.

"Exactly so," said Drew in disgust. "I'm very much afraid my incorrigible sister has tricked us again. I . . . I'm sorry, Lady Rowle, I don't know what to say . . . except to express my regret that I'm related to such a meddling ninnyhammer. There seems to be no way to control her machinations short of strangling her." He gave Gwen a small smile and bowed stiffly. "If you'll excuse me, I'll go to find her right now and do that very thing. My fingers itch to wring her neck."

Gwen, scarcely aware of what she was doing, held out a hand to him. "No, please," she said, "don't go—"

Drew paused at the door and turned to her with a quizzical look. "My dear Lady Rowle, surely you have not taken me literally. You need have no concern. Monster I may be, but I draw the line at murdering my own sister."

Gwen reddened to the roots of her hair. "Drew! I didn't mean—! Surely you don't think I could ever believe—!"

Drew laughed shortly. "No, of course not. I couldn't resist the jest, but it wasn't a very kind one. I apologize. I'd better go, before I say . . . that is, I . . . Good day, ma'am."

"Dr—Lord Jamison, could you not spare me a moment? Since fate—or rather, your sister—has seen fit to throw us together like this, it seems a good opportunity for me to say something I've wanted to say for many weeks."

Drew hesitated. "I think I know what you want to say and, believe me, Lady Rowle, it is not necessary."

"Not to you, perhaps, but very necessary to me."

Drew shrugged. "Very well then, ma'am. I am at your disposal."

"Won't you sit down?" Gwen urged, patting a place beside her on the graceful white sofa.

"No, thank you," Drew answered, unyielding. "I'll stand here, with your permission."

Gwen glanced up at him briefly, then lowered her eyes to the hands clasped in her lap. "Lord Jamison, I have become painfully aware of late that what you said about me that day at the Rose and Crown was true."

"What I said about you? I'm sorry, but my recollections of that night are quite hazy. I don't seem to recall—"

"You said that I make great errors in my judgment of the character of the men in my life. You were quite right. I learned that night how very great those errors were."

"There is no need to dwell on past mistakes. No great harm has come to you, after all."

"Hasn't it?" She glanced up at him, but he quickly looked away. This conversation was making him feel uncomfortable. He edged toward the door. She saw the movement and tried again to hold him there. "I don't want to make those errors again. Lord Jamison, can you forgive me for—?"

"Lady Rowle, please! You've already apologized for the events of that day."

"And for all the rest? May I do so for all the rest?"

He sighed. "There's no purpose in pursuing all this."

"Is there no purpose in my telling you that I now understand that you intended Sir George no real harm that day?"

"No, ma'am. No purpose at all."

"And no purpose in my saying that I now realize that you were not responsible for Tom's accident, either?"

"It is not necessary to tell me that either, Lady Rowle."

"Or in saying that my assessment of your character— what I thought of as your propensity for violence—was in error from the very beginning?"

"I see nothing to be gained by any of this," he insisted.

She stood up and took a step toward him. "Then let me at least say that I must have been blind not to have seen all along that you could never have murdered Edward in cold blood."

Drew looked at her sharply. "My sister has *indeed* been busy in my affairs," he muttered in annoyance. "When did she reveal the details of the duel to you? During your stay at the Rose and Crown?"

"Those questions are not pertinent to this conversation," Gwen said primly.

"I wish I could determine just what *is* pertinent to this conversation," he said irritably. "See here, Gwen, I want you to cease this uncharacteristic humility. There's no purpose in going over all this!"

"Isn't there?" she asked with a slight smile. "At least you've stopped calling me 'Lady Rowle' in that odious way."

Drew could feel himself being pulled back into her web. "What are you up to, Gwen? I warn you—I swore I wouldn't permit myself to become entangled with you again!"

"But I'm only trying to apologize to you . . . to clear my conscience," she said innocently.

He raised an eyebrow and scanned her face with a doubting look. "Very well. But if we're to continue with this fruitless conversation, please go back to the sofa and sit down. I want to keep a safe distance between us."

Gwen's smile became teasing. "That doesn't seem at all necessary, if our conversation is as *fruitless* as you claim."

"If you mean by that remark that you believe I am at all affected by your meaningless apologies, you're very much mistaken, my girl," he declared defensively.

Gwen knew she was not mistaken—he *was* affected. If not by what she said, he was affected by the sudden awareness that she was no longer hostile to him. And her instincts told her that he still cared. Her skin tingled and her pulse raced with an excited anticipation. He was being stubborn. He was defending his pledge to himself. But hadn't she heard that love was like war? If one side was on the defensive, then the other should attack.

She lowered her eyes shyly. "I'm sorry my apologies are meaningless, sir. Would it be more meaningful if I said that, although I believed you to be a murderer, I have . . . I have loved you . . . in spite of it?"

He eyed her skeptically. "Well, I suppose . . . Yes. Yes, I would say that those words are . . . more meaningful," he said carefully. "But I wish you would return to the sofa. We are somehow moving rather too close together."

"Nonsense," Gwen said, her smile widening. "There's half a room between us . . . almost . . ."

But Drew now wanted to return to the subject. "Is there . . . anything else . . . meaningful . . . you want to say to me?"

"Yes, Drew, there is," she said, suddenly serious. "You once said that you wanted me to love you enough to believe you innocent even though—as you put it—you came to me with hands dripping with blood. In that I failed you. But when you did appear before me with bloody hands, I loved you believing you *guilty*. Oh, Drew, is *that* love meaningless?"

Drew's eyes, incredulous, searched her face. "Did you *indeed* love me then?" he asked softly.

"Yes, oh yes!" she said breathlessly, crossing with two quick steps the space that still lay between them. "I wanted so much to take your bloodstained hand to my face, like this . . . and offer my lips for you to kiss . . ."

"Oh, Gwen!" he said with a groan and pulled her into his arms.

Half-an-hour later, Hetty tiptoed down the hall. She paused at the drawing room door. It was tightly closed, just as she had ordered. There was no sound. She looked up and down the corridor, but no one was in sight. She put her ear to the door but heard nothing. One more glance down the corridor, and she knelt and peered into the keyhole. She could see nothing. She stood up and, with the greatest care and delicacy, she turned the knob. There was no sound. She pushed open the door only an inch and peeped in. Standing in the middle of the room were Gwen and Drew, locked in an embrace. She could not see Drew's face, for it was buried in Gwen's hair. But Gwen's head, nestled in Drew's shoulder, was turned toward the door. Her eyes were closed, but her face had a look of such radiance that Hetty felt her throat constrict. Silently, she pulled the door closed and carefully released the latch. She backed away on tiptoe. Just then the front door opened and Selby entered. "Hetty, what are you doing?" he asked suspiciously.

"Sssh!" she hissed. Tiptoeing to him she put her hand on his mouth. "Don't say a word," she whispered. "They're in the drawing room."

"Who?" he managed to say through his wife's fingers.

"Gwen and Drew."

Selby's eyes flashed and he pulled her hand from his mouth. "You devil! Have you been meddling again when I expressly forbade—!"

"Selby, hush!" she pleaded. "Don't scold. I've *done* it, you see! It worked!"

"Couldn't have," Selby said stubbornly. "I told you it was a corkbrained scheme. It *couldn't* have worked."

"But it did. Go and see for yourself!"

Selby marched firmly across the hall, his wife at his heels. He pushed open the drawing room door unceremoniously and stared. The lovers stood just as they were when Hetty had seen them. Selby gaped, swallowed, and started to back out of the room when Drew's voice stopped him.

"Go away, Hetty," Drew said without lifting his head. "I'll see to *you* later!"

Gwen smiled, but she neither moved nor opened her eyes. Selby tiptoed out and closed the door. Hetty was beaming at him. "See? I *did* it!" she chortled jubilantly.

Selby was forced to smile. "Well, well, whoever would have guessed—?"

"*I* guessed!" Hetty bragged. "*I!* Not so corkbrained after all, am I?"

He put a plump arm around her and they strolled together down the hall. "Corkbrained? Not at all, my dear," he said. "You're a clever little minx. Very clever. Haven't I always said so?"